Sahmara

JEAN DAVIS

ISBN: 1-5374-6462-0

September 2016

CHAPTER ONE

Tall grass ripped at Sahmara's bare legs as she dashed across the moonlit field. She glanced over her shoulder. The shadowy forms of her recent captors had grown distant, their voices no more than whispers on the cool wind. Desperate to catch her breath, she slowed and bent low in the thick blades. Her chest heaved.

Her sprint to freedom had saved her yet another night of drunken fondling by her captors. But alone now, in the autumn winds and far from home, dressed in only a tattered shift, with no food, water or weapon… The Mother save her, she may have sentenced herself to death. She clamped a trembling hand over her mouth to stifle the sob.

Wasn't this where Zane was supposed to ride and whisk her away? That's how rescues happened according to the storytellers that had graced her father's hall. But Zane's sword hadn't saved her when the Atherians burst into her home, and the only time she'd seen his blue eyes and silly smile in the past four months was in her dreams.

She hugged her knees to her chest. The storytellers had lied. No one was coming to save her.

They were too late anyway. She wasn't worth saving anymore.

Tears streamed down her cheeks. She had to keep moving. If the Atherians caught her, they'd throw her to the ground and form a line. At least back in camp, she only had to deal with one soldier a night. Memories of their dirty hands and rank breath made her shudder.

Staying low, she crept forward. Her bare skin turned to gooseflesh now that she'd slowed. She trudged onward into the low rolling hills until the blush of dawn edged the skyline. There she sank into the grass and curled into a tight ball. The grasslands couldn't go on forever. Eventually, she'd run into the ocean. And home. If she lived that long.

❧❦

Sahmara's cheek itched. She wiped at it, still half asleep and dreaming of the weight and warmth of the white furs atop her bed. Her hand met with something small and hard, followed by a sharp prick on her finger. Her eyes snapped open.

A large black beetle had its pronged mouth buried in her flesh. Blood dripped from the wound. Sahmara ripped the beetle from her skin and flung it into the grass. She sprang to her feet, but her sleep-fogged mind woke in time to remind her to keep low. With her bleeding finger thrust into her mouth, she scanned the grass for any sign of the soldiers.

Nothing but the wind stirred the sea of blades. Either the soldiers were still sleeping, or they'd abandoned their search.

Hunger pangs seized her stomach. The mug of thin broth she'd had the night before hadn't been enough to fill her then, let alone after a night of running.

Morning dew clung to her matted hair and bare skin. She rubbed her hands over her body, trying to generate warmth. Her rush through the grass had covered her feet in cuts. For just a moment she wished for the warmth of the other women she'd huddled with on the Atherian wagon that had brought her here. The soldiers had considered her valuable, and like others in the wagon, had reserved her for the officer's use. Those that walked beside the wagon had served lines of hungry-eyed soldiers. Most of those women were dead. Like she would be if she didn't keep moving.

The sun rose overhead. The chill of the morning turned to searing heat. Her feet burned. Her body ached.

Her father had thought her valuable too, as a trade item for marriage. He'd even gone so far as to purchase an expensive Ma'hasi bodyguard for her. The numerous offers for her hand had affirmed her worth. The Atherians had assigned her value thanks to that same Ma'hasi.

More valuable would have been the knowledge of the land from the starving children who had wanted to play with her. But she'd been too busy being proper throughout her childhood for that nonsense. Knowing how to start her own fire or find food seemed priceless now. Since being torn from her home, there was a distinct absence of bells to ring in order to summon anyone to assist her.

She muttered curses under her breath. As much as she loved her parents and Zane, it was their fault she'd been carted away, cursed, scarred and raped. Had she been one of the commoners, she would have suffered a far shorter time. And she would have been dead.

Maybe it was her mother's fault. If Sahmara had been a boy, none of this would have happened to her. Then again, they probably would have killed a son outright. She stubbed her toe on a rock and swore at it.

At least she was alive.

The sun took its time warming the air. She trudged onward, glancing over her shoulder now and then and jumping at the slightest sound. Tiny yellow songbirds flitted over the tall stalks of grass, while larger brown and white birds soared overhead, neither of which she recognized.

Sahmara tried to envision the maps of her father's trade routes. Some of them ran between Revochek and distant lands beyond Atheria which lay across the narrow stretch of land that bridged the two countries. Blue ripples of water had surrounded the two bulbous brown masses of land. Why couldn't her parents have held reading maps and knowing what was edible in the wild as valuable as knowing the important families of Revochek, or organizing a household and keeping accurate ledgers?

Atheria was the enemy. They seized ships and plundered trade routes. More detail of the surrounding world and politics had never found its way to her delicate ears.

By the time the sun was high overhead, sweat dripped down the sides of her face. She made out the cries of distant gulls. She had to be close to the shore. Her stomach knotted, whether from hunger or fear of being caught, she didn't know. Thirst was the only thing she was sure of.

Though she'd never been one to light candles in the chapel or to sit through droning services on beautiful mornings beside her mother, Sahmara closed her eyes and turned her face upward to the sun. She offered up a prayer.

"Please, Mother, let this be the ocean that leads me home. I am alone and tired. Please help me. I'll do anything." The required words her mother had taught her as a young girl had slipped her mind years ago. Was she supposed to be kneeling or standing? Did she need to burn incense? Her mother had always returned from services smelling of sweet smoke.

Sahmara opened one eye and looked around. Finding nothing to burn or offer up to the Mother, she knelt on the ground and bowed her head. Something sharp bit into her knee. She yelped. Hot blood met her fingers as she examined the wound. Of all the places to kneel, she'd picked the one with a sharp rock. Tears came to her eyes.

"I'm sorry, Mother," she said in a broken sob. "I have nothing to give you. Please, please help me get home."

She knelt there, waiting. For what, she wasn't sure--maybe a voice in her head or some indication that the goddess had heard her wayward servant.

All she received from the heavens was silence.

With a sore and bloody knee, she got to her feet and staggered onward. After hours, she saw the deep red sky overhead reflected on water. Golden grass gave way to shifting sands and thin green grasses like tiny whips that tore at her already scabbed legs and feet. Sand-worn strands of grey-brown rock offered steadier footing but their ambiguous edges nearly led to twisting her ankle. She limped toward the water only to realize, as she reached the edge of a cliff, that it lay far below her.

Looking down, she made out a wooden hovel tucked against the wall of crumbling rock. A rough path had been carved into the cliffside, leading downward. Before she lost the day's light, Sahmara started down the trail.

The view from the wind-whipped side of the cliff wasn't what she'd wanted to see. There was no sight of the narrow bridge of land that would lead her home, only endless water and a long stretch of sandy shoreline. At least she'd found water. She licked her parched lips.

Sharp rock shards bit into her bare feet as she slowly made her way down the narrow path. The wind was much colder at the bottom and the sand icy now that the sun sat at the edge of the world.

A rough voice greeted her in Atherian from the shadows along the rock. "You're a ragged mite, are ya not?"

Sahmara froze and frantically looked for a place to hide. The beach was wide open but for the shadows along the rocks where the voice had come from. At least she knew enough Atherian from her captivity to respond if she had to. That might just keep her from being discovered as a slave.

"There's nowhere to go out here, mite. Come on, you'll freeze by morning. Best get off the sands." A bony hand grabbed her arm.

Sahmara shrieked. She jerked her arm away.

"No need for that. I ain't gonna hurt ya. Come on now." The hand beckoned her toward the shack.

Too tired to resist, Sahmara followed the hunched figure. She walked through the doorway of cobbled together scraps of wood and immediately appreciated being out of the cool wind. The sputtering light of an oil lamp illuminated the ramshackle single-room structure.

Driftwood and broken, painted planks of ship lumber formed the walls that butted up against the face of the cliff on one side. A worn pallet, pierced by moldy straw at the ragged seams lay in the corner. A wooden table and bench occupied the rest of the space.

Next to the stone wall sat a jumbled circle of blackened

rocks. Warmth emanated from them. Sahmara crept closer. Glowing embers winked at her.

"Go on mite, you're like to be half frozen. I'll make some tea." A gentle shove pushed her toward the low fire.

Sahmara crouched down near the warm stones and fell unceremoniously on her backside as her legs gave out beneath her. Embarrassed, she turned to see if her host had noticed.

Thin white hair hung in wispy tufts from the backside of a brown scalp. The thickly-bundled figure puttered at the table with two wooden cups and a leather pouch.

Her savior turned and drew near, carrying the cups in spotted but steady hands. "Let's have a look at ya then."

One white eye stared forward while one dark eye raked her over as though she were for sale at market. A frown formed on the old woman's weathered face. "Came down the wall, didn't ya mite? A slave run off then is it?"

A wracking cough interrupted her assessment. She doubled over, then finally gasped a deep breath and cleared her throat. "I can give ya a day but then you'll need to move on. They'll be looking for ya, and I don't need no trouble."

Sahmara forced a weak smile, grateful for any respite she could get. She winced as her lip split. "Is there a port nearby? I'd like to find a ship to take me home."

"You've got coin for passage, enough they'd overlook ya being a run off slave?"

She sighed and shook her head. "No coin at all."

The woman sucked on her lip a minute, staring just over Sahmara's shoulder with her good eye. "Not supposed to be here, I think. South for ya then. Follow the shore."

She pulled a kettle from the hook over the fire and poured steaming water into the cups.

Taking the chipped cup in shaking hands, Sahmara swirled the pungent mix around. The steam soothed her wind-chapped face. "Thank you." She gulped it down. "It's very good."

"I have some cheese." The old woman hobbled back to the table and pulled back a thick stained cloth. Using a well-worn knife, she cut off a thin wedge of yellow cheese, tinged with grey at the edges. She worked her way back to the fire. "Here ya are then."

Sahmara ignored the heavy odor and took a big bite. She didn't even taste it. The second hit her with a sour earthen edge.

"That's right. Eat it up." The old woman gave her a toothless smile. "Finish your tea now. It's time for bed." She pointed to the narrow gaps in the boards. Darkness had taken over the sky.

Sahmara nodded. "Thank you."

"You're welcome, mite. Ya might be a slave, but at least ya got your manners." She cackled and then took a deep drink from her cup. "They call me Reva. I suppose you can too."

"I'm—"

"Yours don't matter, mite. Better if I don't know." Her toothless smile held the ghost of motherliness, making Sahmara miss her mother horribly. With a sniff, she nodded and tried to keep her knotted stomach from purging the cheese. She held out her empty cup.

"There now." Reva took the cup and set it on the table. She went to her pallet and pulled a tattered blanket from it. Reva draped it over Sahmara's shoulders. "Ya can sleep here by the fire."

A tear slipped down Sahmara's cheek as she lay down and pulled the blanket over her.

Reva put out the lamp. Seconds later the pallet rustled as she got comfortable. "Good night, mite."

Warm and safe as she could be under the circumstances, Sahmara closed her eyes and drifted off to sleep.

The hall was tainted by the metallic tang of her father's men being put to death by Atherian swords. True to his Ma'hasi training, Zane stood in front of her, his sword at the ready. At the other end of the hall, her mother screamed as soldiers pinned her to the ground. Her Father bellowed threats from where two men held him back. A third held a knife to his throat.

They kept asking her father questions, but Sahmara

couldn't understand them. He spat in their faces. The soldiers punched him in the gut, dropping him to his knees.

Others came at Zane. Glorious, beautiful Zane, her protector. He fought them until they dropped at his feet, unmoving. No matter whom her father married her off to; Zane would come with as her guard. She'd never be without her secret lover.

She held onto his back, her neatly trimmed nails grasping his smooth leather shirt. She felt faint. The scent of blood made her nauseous.

"It will be all right," Zane assured her.

Six men approached. They all had swords. So many footsteps all at once. Her father shouted. Her mother screamed.

A hood slammed over her head. Blind, she screamed. Swords rang out. Men grunted. Metal clanged on the floor. The melee ceased.

She reached out, feeling for Zane. Her arms were wrenched behind her back. Something hit her head.

Sahmara woke with a gasp. Reliving those last moments with him had tormented her nights since she'd been torn from home and Revochek. They wouldn't have killed Zane, would they? Or her parents? She pressed her eyes shut and rubbed them with the heels of her hands. She wasn't alone in the world. She couldn't be alone.

"About time ya woke up," Reva said from the table.

Her eyes took a moment to focus after all her rubbing. Something smelled delicious. The old woman sat on the bench, sipping from the chipped cup.

"I got some work for ya. Not as young as I used to be." Reva beckoned her toward the table. A steaming cup sat waiting for her. "In return, I'll give you a few things for your journey. Can't very well send you off like this."

Sahmara itched her scalp as she did nearly a hundred times each day and eyed the cup hungrily. She tucked her matted locks behind her ears as she went to the bench and sat.

"Break your fast first and then on to your tasks."

The gruel in the cup was a far cry from fresh, warm bread, fruit, and eggs but it beat waking up to a filthy soldier beside her. The contents of the cup filled her stomach with warmth and brought her a measure of comfort she'd not felt since leaving home.

"Feeling better?"

Sahmara nodded. She drained the cup in short order.

"Good. Get into the sea and give yourself a good scrub. You're smelling up my house." She pointed Sahmara to the door. "Leave them rags here. I'll see if I can't find ya something a bit more respectable looking. Ya won't get far looking like ya do."

"Thank you for helping me."

"You'll be helping me too, mite." Reva cackled merrily. "One thing before ya go." The old woman grabbed her knife in one hand and Sahmara's wrist in the other.

Sahmara jerked her hand back, but the old woman held on with surprising strength. She slid the tip of the knife against Sahmara's finger.

Sahmara watched in horror as Reva thrust the bloody finger into her mouth and sucked at it ravenously. Her shock wore off a second later and she managed to yank her finger back from the wet, toothless maw.

Reva lapped a drop of blood from her chin with her long, red tongue. "Eager enough for my help, but so reluctant to pay? You're all the same." She shook her head, sending wisps of hair floating through the air like sea foam. "Go on then, the water is waiting."

CHAPTER TWO

Unable to get away from the old woman fast enough, Sahmara wrenched the wooden door open. The remains of her threadbare shift caught on the latch and ripped from her body as she fled. Her feet dug into the cool sand of the beach, sending sprays of sand out behind her with every step. Naked, she leaped into the white-capped surf.

She spent a few moments scrubbing wet sand over her skin until she felt slightly less unclean. While she worked, the current pulled her further from shore. Suddenly the bottom went out from under her feet. Salty water rushed into her mouth. She came to the surface, sputtering.

The chill of the neck-deep water took her breath away. At least she was still breathing, she thought as she fluttered her arms and sought out footing on the mushy sea floor. Hearing a voice over the cries of the gulls and crash of the waves, she looked to the beach.

Reva held up the tattered rag that had been her shift. The old woman's lips were moving, but Sahmara couldn't make out the words. She scuttled back inside the shack.

A tingling sensation started in her finger where it had been cut. At first, Sahmara thought it was the ocean salt but when she examined her finger, she found the cut had vanished.

Caught in her amazement, she didn't notice the giant wave coming at her until it knocked her off her feet. The torrent of water dragged her under. Sahmara panicked, raking the water with her hands to no avail.

The wave passed over, allowing her feet to again settle on

the bottom. Silt squished between her toes as she thrust her head above the water. She coughed and gagged until the sea had cleared from the lungs. After several ragged breaths, she lurched her way back toward shore. Naked on land was better than drowned in the sea.

The sand and sky were out of focus. Disoriented, she stumbled onto the sand and sat down with a heavy thump. The gulls seemed louder than before. The waves hummed as they washed into the shoreline.

Sahmara clutched her knees and rested her forehead on them. She took a deep breath and picked up her head, letting the breath out slowly and steady through her nose. There, that was better.

She looked at her finger again, smooth and clean now. Had she imagined the old woman cutting her and sucking her blood? Sahmara reached up to wring the water from her hair. Her hands met with a smooth scalp.

She screamed as she ran her hands over her bare head. Hysterical laughter escaped from her lips.

A soft voice called out, "Ya needed to be cleansed."

She whirled around but no one was there. Great, now she was imagining voices. Using her hands, she covered herself as best as she was able. She scanned the upper cliff and the path and Reva's home. Still, she saw no one. She wasn't prepared to be crazy.

"Who's there? Where are you?"

The voice returned, sweet and filled with the ocean breeze. "I am everywhere."

"I don't understand." Sahmara crept toward Reva's shack. Even a bloodthirsty old woman was better than an otherworldly voice from nowhere.

"Go inside. All ya need will be found there." A light tinkling laughter fell around her. "Remember little mite, the ocean is your friend."

"Reva?" The voice was all wrong, but a feeling of ease and surety came over her. Sahmara pushed open the wooden door. There was no sign of the old woman or the rags she had picked up off the beach.

A neat pile of folded clothing sat on the table. Freezing, Sahmara grabbed the top piece and shook it out. It was a soft, thick, linen shirt. She slid it over her head and pulled it down, working her arms into the long sleeves. The shirt hung loose and halfway to her knees, like the shirts her father's workers wore. At the moment, she didn't care that it wasn't a fine silk dress. She was warm, and she was grateful.

The next item was a pair of loose woolen leggings and beneath them, thick, woolen socks. Warmer and more comfortable than she'd been in months, Sahmara smiled.

"Thank you, Reva, wherever you are." The feeling of rightness enveloped her once more.

Tall, brown leather boots sat on the bench. They were worn, but the soles were in good shape. She slipped them on. They fit perfectly.

Sahmara stood, taking a few tentative steps in the boots. They were very different than the silk slippers she'd worn all her life, tight and unyielding. Far different than going barefoot as she had been as well. By her third practice lap around the table, she realized that her bruised, cut, and perpetually sore feet were quite comfortable.

"You're welcome." Tinkling laughter taunted her like a half-heard whisper.

Sahmara examined the rest of the shack. She was alone. Nothing was out of place. The fire was cold. There was nowhere for anyone to hide. She went back to the table and sat down on the bench. Something clunked onto the floor.

Peering beside the table, Sahmara saw a long, intricately carved wooden bow lying in the dirt. Propped up next to the table, beside where the bow must have been sitting, was a quiver full of finely fletched arrows.

She sucked in a breath, running her fingers over the ridges and valleys of the carved bow that she swore hadn't been there when she'd put on the clothes. Setting the bow on the table, she stared at it. The design was beautiful, but she couldn't decide what it actually was. It was as if it blurred right before her eyes, giving her only the impression of being a work of beauty.

Sahmara dropped her head into her hands, where they met with her unfamiliar smooth scalp. Tears of confusion ran down her cheeks. Wasn't it bad enough to have been ripped from her home and defiled? Now she was crazy and bald, and voices and weapons came from thin air. And she was still lost, alone, and who knew how far from home.

She sighed and reached down to grab the quiver. Her hand met with something hard and cold instead. She yelped.

Peeking downward, she saw an earthen jug with a leather strap sitting next to the quiver. She picked it and the quiver up, setting them on the bench beside her. Sahmara removed the stopper to find it filled with water. She lifted the jug and took a long drink.

Suddenly, a wonderful smell assailed her nose. She set the jug aside to see a wooden plate of steaming, browned meat and a loaf of warm, dark bread had appeared on the table where the clothes had been. The clothing hadn't hurt her and the bow and jug would be of great help. No matter how out of sorts she was, the gift of a much-needed meal wasn't something her stomach was willing to turn down. She tore into the feast set before her.

With her stomach full and her body warm, the urge to take a nap overwhelmed her. Sahmara retrieved the blanket from beside the fire and lay down on the pallet. She closed her eyes and wished that when she woke, all would be right with the world again.

As she lay here, half-asleep, she pondered what exactly was right anymore. Would she be happy to see Reva sipping from her chipped cup or would it take waking in her own bed, safe and surrounded by thick doors and a servant to attend to her needs? Given what she'd been through over the past months, would it be enough just to wake at all?

ଧଓଖ

Sahmara woke to the sight of the bow on the table and the skittering of a mouse finishing off the bread crumbs she'd left on the plate. She sat up on the pallet to discover she was still dressed like a man, albeit a very skinny one.

Without her hair to weigh her head down, she felt lighter than ever before and the uncomfortable itching that had accosted her a week into her captivity was gone.

She got up and went to the door. The sun shone brightly in the lower half of the sky. Reva's warning of only staying a day echoed through her mind.

It seemed Reva and the voice were one and the same. Losing her hair and a little blood were only two more things to add to her list of losses in this land. At least she gained something this time. The old woman had said for her to go South. Toward home. She wasn't about to argue with that.

Sahmara slung the water jug over one shoulder and the quiver over the other. As she reached for the bow, she looked longingly at the blanket. If she was right, Reva wouldn't need it. Sahmara picked up the blanket.

It struck her that there was not a single white hair on it. Even more disturbing, there were no footprints in the dirt around the pallet other than her own. Her heart beat faster and her mouth went dry.

The cups and the bag of tea leaves, she thought, surely those would prove Reva had been there. She scanned the table and the crooked shelf on the wall. No cups. No bag of tea leaves. No sign of the knife that had cut her finger. And the cut had healed. Had she wandered to the shack in a fever dream? But the bow beckoned her from the table, confirming that something had indeed happened here and it hadn't been a dream. A nightmare, perhaps. Only time would tell.

She grabbed the bow and the blanket and headed out into the sand. Snippets of the dreams she'd had the night before flooded her mind with the sunlight. She'd seen Zane, a slave with the mark of a whip on his back. Chains bound his feet and despair colored his eyes. She'd seen a band of weary and filthy soldiers fighting men in Atherian uniforms. She'd seen many things, buildings and fields set afire, bodies laying in the streets and swords glinting in the sunlight.

A feeling of urgency tugged at her heart, pulling her down the shoreline. That was where she needed to go. She was sure of it.

She eyed the cliff wall and then the beach. The voice had said the ocean was her friend. Closer to it had to be better, even if the walking was more difficult.

After an hour of walking on the shifting grains, her legs grew tired. She began to question her choice, but the rocky cliffs remained steady to her side and a convenient trail to follow upwards didn't appear. Sand had worked its way into her boots and shortly thereafter into her socks to scrub against the soles of her feet with each weighted step. How did her father's men caravan for weeks? She paused to switch the quiver and the water jug, swapping the heavier burden to the other shoulder. With the blanket tucked around the strap of the water jug, she set off again.

Sahmara glanced over her shoulder. No sign of Reva's shack or the rocky cove that protected it remained. Only shoreline, sand and the glimpse of grasses atop the cliffs to her left kept her company. There was no point in looking back. She straightened her back and strode forward.

By nightfall, the land bridge was nowhere in sight but the shoreline was constant to her right. The feeling of rightness was still firmly lodged in her heart. She wasn't lost. She was just far from home…without any shelter and in enemy lands.

She spotted a hefty log, thrown upon the shore by some ambitious wave. Sahmara set down her meager belongings and used her hands to scoop out a shallow impression on the far side. With her quiver, bow and water jug tucked up against her, she drew the tattered blanket over her tightly balled body and slept.

Morning found her reasonably well rested, though sore from her cramped sleeping conditions. She took a drink from the water jug to calm her hungry stomach and gathered up her things. Her stomach growled again. She couldn't exist on water alone, not if she had to stay on her feet for days.

Her friends and mother had always poked at her, saying she had a little extra meat on her bones. Several months of barely eating what little the Atherians had offered had taken care of that. She ran her hands over her baggy shirt, feeling the prominent ridges of her ribs. If only they could see her now. If only she could see any of them now. What had become of her friends when the Atherians took the city?

She tried not to think about it. It was bad enough to be out here alone, she didn't need more dire thoughts racing through her head. They were home, sitting beside their fires, doing their needlework and waiting to whisper all the best gossip. That at least brought a smile to her chapped lips.

Spoiled by the big meal of meat and bread the day before, her empty stomach rumbled again. She needed to eat. If not now, soon. Sahmara took the bow from her shoulder and examined the taut string.

She'd seen men practice with bows, launching their arrows at straw-filled burlap in the courtyard. She pulled the string back as she'd seen them do. It was much harder than she'd imagined. Her arms shook. She let the string go. The smooth fibers bit into the tender underside of her forearm.

"Ouch!" She dropped the bow and rubbed her arm. After a moment to regain her determination, she retrieved the bow and pulled the string back again. The carved wood arced silently. She pretended to take aim and then eased up on the string slowly.

Feeling daring, she chose an arrow from the quiver and backed away from the log. She kept her fingers far from the sharp metal tips and nocked the arrow. She pulled the string back again. With the log twenty paces away, it seemed as good a target as any. Sahmara aimed and then loosed her arrow. The string thwapped her arm and the arrow flew three feet and fell to the sand.

Sahmara set the bow down and rubbed the red welt on her arm. The stupid men in the courtyard had made it look so easy, shooting off arrow after arrow and sinking them into the straw-filled targets. Why, when she needed to feed herself, did it have to be so difficult?

She set the quiver in the sand next to her and got another arrow ready. Her arm shook as she pulled the string back.

The arrow launched into the air, making it halfway to the log. She blew upward, realizing it was a silly thing to do since the only hair on her forehead was imaginary. She let out an aggravated groan instead and nocked another arrow. By the last one, she came to the conclusion she might be going hungry for awhile. Only one had made it to the log, though at an angle that caused it to bounce off ineffectively into the sand near all the others. She consoled herself with the fact that they were at least all pointing in the right direction.

Sahmara retrieved the arrows and then gathered up her things. Setting off down the shoreline, the muscles in her arm protested any movement as she walked. Her welt-covered forearm throbbed. Her shoulder ached and her back hurt no matter which side she carried the water jug on. Her stomach loudly complained about her lack of hunting skills and wasn't satisfied with the cool, sweet water in the least.

She took off her boots and rolled up her leggings. Taking a single arrow with her, she waded into the water. She stared hard into the ripples, searching for a fish to spear. She stood there, hunched over until the glare of the sun burned her eyes and her back screamed and still not a single fish appeared. Mumbling curses to every living thing in the sea, she made her way back to shore, gathered up her things and headed down the beach.

By sunset, she was ready to fall over, as exhausted as when she'd escaped into the grasslands. But she'd seen no sign of pursuing soldiers and she had warm clothes. She had to admit, she was a little better off. She spent the night in a thick patch of dune grass huddled beneath her blanket.

Morning light revealed a waist-high bush nearby, covered in purple berries. Sahmara reached into the deep green leaves to grab a handful of the plump fruit. Thorns raked her bare skin. She cried out and dropped the berries.

Sucking her sore finger, she was eerily reminded of Reva. She pulled the finger from her mouth and took in her new surroundings.

The cliffs were much lower here, drifting into soft dunes further down the beach. Small round rocks littered the sand, and the beach was wider than she'd seen since leaving Reva's cove.

Two smaller bushes flanked the berry bush that had attacked her. Thorns adorned all of them. She took a deep breath and reached carefully back into the bush, plucking a single berry at a time. When she had gathered a handful, she sat on her blanket and popped one in her mouth.

A familiar tangy sweetness hit her tongue. The family cook had made pies with these before. She threw several more in her mouth, near laughing with the joy of it. Sahmara took a drink from the jug and dashed back to the bush to get her fill of the purple berries.

With her stomach full, she turned her attention to the bow. Nothing presented itself as a target so she settled for seeing how long she could shoot into the open sand.

Three of her twenty arrows flew straight. Two even ended up point down a good distance away. Pleased with her efforts and with only one new welt on her arm to show for it, she gathered up her things. Just before leaving, she plucked two handfuls of berries from the bush and wrapped them in the blanket. No need to go hungry later if her skill with the bow didn't dramatically improve before nightfall. She again headed down the beach.

By late afternoon, her legs hurt and she didn't care to ever see sand or hear waves crash again. When the sound of children playing drifted her way on the wind, her feet moved faster. Dressed as a man she wasn't as concerned with being discovered--as long as she didn't have to talk much. Everyone needed work done, maybe she could find an afternoon job that would afford her a real meal.

A ragged band of laughing children ran screaming after one another at the edge of the surf. Behind them, a cluster of houses formed safe haven on the shoreline. Beyond the children sat a line of boats tied to stakes high up on the beach by thick ropes. Other boats were just coming to shore. Sahmara didn't care if they were the enemy, it was the most welcome sight she'd seen in a long time.

The children were short and brown. The bellies on the shirtless boys looked full. That was a good sign as far as she was concerned.

As she drew closer she could make out men with thick black beards, bringing in nets from their boats. Women rushed out to meet them. The frenzy of sorting fish and reunions of couples helped to mask her entrance into the little village.

A wagon rode out to meet the fishermen, stopping where they had opened the nets high up on the shore to sort their fish. Five Atherian soldiers, swords hanging at their sides and daggers tucked in their belts, hopped down from the wagon and circulated amongst the people with woven baskets in their arms. Sahmara broke out in sweat.

With scowls and dark looks, the fishermen filled the baskets and carried them to the wagon. The armed men watched them like hawks. Once their wagon was full, they left the village.

The villagers muttered in their wake. Sahmara stood and turned to one of the women who were picking the last of the fish out of the nets. She pitched her voice as low as she comfortably could. "Hello."

The middle-aged woman looked her over, her gaze lingering on the bow on Sahmara's shoulder. "What do you want here?"

"I'm hungry." She nodded to the net. "Work for a meal?"

The woman smiled. "We always have work." She pulled out a long needle from a pouch at her waist. "You sew?"

Sahmara nodded.

"Good boys always know how to sew, even ones with weapons." The woman chuckled. She pulled out a spool of heavy thread. "All these holes. After I check it, you'll get fed."

"Thank you."

The woman carried the fish to a set of tables where other

women were cleaning them. Sahmara found a spot in the shade and got to work. Mending a net was much different than sewing silk threads through linen. At least she didn't have to worry about getting the stitches even enough to appease her mother.

"Very good." The woman smiled while checking the last of the mended spots. "We'll eat now."

Once the thought of spending an evening in the company of people who stunk like fish would have been utterly repulsive, but now Sahmara had no complaint. The woman stopped her at the door. "You eat here." She pointed to the step. "When you're done, you go."

Sahmara nodded, trying to mask her disappointment by setting her belongings on the step. The woman returned with a bowl filled with rice and fish. Sahmara ate with her fingers and listened to the family chatter about their day inside. As she chewed, she did her best to follow their conversation and mouth the words to herself.

When she'd finished eating, she left the empty bowl on the steps and set off down the beach. She didn't blame them for their distrust of a stranger. She wouldn't have given a second thought to the beggars on the street. Now she was one of them and without even street to beg on.

Early afternoon on her third day of walking, found Sahmara with an empty water jug, berry stains on her blanket and more sand in her boots than seemed possible. She'd spent the morning practicing with her bow which again left her arm and shoulder sore, but she was growing used to that.

She sat down in the dune grass and pondered the empty jug. *How am I supposed to find fresh water if I to follow the shoreline?* She glared up at the sky. "Didn't think of that did you?"

The urge to pray hit her hard. She'd never felt anything like it, a compulsion much deeper than the feeling of rightness she'd encountered when first setting off down the beach. She dropped to her knees.

Thank you, Mother, who comforts us when we most need it.

Who feeds us when our bellies cry out.
Whose waters give us life when we have not.
Our blood is yours for the life you have given us.

Her finger tingled. The hair on the back of her neck stood up. She glanced around, half expecting to see Reva's bloody lips smiling at her from the dune grass. The fact that she didn't see anything of the sort didn't settle her nerves either.

She quickly picked up her things and started off. Two strides later, a surprising weight on her shoulder brought her to a dead stop. She pulled out the stopper on the water jug. It was full again.

"Thank you, Mother," Sahmara whispered, both her fears and hopes confirmed. She had asked. The goddess had answered. But she'd never heard of the hands of the gods playing such a personal role in the ways of men. Why her, and was a little blood from her finger all she had to pay?

CHAPTER THREE

A male voice came from the dune above, interrupting her morning bow practice. "Hey, what are ya doing there?"

After four days of silence since she'd left the fishing village, the sound of another human voice made Sahmara jump. Her arrow flew wild, sending the flock of seagulls she'd been aiming into skyward.

She whipped around to see a tall, muscular man making his way down the dune with a hand on the sword hanging at his side. His dark hair was cut raggedly just below his ears and several days worth of beard darkened his cheeks. He reminded her of the mercenaries her father often hired to protect his caravans.

She gripped her bow so hard that her knuckles turned white. "I was practicing until you scared off all my targets."

He wore leather armor on his chest and arms but if it had borne markings of either army, it had been scratched off long ago. His clothes were dark with sweat and dirt and possibly blood. She debated whether or not to reach for an arrow, but kept the bow in hand.

"Men don't usually lie still in the sand, waiting to get shot." He looked her up and down and appeared to find her wanting. "Atherian or Revocheki?"

She forced her voice to remain low and steady, though she was trembling through and through. "Depends. What about you?"

He grinned, revealing two chipped front teeth. "Scrawny, but you've got a bit of spark." He shouted over his shoulder,

"Roy, I think we'll be needing your opinion on this one."

The thought of two men against her, armed only with a bow she'd yet to hit anything living with, set her heart pounding erratically.

"I think I should be going." She shouldered her water jug and the blanket.

"Oh no ya don't sparky. Stand your ground. We'll let old Roy take a look at ya and then maybe we can all be friends."

"But I…" The words died on her tongue when Roy, dressed in a Revocheki priest's robes, albeit filthy ones, descended the hill.

Roy had the hair of a priest of Hasi, long and braided, bound with red wooden beads at the ends. His face was hard but his eyes were kind. "Don't be afraid. Yanis, quit scaring the girl." He shook his head. "She's one of ours."

Sahmara wanted to cry. Even bald and in a man's clothing, they'd seen right through her ruse. As a boy, they might be happy enough to have her tag along, but as a woman… She didn't even have the value the Atherian soldiers had assigned her anymore. She'd lost most of her curves and the scars they'd given her left her far from pretty.

Roy waved a hand in the air. "Come on out the rest of you, it seems we have another to add to our number." His gaze landed on the bow on her shoulder. "Maybe you'll make up for the two we lost days ago, eh?"

"Only if one of ya plans on training her." Yanis snickered. "She's put the fear of Hasi into the sand, but the Atherians are made of tougher stuff."

Roy approached her slowly, squinting at the bow and then finally shaking his head. "That's quite a bow ya have there. No common man would own such a thing and it would take quite a craftsman to carve it. Steal it from a temple, did you?"

"I didn't steal it." She stood still, her back straight and her hand tight on the carved wood. "It was a gift."

He raised a doubtful brow. "What are we to call you?"

They might be friends or they could be lying. They were men after all, and the majority of them were foes no matter what side they were on. "Spark will do just fine."

Yanis waved her toward the dunes. "There's a patrol of Atherians only a few hours behind us, been there since the last run in. As ya may have gathered, that didn't go well on our end." He ushered her toward the low voices she heard there. Roy took up a place at her other side.

"How do you know I'm one of you?"

He fingered one of his beads. "I see with Hasi's eyes."

Sahmara sighed. There seemed to be no getting away from gods once they were invited into your life. She knew little of the Mother's twin, her father's god, other than he was worshiped by the men of her country, especially soldiers. Hasi's priests were warriors of a sort. Roy carried a sword like all the others around her. Since he was still among the living, he must have the protection of his god or at least be good with the steel at his side. Zane had been sworn to Hasi as well, and the god hadn't helped her then. She rather doubted he would now.

The others, a motley bunch, met her with nods and unimpressed looks. Some wore bloodstained Revocheki armor, carried battered swords, and bore scars and a few new wounds to prove their allegiance. The other half of the thirty men had the look of those who'd lost everything and were desperate to make someone else pay.

As much as she didn't relish the thought of their company, they greatly increased her chances of making it home alive. Sahmara stuck close to Roy, his being the only somewhat friendly face in the bunch. She struggled to keep up with his fast march. "Where are you going?"

"Home."

She chewed her lip, working up the nerve to ask, "Have you seen Sloveski? How does it fare?"

Roy shook his head causing the wooden beads to clink together. "Yanis and I were days from the border, near Antochecki, when the Atherians fell upon us. They flowed further inward after that city fell and no men have come outward to join us."

"But the city still stands, doesn't it?"

He scowled as her father did when she pestered him in the middle of his work. "We don't know, but we can hope."

"Are you going there? To the capital?" she asked.

"If all goes well. Hasi and the Mother have charged us with retaking the land they have claimed. Our land. It is their uncle, Ephius that the Atherians follow. He must not be allowed to take root in Revochek. He will become too powerful and there will be a bloody war amongst the gods."

"There's already a bloody war among men, can't the gods fend for themselves?"

Roy halted and grabbed her shoulder. "The blood they shed in their war will be ours."

She thought of Zane and her parents, her friends, the bodies she'd dreamt of lying in the streets. "They're already spilling our blood. Can things truly be worse than this?"

"Do not be so careless with your words." He stared into her eyes and then let her go. Men filed past them, giving Roy a wide berth. "Hasi and the Mother have been allowed to rule side by side because they are twins. Neither can hurt the other without suffering themselves. The rest of their family is divided by greed, kept only in balance by the fact that until recently, they have all been equal."

Sahmara followed after the men, not wanting to get left behind. Roy stuck right by her side.

"If that is true, how was Atheria able to attack with our gods protecting us?"

"One does not question the gods," Roy snapped.

Hasi's brusque priest said little to endear her to the Mother's twin. She'd trust the Mother to keep her safe. Sahmara sped up until she found a clear pocket in the crowd of men. Roy didn't follow, but she could feel him watching her and it made her skin crawl. His utter and imposing conviction made her remember why she'd left her mother to her religion and found other things to busy herself with during devotions.

He might not be the ally she wanted, but he seemed to be in charge and if she wanted the others to leave her alone, she'd need Roy. Which meant she'd need to find a way to truly gain his favor.

Walking alone for days at her own pace was one thing, but near jogging amidst the odor of thirty unwashed men was quite another. They cast envious glances at her water jug each time they paused to rest for a few moments. She didn't dare share. What if they didn't hand the jug back? Already at the bottom of the ranks and with her only ally annoyed with her, she couldn't afford to take any chances.

Evening brought a new level of discomfort as the men hovered around the embers of the cooking fire sharing conversations while she ate. The occasional glances in her direction confirmed their topic of discussion. Roy sat among them, scowling. Occasionally he spoke, but she couldn't make out what he said.

Sitting in the dirt with her back against a tree, apart from the group, she ate the barely cooked strip of meat she'd been offered. She kept her belongings close. If they started coming after her, she'd run.

Yanis broke from the group. He didn't meet her gaze or even seem to notice her as he walked over to sit down nearby. Nor did he say a word as he wrapped his cloak about himself and lay down with his back to her.

He might not have been the most friendly of men, and he had made fun of her lacking archery skills, but at least he wasn't ogling her or demanding that she do anything in return for traveling with them. With his arrival, the others stopped leering in her direction and slowly drifted to their belongings and settled in for the night.

She covered herself with the blanket, wishing it were a thick wall with a barred door and watched the men until the embers faded, leaving them all in darkness. Even then, she listened but heard nothing other than a gentle wind through the branches and someone's snoring. Her muscles knotted up so tight that her head would barely turn.

Though the air was warmer here, farther from shore, her blanket didn't begin to subdue the chills that racked her body. She put one hand on her bow and wrapped the strap of the water jug around the other. If the Mother truly was watching out for her, she wouldn't let the men touch her, would she? Sahmara whispered a quick prayer and fell into a restless sleep.

A hand shook her shoulder. "Come on, Spark. We must be moving."

Her eyes sprang open to darkness and a shadow looming over her. She swung the bow at the would-be attacker.

Yanis jumped back. "Glad to see ya wake into action." He helped her to her feet. "We'll make the border today if we don't meet with trouble."

Home. That one word urged her on. Soon she would be back in her house. Her father would know where to find Zane. The Mother must have meant for her to find these men so that she could get there safely. Yet, the feeling of peace that she expected with that thought did not come.

A two-hour march through shadowed hills delivered them into daylight. Roy moved amongst the men with an opened cloth in his hands. When he came closer, Sahmara saw that he was handing out biscuits. He handed her half of one. She took the hard, heavy lump and sunk her teeth into it.

A peculiar taste made her pull the biscuit back to examine it. Green bits of mold speckled the surface. She spat out the bite in her mouth.

Roy's thin lips scowled. "Don't waste it. That's all you'll be getting til dinner."

"I won't. Just surprised me, that's all." She forced a second bite into her mouth and chewed. Even the watery broth she'd eaten as a slave was better than this, but if she angered him more, he might leave her behind.

"Good. We'll be at the border soon. I expect you to keep a lookout. You're the only archer we've got. I hope you can hit something other than sand."

Sahmara bit her lip as Roy walked away to continue handing out their meal. She spotted Yanis up at the front. That was far too close to danger if they were attacked. She found an open space towards the middle of the group and did her best to keep pace with the others.

The thought of an actual battle petrified her. She was supposed to be working on the set of fine embroidered linens in preparation for an auspicious marriage and a new home. She should be sitting near a window to catch the morning light, dreaming of the man her father would choose for her and blushing over what Zane had taught her the night before when they'd snuck off together. Sahmara certainly wasn't supposed to be wandering the Atherian countryside in the company of coarse soldiers. She gripped the swaying jug with one hand and her bow with the other to hide her trembling hands.

Loosely wooded stretches gave way to open windy flatland. Moist air signaled that they were getting closer to the coastline again. An arrow hissed through the air. It sunk deep into the shoulder of the man to Sahmara's left.

"Spark!" Someone shouted through the pounding in her ears. "We need some help here."

Sahmara stared dumbly as another arrow found a home in the dirt at her feet. She mouthed a prayer to the Mother and slid the bow from her shoulder. Men spilled from the trees. She fumbled for an arrow and brought it to the string.

The man to her right let loose a battle cry that sent chills up from the base of her spine to the top of her scalp. She wanted to run, to hide, to be anywhere else but here, but there were men and swords surrounding her and short of turning into a bird or a burrowing creature, there was nowhere to hide.

She set her feet firmly in the dirt and pulled back the string. Sahmara aimed at the men running toward them with swords in their hands.

One of the enemies fell. Then another and another as her arrows flew. The words of the prayer to the Mother tumbled through her mind and out of her mouth with each arrow she loosed.

"It's over, Spark," Roy's voice broke her trance.

She shook her head, chasing away focus the Mother had given her. Men rolled in the grass, clutching at wounds. Members of her group went among them, slicing throats and scavenging weapons, armor and coins. Her arrows stuck out of many of the dead and dying. Only two remained in her quiver. If she meant to fight again, she'd need them.

With bile rising in her throat, she crept over to her nearest victim. The others appeared cold and callous as they went about their necessary business. Sahmara tried to be the same. She yanked the arrow from the man's ribs. Her finger tingled.

The man let out a horrible, low rumbling groan. Her stomach heaved, sending the moldy biscuit into the grass beside him. "I'm so sorry."

She left him to the others, having need of nothing more than her arrows and to get her task done as quickly as possible. With the red tipped arrow gripped tightly in one hand, she moved to the next man. Her arrow had pierced his neck. Not seeing any sign of life, she took a deep breath and pulled. His entire body spasmed. Blood shot from the wound, spraying her chest and arm. Again her finger tingled. His mouth opened and closed several times as his blue eyes looked at her beseechingly. Hot tears ran down her cheeks. Her stomach threatened to heave again. She breathed through her nose and continued on.

The next arrow was lodged in a chest. Vacant eyes stared up at her, a woman's eyes. From her smooth face, Sahmara guessed she was only a few years older than herself. Tears welled, but she refused to let them fall. Would this woman have cried over her dead body? Doubtful. It wouldn't be good for the others to see her weeping over the enemy.

Her hand filled with arrows. Sahmara noticed the men looking at her warily. She resolved to do whatever she could to make them think twice about laying a hand on her.

Each bloody arrow brought the now familiar tingle to the finger Reva had cut open. Was the Mother sucking the blood of each of Sahmara's victims just as Reva had lapped at her finger? She'd never considered that the line about blood in the Mother's prayer might be quite so literal.

Yanis came to her side. "Wipe the blood off in the grass. Quickly. We must go."

Sahmara dutifully wiped the arrow heads on the deep green blades until they were mostly clean. With her quiver again full, she rejoined the milling men. They continued onward, making their way to the land bridge that would lead them all home.

The sun had just passed overhead when she made out the crashing of waves on a rocky shore. Home was within reach.

She turned to look behind her, to say farewell to the land that had treated her so cruelly, but circling birds caught her attention. She felt sick all over again, envisioning the carrion birds feasting on the fallen. That she could well have been one of them did nothing to soothe her nerves. The border might be near but her home lay many days away, and the birds weren't far behind.

CHAPTER FOUR

Roy fell into step beside her. He cast her a sideways glance. "Well, well little Spark, it seems you have a gift with that beautiful bow after all. Where did you learn how to use it?"

"Nowhere."

Gulls circled overhead signaling the sea was again near. The wind carried moisture and a chill that settled under her skin. After the battle and the long walk, she wanted to be left alone. Even better than being alone, she wanted a bath to wash off the blood that had splattered on her arms and dried. A hot bath, steaming and slick with fragrant oils, oh how she missed those. That would make the blood go away, wouldn't it?

Roy's steps were solid and sure in the loose sandy soil. His robes blew against her legs. When she didn't elaborate on her experience, he shook his head. "We'll reach the border soon. Keep an eye out."

She nodded, silently wishing him away.

Roy wandered further up the line to talk with some of the others. She couldn't hear his words, nor did she want to. The distant quiet conversations of others helped to lull her mind, distracting her from the annoyance of the low running prickly vines that snaked through the dune grass, catching on her boots.

When they did reach the land bridge that served as a border, it was nothing as grand as Sahmara had envisioned. The last time she'd crossed over the windswept expanse of rocks and sand she'd had a hood over her head. The only cover the bridge allowed were scraggly, bent trees that had driven their roots into the crevices in the flat grey rock. The bark looked like large scales and short dark green needles sprouted from the branches.

While she appreciated the fact that she was moving of her own accord and could take in her surroundings this time, she longed for some familiar sight of home. There was nothing here that was any different than what she'd been walking through for the last week.

Each footstep ruined the perfection of the wind-etched waves on the white sand. With her head up, she plodded on, keeping her pace steady beside the four others who joined her behind Yanis.

"We gotta move faster," said the grey-bearded man beside her. "Too little cover here. Too easy to spot."

"But didn't we take care of the men who had been following us?" Sahmara asked.

"Could be more. Them Atherians like to break into small groups. Could be some after us yet."

Word came up from Roy to halt for a short rest. The old man beside her scowled and shook his head.

Yanis turned, looked at the sky and then their surroundings. "Can't stay long but a few minutes rest would be welcome."

The men around her nodded and set about shifting their weapons or packs to less sore shoulders. Some attended to wounds, while others washed their faces and arms in the water.

Sahmara set her things down and went to the shoreline. Like she saw the others doing, she grabbed a handful of sand and set to scrubbing the blood from her arms. But even after she could see they were clean, the tight sensation of dried blood on her skin wouldn't go away. She longed to shed her clothes and dive into the surf in the hopes she'd come up clean like she had on Reva's beach, but there were too many men here. Going into the water clothed would mean walking for hours with wet clothing to weigh her down and that didn't sound like a good idea either.

She brushed the sand from her knees and went back to stand guard over her belongings, her shoulders grateful for even a few minutes of reprieve.

Yanis pulled a tattered rag, stained shades of brown and red, from around his forearm and grimaced. Fresh red blood stood out in the sunlight. Though he said little to her, he spent each night nearby. Whenever he was around, the others left her alone. She couldn't afford to have him fall in the next attack if he were too weak from his wound.

She made her way over to him. "Do you need help with that?"

"I'll be fine," he said through clenched teeth. Yet, he didn't protest when she reached out to take the bandage from him.

Sahmara caught a glimpse of a deep cut. Blood oozed from it. "You should wash that out." She glanced at the milling men. "Is there a healer among them?"

"Not anymore." He glared at her. "You're a woman, or near enough. Don't you know something?"

The edges of the skin around the cut were deep red and swollen. Dark tendrils darted away from the wound.

"I…here, let me wash it." She fumbled with her jug, splashing some of the clean, clear water onto his arm. The few things she knew of healing could be counted on one hand. He needed far more than her.

Yanis gasped as the water flooded into the open cut. Sahmara took his filthy bandage between two fingers and held it up. "Do you have anything not so dirty?"

"Everything is dirty," he snapped. "If you hadn't noticed, we're on the run. Anything clean was used months ago. Just wash it out. Hurry, the others are tired of waiting. If we take much longer, they'll leave us behind."

"They won't leave you behind." She'd seen the men look to Yanis. Though he didn't appear to give the orders, they respected him as much as the priest. She poured water from her now half full jug onto the filthy cloth with little effect.

"We don't have time for this." He wrenched the water jug downward, sending a torrent of water over her arm and the cloth.

Her sleeve was soaked and her jug empty. She could fill it with a prayer, but he didn't know that, and yet, he'd used it all. And here she was, only trying to help him. "You used all my water."

"You'll be thirsty like the rest of us then." Yanis yanked the dripping bandage from her hand and hastily wound it around his arm. "Move it." He shoved her toward the others who were already leaving.

He lagged behind, leaving her to find her place in the middle of the pack. Just as well, she didn't want to be near him anyway. Unless it was night. And he didn't want anything from her. A cold sweat raced over her skin. What if he didn't sleep near her anymore? Who would come at her next and how many at once? She couldn't very well use her bow at night if she couldn't see an attacker. She needed a dagger. Next time, if she survived the next time, she'd join in the plundering of the dead and find one.

The longer they jogged onward over the sand, the more she wished just a few Atherians would appear from the water to attack them. Even just one, as long as he had a dagger. Her palm itched for the feeling of a solid hilt that promised a bit of safety for the coming night.

Waves crashed around them, making her thirsty, but the salty water would do her no good. Neither would having a full water jug when Yanis knew it to be empty. She bit back the prayer on her tongue.

Several hours of on and off jogging earned her aching legs, sore shoulders, and a dry mouth. She fought to keep up with the rest. Even having been on the run for longer than she, they were used to this pace and seemingly built for it. Hungry, miserable and incredibly tired of walking, she daydreamed of a fine carriage.

Her dreamy thoughts reminded her of all the bedraggled faces that had peered at her through the gauzy curtains of her father's carriage. She was one of those faces now. There were no cushions to soften the bumps, no cheery tinkle of the horse bells. More than the bells, she missed the familiar deep laughter of the coachman who always had a little surprise for his favorite girl. Was he home waiting for her, driving through the streets filled with bodies, searching for her?

Her heart yearned to go home, to see her parents again. They would be there. They had to be there. The Mother had shown her Zane in need of help, but not them. They had to be safe, but would they want to see her? One look would tell them what the Atherians had done. Her only remaining value lay in the bow on her back and the Mother's gift to use it.

A lump formed in her throat. Tears threatened to fall. She blinked them back, knowing they would leave telltale streaks down her dirty face.

She would go home. She would see her parents again. What had been done to her, she'd deal with that later.

Because she wanted Atherians to attack, none did. By the time the sun faded and Roy called them to a halt within a copse of trees already bare of leaves, she resolved herself to the fact that a dagger was not in her immediate future. She sought out a rock instead. Finding one she could easily carry in her hand, but with enough weight behind it to give a man pause should she hit him, she sought out a place away from the others to lay out her blanket.

Men settled on the ground, some creating shelters by leaning branches against fallen logs, others simply sitting against the trees with their cloaks wrapped around them. One went looking for water, others checked their wounds or sharpened their blades. All of them looked tired and on edge. Roy wandered past tossing a thumb-size portion of rock-hard biscuit into her lap. "This the last of them. We'll be hungry in the morning unless someone comes up lucky."

She wasn't sure which was worse, going hungry or putting the moldy lump into her mouth. A shout sounded in the distance. The pounding of a multitude of feet rushed towards them. Sahmara uttered a quick prayer to the Mother and threw the biscuit and rock aside. She threw her blanket over her jug and jumped to her feet.

With her bow ready, she waited for the first target to come

into view. But was he target? How did anyone know? They weren't wearing uniforms like the last ones. These men appeared as worn as the ones she was with.

A raised sword in the hand of a charging man served as the sign she needed. The ringing clash of steel filled the evening air. Beside her, exhausted men weren't fighting with the same gusto they had earlier. Two went down quickly, leaving a clear path to where she stood.

Panicking, she fumbled with her next arrow. Time seemed to slow and the sounds of the battle faded into nothing more than her heartbeat that matched the heavy footfalls of the narrow-eyed men coming directly for her.

Arrows would do her little good in close quarters. She dropped the bow and scrambled over the dead men at her feet, managing to locate the dagger she'd been dreaming about all day tucked into one of their belts.

The only thing she'd ever done with a knife was to cut meat at the dinner table. These men were not on a plate and there was no fork to hold them down.

Two men came at her at once with swords in hand. One man sliced at the scant air that separated them. A line of pain erupted on her shoulder. Sahmara cried out.

She ducked, stepping backward as quickly as she dared amidst the men all around her who were also fighting for their lives. None of them would be coming to her rescue.

Determined not to become breakfast for crows, Sahmara made a mad stab at the nearest man. The blade bounced off his rusty mailed shirt, gaining her nothing but skinned knuckles.

Her opponent laughed, a low, cruel rumble. The second man dodged behind her. She lunged at him again only to find her feet swept out from underneath her. Sahmara landed hard on her back.

She gasped, sucking air back into her lungs, and rolled away from them. They were right on top of her. One jabbed his sword into her shoulder. The other reached for her. She lashed out with the dagger, slicing him in the arm.

The man leaped back, knocking into the other. She got to

her feet, scanning the chaos for a path of escape. A wet gagging noise drew her attention back to the men. One of them held his throat. The other raised his sword to meet Yanis.

Sahmara lunged at him, dagger in hand. While he was busy fending Yanis off, she sunk the short blade into his back. Her finger tingled as he spasmed and dropped his sword. Yanis finished him off quickly.

Before she could gather her bearings, silence fell over the camp. It took a moment to register the pain in her shoulder, and the panting and groaning of men. Familiar faces went among those still living, giving aid or quick death as necessary. Yanis stood hunched over, hands on his thighs, back heaving with each breath.

She went to him. "You should sit down."

He lifted his head, blinking rapidly as if trying to focus. Sweat glistened on his face and dripped from his hair. His sword lay in the dirt at his feet.

She took his good arm and guided him to the ground next to the men he'd just killed. His skin was burning. On her knees beside him, she reached for his injured arm. He didn't protest.

Sahmara pulled back the still damp bandage. The tendrils of infection had wrapped themselves around his arm. She pushed up his sleeve to see they had traveled as far as the cloth would give her access.

Past caring if he questioned her, she ran for her belongings, said a prayer and lugged the now filled jug to his side. She opened it and poured water into his mouth. Maybe the Mother's water was magic. It would heal him. She prayed for that too. He gulped at the water as if he couldn't get enough. Finally, she pulled the jug away and set it beside her.

Roy should be able to help, he was a priest after all. Didn't they know something of healing? She tried to spot him amidst the others.

Yanis leaned against her, his head lolling onto her shoulder.

"Hang on, I'll find help." The Mother's water had to work. If it didn't, Roy had Hasi on his side. Hasi protected his soldiers. Both gods couldn't just stand by and let Yanis die.

One of the others, a younger man with dark skin approached her. "Is he..."

"Find Roy."

He nodded and darted off.

Was it just the old wound or was it something new, something maybe she could do something about? She laid him out on the ground. Without much light, it was hard to determine what else might be wrong. Everything was dark-- sweat, blood, dirty clothing.

She slipped her hands under the leather sleeveless shirt he wore over a linen one. It came out wet. While his chest was visibly rising and falling, she wasn't sure that it would continue to do so for much longer. She tugged the heavy shirt up to the new wound and then gently peeled the wet linen from his skin. Blood trickled from the puncture, running down his protruding ribs and into the dirt. Her finger tingled.

"Don't. You can't have this one," she said to air around her. If Yanis had a pack she would have searched it for something to hold against the wound, but she didn't recall ever seeing him with one. All she had was her blanket. She chewed her lip.

Around her, shadows moved between the fallen, plundering and consolidating belongings. Maybe if she fed the Mother, the goddess would be more inclined to help. She left Yanis's side, yanking arrows from the fallen as she quickly worked her way around the dead. Her finger tingled with each one.

"Take theirs, but not his," she whispered.

Sahmara shoved the arrows into her quiver, slung it over her back and raced back to his side.

Roy stood over Yanis. "Ah, there you are. Are you well enough?"

"No, my shoulder...but him." She pointed at Yanis.

The priest stared down him, scowling. He crouched down and ripped off the sleeve from Yanis's shirt. "You won't be needing that anymore."

He spun Sahmara sideways and wound the cloth around her shoulder. "We do need your bow. Don't let that get infected."

"But—"

His forehead furrowed as he got to his feet. "But what?"

"Shouldn't you pray for him? Can't your Hasi do something?"

Roy shook his head. "That man gave up on his god months ago. Couldn't do anything about it then or now."

Her mouth hung open. "You can't just—"

"Get up, girl. We've got to be moving.

"We can't just leave him."

"He's of no further use to us. Those that are living have to keep moving forward, or we'll be just like him."

The man she'd sent for Roy stood behind him, looking at Yanis. He bowed his head, and after a few seconds walked away.

"Look." She rested her hand on Yanis's chest. "He's not even dead yet."

"If you're so concerned with the fact, give the man his peace. Either way, I need you on your feet." Roy turned away and melded with the others who were shouldering their belongings.

Yanis stirred. "Don't leave me," he whispered.

She looked between Roy's retreating shape and Yanis' helpless form. "Go ahead," she shouted to the nearest shadow. "I'll catch up shortly."

The dark-faced man came closer. "We can't afford to lose you, Spark. Leave him."

"I'll be right there."

He nodded and left her. Sahmara took Yanis's hand.

His eyes remained closed but he squeezed her hand weakly. "I don't want to die alone."

"You're not alone." Would he have stayed behind for her? With a heavy heart, Sahmara watched her safety depart the battlefield and drift away into the night. When she turned back to him, his half-focused gaze was aimed at her.

"What's your real name?"

She figured it wouldn't do any harm telling him now. "Sahmara."

"Thank you, Sahmara." He fought for a breath. The next one never came.

Tears slipped down her cheeks, landing on his still face. The moonlight shone in his empty blue eyes. "You're welcome."

She sat with him, reciting the prayer for the dead. She'd heard it plenty of times that day from Roy.

As stillness settled around her, she became more aware that she was sitting alone in a field of bodies. Her skin turned to gooseflesh. How far ahead were the others? Would they walk through the night or camp close by? A sense of urgency lit within her.

Sahmara stood, intending to leave but the thought of leaving Yanis, who had saved her, to the crows made her ill. The sandy soil was cold but easy to dig.

An hour later, she strained to pull his body into the hole she had made. Once his body was inside, she was disheartened to find it wasn't as deep as she'd thought.

Guilt settled over her for taking what little he had but she knew he'd expect it of her. She set aside his sword, dull and nicked, but useful nevertheless. The tattered scabbard didn't seem quite long enough for the sword it held, but she buckled the thick leather belt around her waist and took a few steps. The scabbard felt awkward against her leg and her elbow hit the pommel of the sword. This was going to take some getting used to. She slid the dagger she'd used earlier between the belt and where it rested snuggly against her thick shirt.

She pocketed his scant handful of coins and left him whatever other secrets he might have carried. The longer she spent with Yanis, the chances of finding the others dwindled. She settled for piling sand on top of him while trying not to dwell on the thought that the wind would likely uncover him in a day or two, only delaying the birds' feast.

She slung her bow over one shoulder and the water jug and quiver over the other with the blanket rolled up in the straps. Feeling quite weighed down with the addition of the sword, she went in search of the trail the others had left behind.

Trampled grasses formed a fairly clear path to follow. While that boded well for her, the ease it offered their enemies made her cringe. Maybe they'd finally managed to kill everyone who was attempting to track them down. The unease in her gut told her not to bet on it.

Sahmara was down to a trudging half-asleep walk when a hand shot out of the night and knocked her off her feet.

"Who goes… Oh, hey, Spark." A man with heavily calloused hands helped her to her feet. "Sorry about that. It's dark and—" He didn't let go.

"It's okay." She shook him off and checked her bow to make sure her fall hadn't damaged it.

"Didn't know if you'd make it back to us."

"Bart, isn't it?"

"Yeah."

"How many did we lose tonight?" She'd known there were too many bodies for them to be all Atherian.

"Eight. Shame to lose Yanis. He was good with that sword of his."

"Yes, he was." The weight of his sword had caused her to adjust her gait, which in turn had made her back ache enough that she felt it over her the throbbing in her wounded shoulder. She wished it was Yanis carrying it beside her instead. Sahmara gazed up at the silver moon, the last thing he'd seen. "He saved my life."

"He saved all of us at one time or another, but I can't say as any of us would have stayed behind for him."

"I guess I'm not like the rest of you." She walked past Bart and found an open spot that offered security of their numbers without men right next to her. Almost all of them were asleep. The hopefully empty darkness called to her exhausted body.

She set down the water jug, bow, and quiver and then laid out her blanket. Sitting on it, she removed the sword from the scabbard. Once she'd wrapped half the blanket over her, she rested her hand on the hilt as she'd seen Yanis do at night. Safe as she could be, Sahmara closed her eyes.

Rumblings of her empty stomach announced that morning

had arrived. Though the sun had barely cleared the horizon, the others were on their feet and packing up their gear.

Roy picked his way over. "Glad to see you made it back to us."

"How long until we reach home?"

He scanned the trees ahead of them and the grassy dunes that they had passed through the night before. "We are home, though we might as well still be in Atheria. They hold control of Revochek, and I promise you they won't be welcoming us." His gaze went to Yanis' sword as she slid it home. "I see you've gained a sword. I hope you know how to use it."

She didn't have the first idea, but that hadn't stopped her from learning how to use the bow. Maybe the Mother would help with the sword as well.

Sahmara joined the others on their fast march set by legs longer than her own. The sword chaffed against her thigh and her shoulder hurt. When Roy called a stop several hours later, she slumped down on the spot and took a long drink from her water jug.

The men alongside her watched her every movement with longing. Bart licked his dry lips. She felt confident that the men knew she was competent with a weapon, yet she wasn't comfortable with them.

She was needed, but not included. A woman who was one of them, but not of them. Making friends had never been her strong suit.

"Would you like a drink?" She offered the jug to the man next to her.

The man eagerly took the jug from her hand and drank deeply. Rather than hand it back to her, he passed the jug to the next man. The jug traveled further and further away. Sahmara's heart sunk. She'd never see the jug again. Just like all other men, these would take without a second thought.

She got up and put some distance between herself and the others. Her jaw dropped when the man who had lingered behind the night before tapped her shoulder and placed the empty jug in her hands.

"Sorry, we drank it all. The men appreciate ya sharing with us."

Refilling the jug took little more than a prayer but having it willingly returned to her was priceless. "You're welcome."

He left her side without another word, leaving her in the space she'd created for herself. When Roy waved them all back to their feet, Sahmara rejoined them. Some nodded in her direction, one mumbled his thanks. They fell into an easier pace and walked onward until nightfall.

Back in their homeland, Roy allowed them a small fire. Someone had offered up two rabbits that now sizzled over the low flames. The meat would likely be warmed rather than cooked, but as hungry as she was, Sahmara didn't care.

The dark-faced man approached her again. "I'm Olando."

She nodded.

He shifted from foot to foot and rubbed the back of his neck with one hand before dropping it to his side and shaking it out. "Would ya like to refill your jug? We found a small stream over there." He pointed through the bushes behind them.

"Yes." She tossed the leather strap over her shoulder and got to her feet. With one hand on her dagger, she followed him. None of the others paid them any mind as they walked past. If he meant to force himself on her, he meant to do it alone. Part of her wanted him to try. Now that she was armed, she could make him pay for what the others had done to her.

He glanced over his shoulder as if waiting for her to say something.

They'd been walking together for days, fighting for their lives. He knew her name. They all did. Saying hello felt silly. It wasn't a pleasure to meet him, and she certainly wasn't in the mood for small talk. Sahmara kept silent and followed him on the narrow trail through the bushes.

"Deer use the path." He stopped and turned around. "Wouldn't have found it if it weren't for the game trail. The water moves slowly here, but it's clean and sweet."

Sweat broke out on her palms. She couldn't see the fire

anymore and she couldn't hear the low voices of the men around it. Would he push her to the ground now? Perhaps press her back against a tree? Her grip on the dagger tightened.

"It's right here." He stepped aside to allow her down to the water's edge. "Watch out, the edge is lined with muck."

Would he push her in? She made sure to keep him in plain sight as she crouched down and dipped the jug in the water. She couldn't see his face in the shadows cast by the trees overhead, but she felt his eyes upon her.

"I saw ya had Yanis' sword. Do ya know how to use it?"

She pulled the half-filled jug from the ice cold stream and braced herself for his attack. "No, but I do know how to use the dagger in my hand."

Olando chuckled. "No worries, Spark. I wouldn't cause ya harm. Roy would have my hide if I did, and Yanis's ghost would haunt me the rest of my days."

"What do you mean?"

"Ya might be a woman and I might be a lonely man, but you're the only archer we got. And a damned good one too. I want to make it home alive and your bow improves my odds. I aim to keep ya alive. Now, do ya know how to use the sword or not?"

Sahmara stood and slung the jug over her shoulder. "No."

He gave her a gentle push back onto the path. "Two choices then. Carrying it around without ever intending to use it is only going to slow ya down. Hand it off to someone who can put it to good use."

"Like you, you mean?" She spun around to face him. His skin was the color of dry mud and his hair black as the sky above. The only part of him that caught the moonlight were his yellowed teeth as he grinned.

"Would be nice, I have to admit, but ya didn't let me finish." He laid his hands on her shoulders and turned her back towards camp. "Or I could show ya how to use it. Help each other out, ya know?"

She'd heard that tone from merchants dealing with her father a hundred times. A bargain had just been laid on the table. "And how does my learning to use the sword help you out?"

"I saw ya earlier today before Yanis stepped in. A dagger is handy, but it's no match for a sword." His words hung in the air, full of implication.

The dagger sat in her hand, useless. Olando wasn't a threat, not at the moment anyway. Men like the ones she'd faced today were. Yanis couldn't save her if she found herself in that situation again. If she wanted power over men bent on hurting her, she needed the knowledge Olando offered.

Sahmara glared up at the moon and hoped the Mother took note of it. She steeled her resolve. "You also said you were a lonely man."

"I did."

"When do we start?" The relief she'd hoped to feel with the sight of the fire didn't come.

"I am a poor man, Spark, but I am a man of honor. We'll start with the sword in the morning. If the lesson pleases ya, I'll take my payment at night."

As they approached the others, men turned to them and then to each other, nodding and grinning. Heat rose on Sahmara's face.

"Sit next to me," Olando whispered. He dropped down in the spot he vacated earlier.

Sahmara took a long look at them all. The men, staring at her, even Roy, all had the look of a dog who'd just caught the scent of its next meal. She'd gone off alone with one of their number, made herself willingly available to him. If she didn't want to suffer the attentions of the entire lot, she had to establish her stance right now.

However, she didn't appreciate being put in that position. Olando had cornered her nicely, but that didn't mean she had to admit it to everyone.

She held her head high and walked past him and all the men around the fire. Whispers and goading followed in her wake. She hoped Olando was squirming.

Sahmara took her time folding her blanket and checking the

bandage on her shoulder before going back to the ring of men to sit by Olando.

"I'm glad ya came back." He wrapped his arm around her waist and pulled her closer.

"Keep your hands off me," she hissed in his ear.

"Trust me, Spark. This is for your own good."

"Is that so? How about I decide what is for my own good?" She shrugged off his arm and stood.

The whispers went silent and the eyes of the entire camp were upon them.

Olando gave her a long look. He threw his head back and laughed. "Come, Spark. You're right." He patted the ground beside him.

The surrounding darkness seemed to crush the firelight, bearing down upon her. Her legs went weak and her finger tingled. "*Sit, stupid mite.*"

Sahmara laughed nervously. "Of course I'm right." She settled back down next to Olando but kept some space between them. Just when she'd found a little power in this world, men and gods took it away.

CHAPTER FIVE

"Wake up, Spark." Olando loomed over her. "Ya sleep like the dead."

Sahmara rolled to her feet with Yanis' sword in her hand. Her heart thudded in her chest. She scanned the camp to see the faint forms of sleeping men in the barest hints of dawn. "What in the Mother's name?" She regarded him with narrowed eyes. He held no sword and appeared completely at ease.

Olando held up his empty hands. "Roy didn't mind if I showed ya how to use a sword, but he won't hold up our march for it. We've got about an hour before we head out. Ya wanna learn? This is the time we got."

Another day of marching but with an hour less sleep. Sahmara groaned. Did the Mother have no mercy? She rested the sword against her leg and rubbed her hands over her face. "Fine. Fine. Where are we to practice that we won't wake the others?"

Olando headed away from the camp. She slung her bow and quiver over her shoulder and followed.

"First of all, put the sword down."

"Why?" She cocked her head. "Am I holding it wrong?"

"Yes, amongst other things."

Sahmara threw him her very best glare, the one she reserved for her mother when told to sit straighter or talk quieter or laugh softer.

He sighed. "Not your fault if ya a never had a reason to learn." Olando handed her a stout stick roughly the same length as the sword. He nodded and smiled softly. "Neither of us needs to get hurt while you're learning."

"Fair enough." Sahmara gripped the stick. For a second she considered hitting Olando upside the head and making a run for it. She was back in Revochek. Home couldn't be all that far away. Soldiers would be fewer here and allies more abundant. Surely there would be people willing to take her in and give her food.

But what if home wasn't like it used to be? The soldiers may have taken her parents away, may have set her home afire. Her father's riches might be gone, and she'd be a penniless, ruined girl all alone on the streets. Perhaps it would be best to keep her current allies for now, however distasteful they might be.

Olando shook his head. "It's not a stick to beat rats with." He came around behind her, adjusting her grip and her stance. "Now swing, like this."

Sahmara ignored his hands on her body and listened to his words, swinging and thrusting as instructed.

"Good. Now let's try it with the sword." He stayed behind her, matching her steps as she switched out the wood for the steel.

The weight of the sword was far different than the stick. It took her a few tries to get the grip right and to copy the three seemingly simple movements he'd first shown her. After seeing men madly swinging swords and crashing them into each other with all their might behind them, she felt sorely inadequate.

"Move your hips like this." He used his hands to twist her body.

She gritted her teeth and tried to focus on what he was showing her rather than his touch.

"Use your feet, Spark. Move. Come now. Men don't stand still while you're trying to kill them."

"I know." She tried again and again but ended up far more frustrated than successful. A bow was so much easier. Pull the string back, aim and release. This sword work required her entire body and it was tired and sore and the cut on her shoulder screamed in agony with each swing.

"That's enough for today." Olando came around in front of her once she put the sword away. He frowned. "Why didn't you tell me your shoulder was bleeding?"

Sahmara looked down. Blood seeped through the cloth on her shoulder. It hurt, but she didn't feel lightheaded or feverish. "It will be fine."

"Can ya still use your bow?"

He ran a hand through his tangled hair. "Roy will kill me if I've ruined our only archer."

"If I can lift the sword, I can lift the bow. It's much lighter."

"But pulling the string back?"

She nodded.

"Show me," he demanded.

Sahmara retrieved her bow and quiver. She pointed to a tree across the clearing. An arrow nocked, she pulled back the string and took aim. She'd grown used to the Mother's assistance but without a living target with blood to offer, a prayer would get her nothing.

The tree across the clearing presented itself as a suitable target. She didn't want to admit it, but her shoulder did hurt bad, and it did make it hard to hold the string back while she aimed. Sweat gathered on her brow. She released the arrow.

It shot past her intended tree with a good foot of leeway. Sahmara swore under her breath. Then she bit her lip. She didn't swear. Swearing was unseemly, the behavior of the lowborn.

Olando paced back and forth and looking at the unscathed tree in despair. "Oh damn. We're all in trouble now."

"So I missed one shot. Not a big deal."

"I've seen ya. Ya don't miss."

"I'm not perfect, Olando. I do miss."

"Not targets that are standing still." He ran a hand through his already tousled hair. "Let's pray to Hasi that the bastards leave us alone today."

"If you're going to pray you might as well ask to have them

leave us alone forever." She slung her bow over her good shoulder and headed back to the campsite.

The others were up and milling about. No one seemed shocked to see her and Olando coming back from the woods together. She wasn't sure if that made her angry or grateful. When they set out, Olando stuck close to her side. She wasn't sure if she was angry or grateful about that either.

Her shoulder ached throughout their march, making it impossible to switch sides for her bow and water jug. Whatever Olando had said to Hasi that morning seemed to have worked. During their midday break, she again shared her water with the men who had none. Evening came fast, perhaps because of the peaceful day. Their one meal consisted of late berries which were mostly dry but full of tangy flavor.

And then came the time Sahmara had been dreading since the night before.

Olando spread out his cloak next to her blanket. She closed her eyes and lay down, not even wanting to look at the man who'd stood behind her early that morning and who had quietly walked beside her all day. His arm snaked around her, pulling her back against his chest.

"There now, Spark. That's not so bad, is it? We will be warmer with the two of us." He tugged half her blanket over himself, leaving her no choice but to stay next to him unless she wanted to suffer the cold of the night.

He lay there for a moment unmoving.

She unsheathed her sword and kept one hand on it.

"I'm not going to hurt ya."

"Maybe it's not for you." And maybe it was. Either way, the nearness of Yanis's blade made her feel safer. If only Olando would be content to sleep nearby like Yanis had.

The men around them quieted down as they all settled in for the night. Somewhere around them, two men remained walking, keeping watch over the sleepers. Were they watching her? The muscles in her neck and shoulders grew as tight as her bowstring.

"Spark," Olando whispered against her neck. "You're hurt

and though we were fortunate today, I don't expect tomorrow to be so kind. Would it please you to resume our agreement tomorrow?"

The muscles in her shoulders eased as did the dread in her heart. "It would."

"Then sleep." His arm remained draped over her and the heat from his body seeped into her own, bringing a small measure of relief to her aching muscles.

For the first time since she'd left Zane's arms, she didn't so much mind being in another's. She drifted off.

The yellow dress her mother had commissioned for Sahmara's birthday fit her much tighter than anything she'd been allowed to wear before. It still covered all the improper areas, but better defined the curves that had graced her body over the past few years. Once her maid had left, she ran her hands over her hips, up her waist and over small breasts. The silken fabric did wonderful things where it rubbed against her skin, something akin to gooseflesh but far more pleasant.

Guests filled the dining room, waiting on her birthday feast. Her mother's friends and their daughters chattered away. Her father sat at the head of the table with a few of the husbands nearby, talking of wool and the going rates for sheep. As she entered the room, her attention flew to Zane's lopsided smile.

His white leathers all but shone in the candlelight and her father's dogs bowed at his feet. Truly a prince, she'd thought, come to save her from a life of boredom.

Her father stood, making the formal presentation of the gift of a Ma'Hasi to his dear daughter, to keep her safe all of her days. It was an extravagant gift. One she was sure he'd made to impress his friends as much as her suitors. Zane's calloused hand took the one she demurely offered, raising it to the slightest brush of his lips.

A rustling noise broke the magic of her dream. Sahmara's eyes flew open to the blackness of night. A thick blanket of clouds muffled the light of the moon and stars. The embers of the cooking fire outlined sleeping bodies between her and the fire's waning warmth.

The rustle came again, a quiet noise, but clear. She came fully awake. Her hand went to the sword. Her back butted against Olando. He stirred but did not wake. Where was the guard? It was probably him, clumsy with exhaustion, shuffling through the underbrush, she assured herself.

The urge to relieve herself hit hard with the chilly night air. Sahmara slid from the comfort of the blanket, took the sword in hand and headed away from the where she'd heard the rustling. No need to encounter the guard while her leggings were around her ankles.

She crouched down and took care of her business. The rustling came again, closer. She suddenly wished she'd alerted Olando of her whereabouts. Gripping the sword with one hand, she fought to pull up her leggings with the other.

A hand clamped over her mouth from behind. Another knocked the sword aside and shoved her onto her back. She squirmed, still trying to pull her pants up.

"No need for that," whispered a voice in her ear. "Saves us some time."

The man who had pushed her down settled onto her hips. "Mighty nice of ya."

She tried for her sword but the knees of the man atop her blocked her access to the blade. He yanked the dagger from her belt and handed it to the man behind her.

She bucked under his weight but couldn't dislodge him. Twisting her head did nothing more than gain her scratches from the hand over her mouth.

"What's the matter, Spark? We not good enough for ya?" Hands snaked under her shirt. "We're a little short on women. I'm afraid you'll have to do for the lot of us."

Another set of hands clamped down on her ankles, prying her legs apart. She tried to yell, but her muffled complaints met deaf ears. Hands cupped her breasts. She kicked hard and succeeded in unseating the man atop her for a second. He hissed something to the man behind her.

A cold line of steel at her throat ended her fight. "Just give us what we want and you'll live til morning." She recognized his voice. Bart.

Tears slipped from her eyes. Bristly whiskers raked across her face. "No more fighting now. We can both have some fun, eh?"

The weight on her middle eased for a moment as she heard him unlacing his leggings. Then his hands were back. He gave her breast a hard squeeze. "You've been holding out on us."

Hands reached for her hungrily, touching her in places she'd sworn no man would touch again. Olando's concern from the morning before came back to her. If he was so worried about causing her harm, would the other men have been warned by Roy too? Did they truly mean to slit her throat if she resisted or was it an empty threat? It was worth the gamble to find out.

Sahmara flung her head to one side. The hand over her mouth took a second to respond. It was just enough time to sink her teeth into the sour, salty skin and bite down hard. Blood filled her mouth as a growling scream escaped around his hand.

A shadow stood over her. The hands on her breast froze. The grip eased and then was gone. The weight on her hips left a second later.

"Get off her," Roy demanded. "Spark is one of us. You dishonor yourselves before Hasi. Go. Pray for forgiveness if there is any left in this land."

Her attackers were gone as quickly as they had arrived. Sahmara spat the blood from her mouth and got to her feet. She pulled up her leggings, yanked down her shirt and felt around until she located her sword.

"Men know no honor," she said as turned from Roy and stalked back to camp.

He followed close behind. "Little slow with the steel, Spark. Suppose that's just as well. If you had Yanis' skill, I'd have been short three men in the morning."

She spun around. "Who were they?" She'd shared water with these men. Ate with them, fought with them. Now she had to face them in the morning. She knew Bart, but if she didn't know who the others were, she'd have no choice but to assume it was all of them. Only Olando and Roy were safe from suspicion. Being attacked by the enemy was one thing, but having to trust her back to these men made her skin crawl.

"You'll know in the morning. They'll be the ones who don't look at you. Just remember, we need them all. Hasi will punish them in his own way."

She had a mind to run Bart and his friends through with Yanis' sword rather than wait for the damned gods to do anything about it. If what Roy had said about the gods fighting each other had even an ounce of truth to it, they had bigger things on their minds than three wayward men. They hadn't cared about Yanis dying. They certainly wouldn't care about men like Bart and the other two.

He coughed. "For your own safety, you may want to work more with Olando and your sword. I might not hear you next time."

She spun around. "You better hope there isn't a next time or you can try your odds without an archer." Too furious for further words, she left him there to digest her threat and headed back to her blanket and Olando.

The only thing Hasi had ever done for her was to send Zane. The god of war, of steel, of all things masculine, meant little to her, and if he were truly the God of War, he wasn't very impressive given the state of Revochek.

The Atherians and their god Ephius had won. She'd had her fill of losing.

She fingered the sword at her side. Sleep could wait. It wouldn't be coming anytime soon anyway. She veered away from where Olando slept and crept into the night.

Sahmara had done her fair share of sneaking around the estate in her childhood. Her parents had thrown many grand parties but children were never on the guest list. The allure of the dresses, the dances and the handsome men all in their finery was too much to pass up. She'd lost her heart many times during those late night spying excursions.

Tonight lacked handsome men, parties, and finery of any

sort, but Sahmara was grateful for her ability to sneak all the same. It was one of the few skills she had out in the wilds that didn't require any help from anyone else.

Listening intently, she picked up angry whispers on the cool night breeze. She headed for the one tree that stood between her and the voices. With her back pressed against its smooth bark, she listened.

Bart said, "Why'd ya run, Jon? If we'd all stood together, we could've told that damned priest that his empty words didn't matter and we could have had our fun."

"He's a priest, ya fool. I'll not cross a priest. Not for ya or anyone else."

Bart grumbled. "With Yanis gone, there's no one to protect her. Him and his claim on our only woman. Like he truly thought he'd be keeping her for himself."

"Bit bony for my taste and I like me a woman with some hair, but she's got all the right bits." The third man sniggered.

"Ya don't have taste, Agis. All ya look for are two legs and pair of teats," Jon said.

"Ah, the legs is optional." Agis laughed.

Sahmara shook with fury. It might have been some consolation to find them actually praying, but to hear them lewdly going on sent her hand to Yanis's sword. Whatever his claim had been, he'd kept his hands to himself and for that, she was eternally grateful. She hoped he was somewhere warm with a full belly after the grief he'd endured in this life.

"Ya think that priest will be watching over her all night? I got me a bad itch for a woman," Jon said.

"Ya do?" Bart scoffed. "She bit me. I have a mind to make her pay."

"How bad ya thinking about making her pay? I got an eye on that bow of hers," said Jon.

Jon had been the heavy man on top of her, she put his name with his face. She'd seen him swing his sword with enough force to hack the head halfway off a man in a single blow. Now he was in league with a man who might want her dead. Bart, she might get her sword into, but Agis and Jon were much larger and stronger and once she'd lost the element of surprise, she'd be overpowered in seconds.

Perhaps if they'd had their heads dutifully bowed in prayer like she'd envisioned, she might have had a chance. Unfortunately, they had little more respect for Roy than they did for her.

In the morning, she'd tell Roy of the threat against them both. He might not have actually seen the men he'd chased off. Though he made her uncomfortable with all his talk of the gods, and he was far more brusque than caring, he had helped her.

She stepped back from the tree only to have a hand clamp over her mouth. Twice in one night was too much to take. She was about to bite down when she recognized the thin, hard body she found herself pressed against. "Not a sound," Olando breathed in her ear.

She knew he meant her no harm, but she'd been too close to men tonight—too many hands on her in too many places. She needed space. She needed air. Her heart beat crazily and every exhausted muscle strained to pull away.

"Stop it." He held her against the tree. "If they hear ya, they'll not hesitate to kill ya."

She knew he was right, but she could hardly breathe. The only way to get the space she needed was to give in. Sahmara went still.

Olando took his hand from her mouth. He reached for her hand, and wrapping his fingers around hers, pulled her away slowly.

When they'd returned to their blankets, Sahmara sunk to the ground and put her smooth head into her hands.

"We need to talk," he said softly.

She shook her head.

"Do you want to go to them?"

"Of course not."

"Then stick by me." He took her hand in his. "I don't know where ya came from, Spark. But around here, there's no such thing as an unclaimed woman. Yanis was the best of us and he laid claim from the moment ya joined. No one dared touch ya."

"So I've heard, but…" She faltered, remembering their meeting and his first crude comments. "He never said anything about it to me. We had no agreement."

"Ya didn't need one with the likes of him. It was his right to ask or not. He chose not." Olando squeezed her hand and let it go. "He was a better man than me."

But Olando was the one still alive, and she needed him. "He wasn't a better talker."

"What do you mean?"

"He didn't say much, and he wasn't very kind when he did."

"He wasn't always like that."

Warmth grew between them under the blanket. She breathed a little easier, but still kept her sword within reach. "Why don't I get any say in this claiming business? It's my damned body you're all groping."

"That's the way things are, Spark. Ya know that."

She did, as much as she hated to admit it.

There was just something about being far from home, after all she'd endured, that made her think that the world had changed. It had changed. In so many ways and most of them for the worse. Why couldn't her future as a pawn change? Though, being her father's social pawn was far better than the situation in which she now found herself. She wanted to cry, but it wouldn't keep men's hands off her and it wouldn't make her feel any better. Tears would only make Olando, who actually did seem to care in his own way, want to offer her comfort. The only thing Sahmara wanted from him right now was to be watched over but left alone. Untouched.

She rather missed Yanis. If he had still been alive, Bart and the others likely wouldn't have even attempted to attack her.

"The way I see it, ya can either stick with me or go to Roy—if you don't mind sleeping with a priest. Most of the men were Yanis's. They follow Hasi and would never dare touch ya if ya had Roy's protection."

"I wouldn't say most of the men." Sahmara took a deep

breath and let it out slowly. "Two of those three, and I doubt they are alone, don't care much about Roy and the gods." She told him what she had overheard.

Olando sighed. "'Tis a sad world we have come to live in. Maybe's it's the loss of Yanis that's turned them away."

"For what it's worth, I'm not in favor of Roy either."

"Then you're stuck with me."

Sahmara nodded. Olando was, in fact, the lesser of the surrounding evils.

"With Yanis gone, I'm the best swordsman we have left."

"And you've offered to help me."

"I have." He nuzzled her shoulder. "We should get back to sleep. There are only a few hours before morning and we have a long day ahead of us."

"I don't think I can sleep."

"Ya need to. I'll keep watch."

"But if you are the best swordsman we have left, you need your rest too. I'll not have you fumbling about in the battlefield with bleary eyes."

Olando chuckled. "Ya have a point, dear Spark." He rolled over and shifted around outside the blanket, sending wafts of cold across her back.

"What are you doing?"

His back met hers and he pulled the blanket tight. "I'm not wild about one sword in my bed, but if it will help you sleep better, we'll have two. That should make them think twice."

"As long as I don't leave your side."

"Well, yes." He nudged her with his elbow. "Just don't leave my side."

"Am I your prisoner then?"

"Spark, that's not what I mean."

She sighed. "I know, but I don't like it."

He fell silent and even after her eyes began to droop, what seemed like hours later, he still hadn't fallen into the even breathing of sleep.

Half into the dream world, she tried to convince herself that it was Zane's back against hers. The hands that had touched her in the woods had been his. It had been his rough cheeks that had brushed against hers. His unbound blond hair had fallen against her face as he traveled down her body, delivering kisses to every inch of her flushed skin. She could smell him, leather and oil, and sighed deeply knowing she was safe. But she wasn't.

Her eyes flew open. Zane wasn't here.

Sahmara ran her fingers over cold, smooth blade beside her. Her fingers wrapped around the hilt, where other, more skilled fingers had rested before hers. She would learn how to use the sword, and she would find Zane. She would feel his touch again.

CHAPTER SIX

The soft breathing in her ear was not Zane's. The smell was wrong too, dirt and sweat. Sahmara came awake in an instant.

"Relax, Spark. It's just me." Olando sat up and stretched. "How is your shoulder?"

"Better."

He regarded her for a moment. "Let me see it."

"Why?"

"I've told ya why." He cast a glance to where her attackers lay amidst the other men. "They might not value your bow, but the rest of us do."

His intentions sounded honest enough and the concern on his face seemed real. "Go ahead." She nodded to the bandage.

"Did they hurt you last night? Your shoulder, any of ya?"

"No more than has been done before."

He pulled the bandage from her shoulder. "I'm sorry." Bowing his head, he turned his attention to the cut on her shoulder. "While ya are mine, no one will hurt ya. I promise."

Though she truly didn't want to belong to anyone, his pledge warmed her heart and brought a smile to her lips. "Does that include Atherians with swords and arrows?"

"Well, I..."

"I'm kidding. Nothing you can do about that."

"I can make ya better with that otherwise useless sword."

"Right." She smiled.

"It is good to see ya happy, Spark." His dark eyes scrunched up at the corners as he grinned. "Ya looked happy this morning, too, smiling in your sleep."

Sahmara's face grew hot. "That's none of your business."

He chuckled. "Your shoulder looks well enough, at least not bleeding. We can hope it stays closed and will heal quickly. We should go easy on it today to be safe."

The need to learn to use her sword outweighed her reluctance to pay for her lesson. "No practice then?"

"Maybe a little, if you truly want to try it."

"I do." She let him wrap the remains of Yanis's sleeve back into place and then got to her feet.

"I'll see if we have food this morning before we begin."

Sahmara watched him cross the camp to speak with Roy. They both glanced in her direction more than once. Olando pointed to Bart and the others. Roy nodded, handed him something and went about packing up his own things.

Olando returned with two apples. He handed them both to Sahmara.

"Where did these come from? I thought we were out of food?"

"Locals leave offerings to Hasi on cairns in the woods."

"Gods don't eat man's food." Though she only knew that for sure because of the tingling in her hand anytime she was around blood.

"Probably not. As Roy explains it, the gods appreciate that people leave something meaningful to them. They're making a sacrifice." he eyed the apple in her hand. "I don't know about eating something intended for the gods."

"Roy said you should eat. You need your strength. Besides, where do you think those biscuits came from?"

"But we were in Atheria then."

"We were. We stole them from offerings to the Atherian's god."

"Good. He's stolen enough from us." If Ephius hadn't struck them down on his own soil, her own gods shouldn't mind that she ate. Besides, if she was strong, the Mother would benefit.

Sahmara bit into one of the apples. Sweet juices ran down

her chin. She wiped them away with her sleeve. Her mother would have been truly appalled. "You're not eating?"

He shook his head.

She held out the second apple. "I don't need both of them."

"We might be in Revochek, but the road to freedom is long. We're to meet up with others in Antochecki. There'll likely be a lot of fighting before we get to rest and we need your help. Now eat."

"That would mean we need you as well, sir best-swordsman we-have-left." She dropped the apple into his hand and took another bite of her own as she picked up her sword. "Best eat so we can get to it."

"We should pack while eating so we'll be ready to go when the others are," Olando said between crunchy bites.

Sahmara slung her bow across her back and the quiver over her shoulder. Once she had the blanket and jug ready to go as well, she still felt like she was missing something. The dagger Agis had stolen.

"How do you think I should go about getting my dagger back?"

Olando chewed a bite of his apple. "Is it important to ya? The dagger I mean? Was it a gift?"

"Hardly. I picked if off a dead man just before Yanis saved me the other day."

"Then do ya need that particular dagger back?"

Sahmara considered his question as she finished her apple. "It's more that I want my dagger back because it's mine."

"And it was taken." Olando nodded knowingly.

"Yes."

He tossed the last bite in his mouth and took his time chewing it. "Thank ya for that."

She nodded. "You deserved some sort of payment. You've been more patient than most men I've known."

Olando looked away. "About what I said before, I don't want you to think of it as payment. I mean, I'll not force ya to do anything ya don't want to do. I'm not like them." He gestured to Agis and Bart who were just waking up.

"I see that." And she thanked the Mother for that fact.

Faced with only men like Bart, she would have taken her chances on her own rather than stay with the group. Instead, she had someone she didn't exactly mind, and he was almost too kind to be a soldier like the rest. Not that she was about to complain. Instead, she patted his shoulder. It was the first time in months she'd voluntarily touched a man other than to push him away. "We should practice."

Olando took his sword with him as they walked away from the others. They found an open space with minimal underbrush and he went about showing her how to deflect his blows. She appreciated his lack of strength behind each swing. As much as she wanted to learn to use the blade, she wanted her shoulder to heal.

Olando paused to correct her footing again. "So what's his name?"

"Whose name?" She swung again, this time getting a nod of approval.

"The one ya were smiling about this morning."

She didn't see any harm in telling him and having someone to talk to was something she'd not had in a long time. "Zane."

"Were you married?"

"No. He was my Ma'hasi."

Olando's eyes grew wide. He swung low and faltered in his footing. Sahmara's swing sent him stumbling off balance. "Ya had one of Hasi's warriors? Your own sworn bodyguard?" He thrust his sword into its scabbard and grabbed her arm. "Tell me truthfully, did ya?"

"I did." She desperately wanted Zane by her side just then. Not to prove that she did have him, but that her life had been normal and wonderful once. She'd been clean and pure, for the most part anyway.

"Who are ya really? One of the king's family?"

"Not quite so grand as that." Though her father played like he was one of the court, and he'd found the coin to act it with his extravagant gift of Zane, he was only a merchant who lived in the capital. And she was only his daughter. And he might not even acknowledge that if he could see her now. She pulled her arm away. "I'm no one."

Sahmara left him there and went to join the others who were on their feet and packing their things. He joined her in short order. Though he didn't question her further, he kept giving her odd glances. She rather wished she hadn't mentioned Zane at all.

Roy set an easy pace for the morning march. It seemed he was well aware that everyone was hungry and tempers were high. He had positioned himself between Sahmara and her attackers from the night before.

After an hour of silence other than the crunch of grass under their feet, Olando said, "I thought Ma'hasi were celibate."

"Is Roy celibate?" It was an honest question. If he was, it would be good to know in case something happened to Olando.

"Not exactly, I suppose, but he's not a Ma'hasi. He's a priest. They have different vows."

She shrugged and then grimaced as her shoulder protested the movement. "Zane was loyal. In that, he was true to his vows."

The woodlands began to clear into rolling meadows. In the distance, she spotted a couple houses huddled together. Burned fields surrounded them. She couldn't see anyone moving, not even livestock. "How much longer will we be walking?"

"Until we reach Antochecki. That's the first town we've had favorable reports from. The Atherians have burnt everything between there and the border to the ground. They don't want us to have anywhere to resupply or mount organized attacks."

"How long until we reach Antochecki?" The name sounded familiar from her father's conversations, but she didn't remember seeing it on a map.

"Four days or more, depending on how many attacks we

have to face."

Sahmara's heart sank. Her legs didn't want to take another step. Four more days of this with no food? "When I get home, I'm not going to walk anywhere ever again. Not even to the next room. I'll hire servants to carry me everywhere I need to go."

"Please tell me you're not a princess."

She laughed. "No. I've never even been inside the castle."

His voice grew quieter. "But you've been outside of it."

"I have." She missed the beautiful white walls with its red cloaked guardsmen and their white-plumed polished helmets. Home was safe. Home had a market where vendors smiled upon her and gave her delicious morsels for free in hopes of gaining favor with her father.

"The castle is rather hard to miss no matter where you are in Sloveski. It was just up the hill from our home and my father often had dealings near..." she faltered, having noticed his pained expression. "Nevermind."

"So ya had a Ma'Hasi and lived close to the castle." He whistled and shook his head. "Sorry to say, my dear lady, we're short on servants, and wagons and even horses. We ate the last one a week before we ran across you. It belonged to Yanis. He was quite unhappy about it, but when the rest of us demanded it, he gave in. He didn't speak much after that."

"Sounds like he was more than unhappy about it."

"He was." Olando stared at the horizon filled with nothing more than the backs of those ahead of them and the same grass and trees they'd been walking through. "We all had horses in the beginning. Those of us that were in Yanis's company that is."

Sahmara nodded. They'd all had normal lives once.

"Mine was an old plow horse, I'd guess. He was a big, brown thing with a horrible lurching gait, but it sure beat walking." He shot her a quick grin.

"I had a beautiful horse. She was a gift for my twelfth birthday." Sahmara lost herself remembering the heart pounding glee she'd felt when her father had taken her down to the stable early in the morning. He'd truly smiled that day. He'd watched her admire his gift and laughed at her squeal of joy when he'd helped her up on the horse's back.

"You didn't eat all your horses, I hope?" she finally thought to ask.

"No. Most of them didn't live long enough for that horrible fate." He walked in silence for a few minutes, following the steps of the others ahead of them as they made their way through the knee-high grass.

"There were many more of us right after the invasion, we'd found each other, smaller units combining into one larger company. We also took in any man who wanted to join us, rich or poor, didn't matter. Some had fine weapons, like Yanis. That sword was the pride of his life at one time. It shone like a mirror, I tell ya."

Sahmara patted the sword at her side, silently promising him that she'd take care of his cherished sword.

"Yanis sent us across the border, hoping to push back while the Atherian forces were away from home. He dispatched scouts. They returned to say that the town looked ripe for the picking. Intent on regaining some of our dignity, we struck hard."

Olando went silent for a short while until she looked over at him. "They'd paid off our scouts. Bribed them, made empty promises, I don't know what it took." His voice shook. "The town was far more prepared for us than we'd expected. Our losses were heavy. Their archers aimed for our horses, and when men toppled from their dying mounts, they were swarmed with swords and maces. We were lucky to get away with as many as we did."

Sahmara let him have his silence for a good while. "Where are you from?"

"Just outside Antochecki." He seemed reluctant to go on.

"What did you do before this?"

"Before Yanis came to town, recruiting men, I tended my father's sheep."

"Did Yanis teach you how to use a sword?"

"He taught me to be better." Olando sighed. "We lived outside the city walls. My family was large and I had many brothers. There was nothing to protect us outside of the walls but ourselves," he said proudly. "My father taught us all how to use a sword when we were old enough to work. Thieves were plentiful and we needed every scrap of wool to pay our taxes and earn a living. As it turns out thieves weren't the only thing we had to worry about."

His face turned glum. "The city got word that the nearby towns were being put to the torch. They closed their gates, not giving any of us the chance to get inside. My father sent me and one of my brothers to hide the sheep in the hills. He said he would send my mother and the younger children into the woods." He took a deep shuttering breath. "When my brother and I returned, they were all dead, slaughtered in the yard. The house was burning. There was nothing to be saved."

"I'm sorry," Sahmara said quietly. "Where is your brother now?"

"Dead. I didn't even have time to bury him." He shook his head. "Yanis was a strict captain, but a good one. He kept us alive the best he could."

"I'm sorry," she said again, feeling that her words were woefully inadequate.

"And what of your Ma'hasi?"

"Alive somewhere. They separated us and took me away." It felt good to hear the words out loud, giving her hope that they were indeed true.

"How do ya know he lives?"

"I saw him in a dream." The look of pity he gave her made her amend her statement. "I had a vision."

He raised an eyebrow. "A vision?"

"Yes, and I know it was true."

He shrugged, but she could tell he didn't really believe her. If she told him she suspected the vision came from the Mother, as did everything else she'd received, he'd run her right over to Roy. Being questioned and preached at wasn't how she wanted to spend her days.

"So this Ma'Hasi," Olando said, "how was it that he let you be taken and yet he still lives? I was told that the Ma'Hasi gave their lives before allowing harm to come to their charges."

Sahmara fumed to hear Zane's abilities taken so lightly. She took her time answering. "He was knocked unconscious during the fight and it was seven against one." She guessed at the details since the Atherians had covered her head.

"Ah. I see. Every man, no matter how dedicated, can only do so much." Still, he sounded unimpressed.

She stared at the ground as they walked. If Zane had lived through the attack, if the vision was real, it meant he must have been unable to help her. He'd loved her. He'd said so. He wouldn't have just let her be taken. Sahmara crossed her arms over her chest and kept walking until her shoulders protested. She shook out her arms and switched her load around, but still maintained her silence.

They came to what remained of an orchard. Men scattered, shoving each other aside for the few bruised apples and pears that remained. Sahmara followed Olando away from the fray. He kicked around a few apples but didn't find anything worth picking up. She shared some of her water with him instead.

"You should trade that thing in for a waterskin next time we come across one. The jug is heavy."

"It was a gift. I'm keeping it." A skin, like a few of the others carried, would be lighter and less awkward, but the ability to summon fresh water with a prayer was worth the inconvenience.

"Suit yourself." He kicked at the dusty ground and gave the others an irritated glance. "Roy doesn't have the hold on them that Yanis did. We shouldn't have stopped here. There's too much open ground to cover. We need to keep moving."

"We've been moving for days. Why can't we take a day to rest up at one of the villages? No one is there anyway. A little shelter, burnt or not, would be welcome."

"Every extra day it takes us to reach Antochecki is another day that the Atherians kill our families, steal our riches and ruin our land."

"Oh." She stared at her own feet.

"How about we see if that bow of yours can find us something better than rotting apples? If the others see your skill at filling the dinner pot, they might be more inclined to leave you alone." He went to Roy before she could answer.

She'd shared water with them and they'd not seen her worth, she didn't see how filling their bellies would be any different. However, learning to hunt was a skill she needed, so when Olando returned, she followed him into the brush.

"I told him of our intentions so he doesn't leave us behind," Olando said. "Let's try over here, away from all the noise." He led her to a stretch of waist high bushes beyond the orchard.

"Why didn't the Atherians burn all this?:

"Crops in the field feed the men and horses fighting them right now. The ashes will make the soil richer for the Atherian's first harvest. Orchards take years to replace. They are brutal, but they aren't foolish."

He motioned for her to be quiet as they crept further into the bushes. Sahmara readied her bow. The sounds of the others enjoying their lackluster feast faded into the chirping of birds and insects.

A brown feathered shape darted from a bush in front of them. Sahmara uttered the prayer she'd held ready on her tongue and loosed her arrow. The bird squawked. Two more birds leaped to the sky. She grabbed another arrow and launched it. One of the birds fell to the ground with a shaft stuck in its side. She shot a third arrow. It missed.

Olando shrugged. "I'm still impressed." He went after the two flailing birds. "How is it that you have such skill with a bow and yet warranted a Ma'hasi?"

No good answer came to mind. "I need to find my arrow." She left him there and went in search of the missing shaft.

When she returned, he was still waiting for an answer. She shook her head. "I'd rather not talk about it."

Olando handed her the arrows from the now limp-necked birds. "You don't seem the sort that needs a Ma'hasi."

"Maybe I didn't always know how to use a bow."

He ducked behind her and she could feel him touching the bow on her back. "It's quite a work of art."

"I guess." She still couldn't figure out what all the carvings were exactly, but she had the impression that he was right.

"So where did you get such a thing? Your father?"

"No." Inspiration hit her. "My Mother."

He raised a single eyebrow. "That's quite a gift."

"It was." In the hopes that he'd drop any further questions, she held her hands out for the birds.

Olando handed them over, but she could feel him watching her back as she brought them over to Roy. As she got closer, she the rest of the men watched her as well. Some focused on the meal in her hands, others had a different sort of hunger in their gaze.

"Thank you, Spark." Roy grinned. "These will fill our bellies tonight."

Unending hunger drove her to ask, "Can't we eat them now?"

"These birds will take time to cook. Best we do that after the daylight hours have been used for their best purpose—to safely cover ground."

The afternoon dragged on. Olando stayed close by but didn't say a word. Her gaze wandered over the men around her, noting their dirty and gaunt faces and the way two of them limped. Roy strode steadily along beside three others at the head of the group, dinner slapping against his back with each step.

Her dagger glinted in the sunlight against Agis's hip. Anger surged inside her. Even though Olando was silent beside her, she was sure he had her back, she made her way to the large man's side.

"I'd like my dagger back."

Agis laughed. "I'd like you on your back."

"It's mine. Hand it over."

"You'll have to earn it." A sparse blond beard spotted his round ruddy cheeks, which grew a shade redder as he chortled.

Bart found his way to Sahmara's other side. "Looking for some fun, Spark? Could've had that last night. Unless you're here to apologize for running off?"

Sahmara copied Agis' sputtering laugh with a huge burst of false bravado. "Actually, I came over here for your apology."

"About that." Bart slapped her on her wounded shoulder. "I don't think so."

Sahmara cringed. Pain shot down her arm and up her neck. There were only two things these men listened to. She mimicked her father's tone that he used when delivering orders to the servants. "If I don't hear an apology right now and get my dagger back, you'll be going hungry tonight. I shot dinner. It's my right to decide who eats and who doesn't."

"That's not how it works." Agis puffed up his chest and drew back his thick shoulders, taking a step closer. "We work together, we eat together."

"Really? I wasn't one of you last night, now was I? That means I don't have to follow your rules."

Agis glanced at Bart. Bart shrugged. Agis stepped back. "We had apples for lunch. We don't need your dinner."

A thin-lipped smile appeared on Bart's face. He shooed her away. "Go back to nipping your master's heels."

Anger drained the command from her voice and replaced it with amazement. "I beg your pardon?"

"You heard me," Bart said. "We'll be keeping your dagger, and you can bet we'll be keeping an eye on you. You owe us."

"I owe *you*?" Her hand went to her sword. It was time for the other thing they understood.

A solid hand slammed down on hers. Olando cleared his throat. "Bart, Agis, I think you owe the lady an apology."

"Oh do we now?" Agis slowed. His hand went to the mace at his side.

"And a dagger." Olando pulled Sahmara out of line with them and filled the empty space with his own body.

Roy appeared at the edge of their cluster a second later. "Is there a problem here?"

Everyone came to a halt. Jon stood apart from the others as

if he were unsure of which group he should be part of. Roy called him over.

"I think the three of you have something to say to Spark. Say it and let's be on our way. We have enough enemies around us, we don't need them within."

"I got nothing to say," said Jon.

"Me neither," said Bart.

Agis laughed. "You want your dagger, little girl? Go fetch it." He pulled it from his belt and tossed it into the bushes.

Olando glared at Sahmara and shook his head. She wanted to yell at him for interrupting her. She wanted to yell at all of them. But she knew it would do her no good.

Agis, Bart, and Jon shared a look and started walking. The rest of the men followed, leaving Roy, Olando, and Sahmara behind.

"You see where your anger got us?" Roy fumed. "I need you, Spark, I'll not lie, but I can't keep stepping up for you."

"No one asked you to." She dashed over to the bush and rooted around for her dagger.

"If he hadn't, one of them would have stuck you through," Olando scolded.

Her fingers landed on cold steel. She grabbed the blade and stuck it in her belt. "I didn't ask for your help either." She glared at both of them. "And Roy, you might want to step up for yourself. Those men have no respect for you or your god."

She held her head high and strode after them, leaving Roy and Olando in her wake. She was proud of herself. Perhaps not exactly proud of having to scramble around in the bushes for her dagger, but she *had* gotten it back.

CHAPTER SEVEN

The men came to a halt just before sunset and went about making a fire. Roy kept to himself, plucking the birds. Olando kept his distance too.

Had she lost her protector? She didn't need him. But she did. There were too many men and too many opportunities for the night before to happen again.

By the time the birds had roasted, lending a delicious, mouth-watering aroma to the night air, Sahmara came to the conclusion Olando wasn't going to come to her. She swallowed a bit of pride, joined the others at the spit to carve two handfuls of hot, juicy meat, and walked over to him.

"Here." She handed a thick slab of breast meat to Olando. He took the meat but remained silent. She had no plans to apologize for sticking up for herself. She ate in their shared silence. When she finished, she unfolded her blanket and handed it to him.

He looked at it a moment and then handed her his cloak. She spread it out on the ground and lay down. He sighed loudly and stretched out next to her, spreading the blanket over them both.

"You're trouble. Ya know that, Spark?"

She stared up at the moon, wondering if the Mother was looking down on her. Did the gods think she was trouble or was that her purpose? What did the Mother want with her?

Olando interrupted her thoughts. "Can I ask you something?"

"Maybe." At least he hadn't started groping her yet. After two practice sessions, she was sure he'd be after more payment than an apple.

"What happened to your hair? I've not seen you shear it, yet your head is smoother than a riverbed pebble."

"It fell out in the ocean." There, let him ponder that, she thought smugly.

"You're beautiful without it, you know."

Beautiful? She resisted the urge to laugh out loud only because he sounded so earnest. "Umm, thank you."

"I would have liked to have seen you in a dress. Probably had a chest full of those fine silk ones with the lace and pearls, I'm guessing."

What had become of all her fine dresses? Nothing but the finest fabrics, her mother had insisted for both of them. Her father had bargained to his best ability to oblige their whims.

Had her home become a burned out shell like all the others she'd seen since crossing the border? But these were without guarded walls. Not that walls had saved her during the invasion. The nightmare of that evening played out again in her mind.

Olando shifted around, searching for comfort on the hard ground. "If you hadn't known of Yanis' claim, why did you stay behind for him?"

"He saved my life."

"I am not a high-ranking soldier, nor have I ever owned a horse or anything beyond the clothes upon my back. Yet, if I were sorely wounded, would you stay behind with me?"

"Until you told me, I thought Yanis was the same." She rolled over and propped her head up on her hand. "Yes, I would stay behind with you."

His long, dark lashes dipped low over his eyes and he smiled as if savoring a tasty delight. "Ya were a lady once, a fine one, I gather if ya merited Ma'hasi. If not for the war, I wouldn't get the chance to say three words to ya."

He had kind eyes and a heart she hadn't expected from a soldier. "Then I am glad for the war, just a little."

Olando turned to her. "As am I, just a little." He kissed her then, lightly, his lips tentatively brushing against hers.

Sahmara allowed him to pull her closer until her breasts were crushed against his hard chest. His kisses grew deeper, more urgent. He kept one hand around her while the other slipped under her shirt.

He was so unlike the eager soldiers who took without asking, and yet, he'd not asked either. Not exactly.

She could feel other eyes upon them. The camp was too still. Every wet sound shared between them seemed to echo through the night air. Sahmara squeezed her eyes shut. If she could endure what the Atherian soldiers had done, sometimes two and three at a time, Olando and his wanting kindness were nothing in comparison.

His hunger turned quickly into long held back lust, his hands devouring her skin as his tongue did her mouth. He had allowed her to keep her shirt, giving her some remote feeling of modesty. Using what she had learned in captivity, Sahmara knew how to make the humiliation stop. All she had to do was give the man what he wanted and the better she did it the quicker his assault would end. In an effort to keep more of her own clothes on, she went for his laces. As soon as his manhood was free she took him into her mouth and employed every trick she had learned. A hand found her head, keeping her right where she was, controlling the rhythm of her movements. Gasps and grunts gave her a good idea of what he enjoyed best and she concentrated on those. A sudden shuddering cry that likely got the attention of every man in camp, signaled his release.

Sahmara returned to her spot on his cloak and reached for the water jug. The Mother's clean water rinsed his taste from her mouth.

She did her best to ignore the lewd whispered comments drifting on the night breeze as she readjusted her shirt. Olando, still breathing heavily held the blanket out to her.

"Good gods, Spark. Where did you learn all that?"

"I think you know. Good night." She turned away from

him and tugged the blanket around her as if it could keep her safe from the entire world.

He let her be until morning when they stole away from the others to practice. Since the rest of the camp was still sleeping, he left his sword sheathed and scrutinized her moves.

"Keep your blade up. I know it's heavy, but ya must try not to make it so easy for the enemy to kill ya."

"I wasn't trying to make it easy." She wanted to throw the sword down and find a quiet space for herself, a few moments of peace to gather her wits and release her frustration.

His hand on hers made throwing anything impossible. "Like this." He moved with her, swinging and thrusting, pulling her with him as he turned and spun around. A sudden hardness pressed against her buttocks.

Sahmara wrenched herself from his loose grasp and kept the sword up as she'd been instructed, holding it between them. "Have I not already earned this morning's lesson?"

Olando looked hurt. "Do ya find me so distasteful?"

"Yes and no." She sighed raggedly as she slipped the sword into its scabbard with trembling hands. "Please, just leave me here for a short while."

"I'd rather not," he said softly. "It could be dangerous for ya to be here alone."

"The others are still sleeping. There has been no sign of the enemy for days. Please, just go."

His head hung low as he walked away.

Silence settled around Sahmara. She stood, alone, listening for a hint of hope, a whisper from the Mother, a bird song to cheer her heavy heart, but there was only silence. The tears that had threatened to fall in front of Olando refused to come. She crossed her arms over her chest, fending off the emptiness of the morning with her own comfort.

Sahmara watched the sun creep higher above the horizon, wondering if she'd be killed today, if the men would turn on Roy, and if so, would having Olando beside her make any difference.

A branch snapped. Sahmara whirled around to find Olando

looking guilty. He cleared his throat. "The others are about ready to move out. I have our things packed." His gaze dropped to the ground. "Are ya coming?"

Sahmara wanted to laugh but the emptiness inside her swallowed the crazy notion whole. "You go on about the dangers of me standing her alone for a short while and then you ask if I'm intending to remain here once the rest of you leave?"

"Roy has enough trouble keeping these men on a unified course. While he would miss your skill with your bow, he wouldn't miss the tension having you among us causes."

"Is that so? You've talked to him about me?"

"Yes and no," he shot her answer back at her with a tight-jawed, stiff-backed, volley.

She'd hurt his feelings. More than that, she was both stunned and amazed he actually had feelings for her and that she had the ability to hurt them. Much like retrieving her dagger, she wasn't exactly proud of that fact, but it gave her a small amount of power and she clung to it.

"And what about you? Would you miss me?"

The tension on his face melted away. "I have nothing more than soot and tumbled stones on a small parcel of unprotected land. My sheep are likely filling the bellies of wolves and soldiers. All I can offer ya is my sword and a promise. I will not force ya to do anything you do not wish to do." He sighed. "Yes, my dear lady Spark, I would miss ya."

A lump formed in her throat. "Then I'll come with you."

Olando nodded. He kept his hands to himself and a polite distance between them as they returned to camp. The others were indeed ready to leave. They started off the moment she and Olando arrived.

CHAPTER EIGHT

Men kept looking at her over their shoulders all morning. Some jealous glances included Olando as well. Despite her newfound self-assurance, she stuck close to his side.

The skies overhead had turned dark grey by the time they stopped for their midday rest. Distant thunder rolled high over the tall, black-barked trees surrounding them.

"These are nut trees," Roy informed them. "Quickly now, search for the bounty Hasi has left for us."

Like squirrels just before the first snow, the men scattered, rifling through fallen leaves and gathering handfuls of the hard-shelled nuts. Sahmara found a few of her own. The dirt colored shells didn't contrast from her hands near as much as she would have liked. She'd never been so filthy in her life. Or hungry.

"How do we eat these?"

Olando took out his dagger and set the nut on a fallen log. He showed her how to smash the shell with the pommel and pry out the tender nutmeat inside.

The earthy and bland nuts did little for her tongue, but her starving belly didn't mind. When she'd finished eating what she'd found and the couple Olando shared with her, she went off to search for more. Olando stayed close behind her as they moved through the trees and milling men with steel in their hands.

Agis, standing with Bart and Jon called out to her. Though she knew it would be better to ignore then, habit made her look up anyway.

"When's it our turn?" Bart asked.

Agis made a lewd gesture. She'd seen plenty of those on her march with the Atherian soldiers, made in jest and otherwise. Without a care for proper decorum and anything but a lady anymore, despite what Olando had called her, Sahmara made a gesture of her own. Their brows flew up and mouths dropped open. She followed up with a few more. Just to make sure they got the point, she mimicked cutting off his manhood and grinned. "Never."

Sahmara spun on her heel and went back the way she'd come. Olando met her at the log where they'd sat.

"You're full of surprises, dear lady. Did you see his face?" His entire body shook with laughter.

"I did." The long unfamiliar sensation of laughter bubbled up inside her and burst from her lips. She leaned against the rotting log and held her stomach until the laughter subsided enough that she could catch her breath.

A sudden serious look on Olando's face brought her to an abrupt halt. "What?" She glanced around, expecting to see Agis or his friends coming after her.

"You're beautiful when ya laugh."

No matter how sincere he looked, the wall was breached and she couldn't hold back. Laughter took her until tears spilled down her cheeks, and a fit of hiccups racked her body. Olando studied her with an amused smile, which only made her laugh harder. She held up her hands. "Stop it. I can't breathe."

"I'm not doing anything," he said innocently.

The laughter filled some of the empty space inside her. Feeling a little more whole again, Sahmara composed herself and wiped the wet tracks from her cheeks.

Roy, looking far less than amused, came over to them. "Are you about done here? We need to get moving again. The rain won't hold off much longer."

Olando nodded. "Whenever you're ready."

Roy leaned in close. "If you're intent on keeping this woman, you best keep her under control." He turned to

Sahmara. "I need your bow, but if you insist on stirring up trouble, I'll make do without it."

She was hardly the one causing trouble, and she had a mind to point that fact out. Olando shot her a warning glare.

The two of them alone wouldn't stand much of a chance if they ran across a patrol of enemy soldiers. Her odds dwindled even further if Olando sided with Roy. She nodded and bit her tongue.

"Let's move out," Roy yelled.

Sahmara shouldered her belongings, and noticing her water jug was near empty, uttered a prayer to the Mother. Her finger tingled and the jug grew heavy once more.

"Do you have any water left?" Olando asked.

She slid strap off her shoulder and handed him the jug. He took a long drink. Water dribbled from the corners of his mouth and dripped from the scraggly whiskers on his chin.

"That is good water. I thought ya were almost out last night. Where did ya find it?"

Her steps faltered as she scrambled for an answer. "There was a small brook where we practiced this morning."

"I don't remember that. The others are out, though, I don't exactly blame you for not mentioning the brook to the others."

She took the jug back and hung it over her shoulder. Raindrops hit her face. Sahmara pointed to the sky. "Think they can find this by themselves?"

Olando laughed. "We should find shelter before we get too wet. Come."

They followed the others to a thick stand of tall pines. Olando tugged her toward one of them and lifted the lower boughs. "We will have a better chance of not getting soaked under here."

She looked dubiously at the thick layer of sharp brown needles on the ground. "A tree is hardly a water-proof shelter."

"Would you rather stand out there?"

The day had suddenly turned to night and lightning arced through the sky. She ducked under the branches with him. Rain pelted the tree but far less of it ended up on her. "No.

This is fine."

"I thought ya might say that."

Wedged in the cramped shelter, her bow crushed her shoulder and the water jug dug into her back. "I take it we're going to be here for awhile?"

"Quite likely. From the look of the clouds earlier, this storm has been building all day."

Sahmara rolled onto her side and removed her bulky belongings, setting them behind her head near the trunk of the tree.

"Cover your eyes," he said.

"Why?" He had better not start undressing, she thought to herself. It would just figure if he did even after all he'd said that morning.

"I'm going to break off some of these lower branches so we have more room. Unless you want needles in your eyes?"

"Oh." Sahmara rolled onto her stomach and covered her face with her arms. Old, brittle needles showered down on her, tickling her scalp and neck and sneaking under her wet shirt to irritate her skin.

Loud snaps sounded above her. A branch slammed into her back.

"Sorry about that." He whisked the branch away. "That one was deader than I thought."

The wind picked up, whirling around outside the safety of the boughs and blowing needles into her face. Sahmara rolled onto her side.

Instead of tossing the branches out as she thought he was doing, Olando was busy weaving them into the remaining branches to make a windbreak.

Relief washed over her as he put the last one into place, blocking most of the wind. The needles poked into her clothes, seeming to make every effort to stab her with their tiny points.

"There, now we have a nice private spot all to ourselves. That's better, isn't it?"

So he'd sensed her discomfort over fulfilling her end of the bargain in public. That was a step in the right direction, but she would much rather not have to fulfill it at all.

"You'll have to wait until I'm warm and dry if you expect anything from me."

"I don't expect anything. I just meant it would be more comfortable. You'll want to take your wet clothes off. The blankets are mostly dry. If we're lucky the water will stay out there and our clothes will have a chance to dry a bit. I thought you'd appreciate the privacy."

She studied his face, and finding it earnest, offered him a tenuous smile. "I do. Thank you."

Without another word, Olando squirmed out of his shirt and hung it on the branches above them. His leggings followed a minute later. Her cloak wasn't all that dry but it did serve to blunt the needles they laid upon. Sahmara took her blanket from her things and pulled it over her. Under the safety of the tattered wool, she shed her damp clothes. Olando hung them from the branches and settled down next to her. He reached for the blanket.

"What are you doing?"

"Getting warm."

"I'd rather you didn't."

"What, you'd rather I freeze?"

"No, but I don't feel comfortable with you laying naked next to me."

"Spark, I… It's cold."

She sighed. "I know."

He wasn't so bad, certainly not like the soldiers that had hurt her or like Bart, Agis or Jon. He'd been kind and she was far better off by his side than alone within the group. Even Roy seemed to respect Olando. After all, the priest hadn't demanded that she be left behind just yet. Or maybe that was because Olando had pleaded her case.

"Fine, but stay over there." She made a definite indentation in the blanket signaling her half and his.

"We'll be warmer if we lay together."

"Likely story."

"I'm not lying to ya, dear lady."

"Quit calling me that." She shivered. Random drops fell and landed on her head, face and neck. She pulled the blanket around her tighter.

"It would seem that you're not fond of rain."

Sick of staring at the tree bark, and she was pretty sure she could see insects traveling up and down its surface, she rolled to face the man intent on holding her attention. "It is wet, dirty and pokey in here. The word that comes to mind is: miserable. This storm is also keeping us from getting home."

"I see. It is wet and it does delay our travel, but why be miserable? Think of it as an extra time of rest. You've been complaining of sore muscles since we met. Relax and enjoy lazing around in bed." He grinned.

He was right about always being sore. She couldn't remember a time when her muscles didn't ache. "If this were truly a bed, I might enjoy it more."

"Used to a soft bed, eh? I'm sorry this is all I can do for ya right now. I shall search for more pleasant lodgings next time." His eyes twinkled.

Sahmara found herself giggling. "Yes, please—the best room in the inn, with a steaming hot bath and a maid to wash my hair."

"If ya had hair, my dear lady, I'd wash it for ya."

"Way to ruin the dream, Olando."

"I'm sorry." But he was smiling. "I think that is the first time you have spoken my name."

She paused, thinking. "I suppose it is."

He leaned over, kissing her gently.

She didn't mind that so much, but she knew he wouldn't stop there. He wiggled closer until his body had crossed over her invisible line. With no shirt to impede his wandering hands, he went right for her breast. She stiffened.

"What is it?" Olando asked.

"You're all just take what you want, don't you?" She pulled away from him, not caring about the cool air washing over her backside.

"I am sorry, my dear lady. It seems my desires got the

better of me." His shy smile brought her back into the warmth of the blanket.

Sahmara's muscles relaxed as they lay side by side. The thunder subsided, taking the lightning with it. Olando kept his hands to himself and after a short while of staring up at her damp clothes, the rain soothed her to sleep.

She woke when she rolled over to find herself against an unyielding warm body. His muscles against her back were just as taut as hers had been earlier.

"Do you seek to torture me?"

It was about time someone else was tortured, and truthfully she enjoyed it just a little. "You're right, it is warmer here next to you."

"Now you're just being cruel." He gave her a playful shove. "Distance or pay the consequences."

She snickered softly. "So much for the willpower of honorable men."

Olando groaned. "Ya have no idea." She heard him roll over, bumping into branches and tipping over one of their windbreaks. He swore under his breath as he put the branch back into place. Once he had settled down, he asked. "Your Ma'hasi, what was he like?"

Sahmara took a deep breath of pine that barely masked the stench of their unwashed bodies. "He has long golden hair and deep blue eyes. He is also very good with a sword."

"At least we have that in common. Let's just hope he doesn't want to fight me for ya."

She rolled onto her back so she could see his face. "Why would the two of you fight over me?"

"If we have occasion to meet, I would like to see just how good this Ma'hasi of yours is. I know I excused his loss of ya before, but truly, a man favored by Hasi as he should be, and doing his sworn duty, would have kept you by his side. Or he would be dead."

"What exactly are you saying?"

His eyes narrowed the slightest bit. "What would your suitors have said if they'd found out about your romps with your wayward Ma'hasi?"

"No one would know. I had no bed maid, well not anymore. My mother walked in on us one morning, and discovering that we'd become much more than friends, sent her away." A lump formed in her throat. She coughed to clear it, not wanting to dwell on how irate she'd been with her parents. She missed them terribly. Being angry with them felt wrong now.

"They were concerned I'd develop 'unmarriageable tendencies'." She rolled her eyes. "Zane's room adjoined mine so that he could guard me even in sleep, as was his duty. And we were careful. I wasn't going to let him get sent away."

"Took his duty a bit too much to heart, didn't he? Celibate warrior of Hasi indeed." Olando scoffed. "Did it ever occur to either of ya that your true husband would be mightily put out to learn he was sold soiled merchandise when he was promised perfection?"

"They would have never known." She remembered her first time with Zane vividly, and she was confident that she could have put on a convincing show for whatever husband her father chose for her. Not that it mattered now. There was no amount of playing coy or demure that could fool anyone. All they had to do was look in her eyes.

"Ya are naïve, dear lady. They would have known. And then your father would know, and ya can bet he'd have something to say about your beloved Ma'hasi then."

"What could my Father say? What was done, couldn't be undone."

His face grew stern and anger lit in his eyes. "He wouldn't have to say anything, not to your Ma'hasi. He'd have a talk with the priest he'd commissioned him from. Your dear Zane would be brought back to the temple in chains and punished publically for his sins against Hasi." He exhaled sharply through his nose. His face darkened much like the storm raging outside their shelter. "Ya do know what the priests do to men who dishonor Hasi?"

Sahmara suddenly wished she'd paid more attention during

the temple services. Her heart beat faster. She wasn't sure if it was because she was worried about what Hasi demanded of Zane or that Olando was this angry on her behalf.

"A man who steals will lose his hand. A man who walks away from his duty will lose his foot. A man who ignores his vows will lose his tongue."

She didn't remember Hasi being so absolute in his punishments. Was there no forgiveness or overlooking what might be considered a sin if good came of it? She and Zane had done nothing wrong. He'd certainly not forced himself upon her. She'd had a choice then, loved for the pure enjoyment of it. She always had until the Atherian's came.

"But Zane is not a thief or deserter. I admit that he may have overlooked a vow, but he upheld the rest. He's not a bad man."

"No men are bad in the eyes of Hasi, dear lady. They only are forgetful and need reminding. That is why they are not to be put to death, but given a reminder of their sins that they may rise above them."

"He never did anything I didn't welcome or ask of him." Anger rose up and spilled from her in a torrent. "What of the soldiers who killed so many, burned our homes and fields and defiled more women than I could count, including myself? What will Hasi do to them? Nothing, that's what. So why is Zane any different?"

Olando's gaze remained intent, piercing. "Soldiers are simply men. They follow their hearts, be they good or evil, and do the will of their gods. They take no vows save to serve the men who lead them. They may follow the teachings of Hasi, such as many of us do, but we are not avowed of him. Not like your Zane."

He shook his head and his voice grew flat. "He stole from your father his most valuable possession. He deserted his charge, his single duty. He violated his vows of celibacy to lay with ya."

Olando gave her a long hard look. "Did it ever occur to ya that your beloved Ma'hasi saw the invasion as the perfect time escape punishment? If ya had been allowed to marry, he would have been found out. Your beautiful man would have lost a hand, a foot, and his tongue, and if I were your father, I would have demanded that the priest relieved him of his manhood as well."

Sahmara gasped. "How could you say such a thing?"

"With my tongue, which I still have."

"But you have made no vows, so that means little."

"I made a vow, to ya, dear lady. Unless my words mean so little that ya have already forgotten them."

How dare he compare himself to Zane? Sahmara wanted to rage at him, to get up and storm away, to never have to speak to him again. But there was nowhere to go and she was naked, and if she left his protection, she'd likely never see home. Instead, she rolled over, yanking her blanket with her. If he wanted to be an ass, he could be a cold and wet one.

"Spark."

She held her jaw clenched shut and stared at the tiny insects on the bark mere inches from her face.

He tugged on the cloak underneath her. She stayed put.

"I didn't mean to make you angry, but ya need to see the truth of things."

It wasn't the truth. Her father would have never harmed Zane. She wouldn't have let him. But she'd had no say when they'd sent Brenna away. Her pleading had fallen on deaf ears, earning her nothing more than looks of pity mixed with disdain from her mother. That hurt so badly that she hadn't dared speak to her Father about Brenna. Would Zane have fared any better?

"Spark." His voice was softer this time. His hand clutched her shaking shoulder.

Sahmara realized she was crying. She was sick of crying, both inside and out. She sniffed and willed the tears to stop.

"Come here and share your blanket, ya cruel woman." Olando gently pulled her closer.

When he tugged at the blanket, she let go. He dove back underneath the woolen warmth. Within seconds his chest was against her back and she was warmer for it. His hand again rested on her shoulder lending her comfort, his body forming a wall of safety from the world beyond their little shelter.

The thunder and lightning had abated but the rain still poured down. More drops filtered through the boughs than before. Sahmara began to doubt that she'd have the comfort of drier clothes by the time the time the rain stopped.

"Your Zane, he was kind to ya?"

"Yes."

"I have seen the scars left by the others who were not so kind." He trailed his fingers down her cheek. "I would like ya to do something for me."

"What would have me do?" She turned to look at him.

"Close your eyes and let me love ya as ya deserve to be loved." His face was filled with kindness, but it was the wrong face.

If she did as he said, she could pretend it was Zane. The others had been too rough, too cruel for the illusion to ever have worked but Olando was trying so hard for a chance to please her. She would try.

His fingers slowly traced the scars on her back. He kissed her shoulder. "These men who have done such things to ya…I would kill them all."

Her heart swelled at his words. She'd imagined Zane saying those very things to her in the dark of the night while drunken soldiers snored by her side. But this was Olando. He was here now and he had a sword and there were plenty of Atherians between them and home. He was an honest man and he'd spoken the words out loud. He *would* make them pay.

She rested her hands on his wiry muscled arms, not to push him away, but debating whether to pull him closer. Would he think she had deserved her fate back in Atheria if she was too wanting now?

His hair brushed over her skin as his lips laid delicate kisses up the side of her neck. "I wish that I could take all the scars away." He whispered, moving slowly toward her mouth. Those were the last words he spoke before he began a sweet assault on her lips that had her lost in her daydream of Zane. Giving herself over, she joined his kiss and for a while, she could have sworn she was back home in her soft bed, the white fur tickling her neck while Zane lay atop her whispering loving words in her ear between lavishing her with deep passionate kisses.

Her body played along with the illusion as well, rising to his touches and waiting anxiously for what was to come. His fingers found her first, making sure she was ready for him and finding that she was, he shifted above her. The moment he entered her, the illusion broke. He moved all wrong, too slow and then too fast. It was too different to maintain the dream. But with relief, she realized that while Olando was not Zane, neither was he causing her pain. It took her a few moments to find the rhythm that he set but when she did the sensations became more enjoyable. Again she closed her eyes, seeking the illusion. Not fully immersed as she had been before but enough so that she didn't give much thought to who she was really with, Sahmara gave herself over to him.

He took much longer than the Atherian soldiers ever had but she wasn't complaining. Rather, she was breathless and near to losing herself as she had only ever done with Zane. When the moment came that she cried out and the world exploded behind her eyelids, she felt guilty, but only for a second. The man atop her drove himself deeply inside her but then quickly pulled himself out to spill his seed onto her belly.

"And that, my dear lady, is how ya should be loved." He said, dropping down to lie beside her.

Unwilling to break the pleasant moment, Sahmara laid her head on his still heaving chest, again closing her eyes. The sound of the rain disappeared in the beating of his heart.

CHAPTER NINE

"Spark." Olando shook her again. "The rain has stopped. We must move quickly before they leave us behind." The moment she was off his chest, he reached for his clothes. Grabbing her own, she was surprised to find that he had been right. They had mostly dried during the time they had spent under the tree. Rather than move the prickly wall he had made, Olando scuttled out above her head once she had moved her bow. Squirming out behind him, Sahmara could see others emerging from various similar shelters. Some looked muddy and miserable while others were much drier and appeared rested. Glad that she was of the later, Sahmara followed closely behind Olando as they joined those coming together in front of Roy.

"We have lost valuable time today. The Atherians must know where we are heading by now. Be on the lookout, especially you, Spark." Roy said. "Any that we can pick off before it comes to swords may save a life. As you see, we're running low on those lately. With Yanis gone, we will be hard pressed to keep them off. We must reach Antochecki soon or we will miss the others. Roger is depending on us. Without all our strength, retaking our cities will not be possible."

Sahmara whispered to Olando, "Who's Roger?"

"Roy's brother. He was on the city council in Antochecki. A good leader that one. Too bad the rest of the council didn't listen to him. The city may not have fallen. They wanted no fight, and seeing the Atherian forces had them far outnumbered, they opened the gates and hoped for mercy."

"I gather they didn't get any?" Having spent enough time

among the Atherians, she knew how they treated their enemies and it had little to do with mercy.

He shook his head and quietly listened to the rest of Roy's instructions.

"Olando, I want your sword up front. Bring the woman with you. The rest of you, keep together. No one goes off alone." Roy waved them all onward.

Sahmara had to run to keep up with Olando as he strode to the front of the already moving group. When they finally dropped into place at the front of the mass of men, she asked, "How likely is it that we'll be attacked before we get there?"

Olando watched their surroundings with every step. "Likely."

"How is it that we keep getting attacked? How long has this been going on?"

"After our first big move that I told you of went wrong, the main mass of us were scattered into much smaller groups. Some of us marched into Atheria to hit their outposts while their forces were out chasing the others. Other's remained in Revochek intent on disrupting the Atherians while they went from city to village as much as possible."

He went quiet as he scanned the trees around them. His feet seemed to cover ground without any effort on his part while she had to tear her gaze from the countryside around them every few strides to make sure she wasn't going to trip over a rock or fallen branch, or step in a hole and break her leg.

"The plan was to fall back to Antochecki once things had settled a bit. The Atherians must have gotten our plans from someone because they've been sending troops to pick us off like they know where we're heading. We don't know how many others made it, and if you ask me, I think Roger and Roy are being too optimistic about any great attack on Antochecki."

Olando fell silent, his face glum. They'd happened across a narrow and game trail that made progress faster, but branches still threatened to slap her in the face if she wasn't careful. The others spread out in a long line behind them, the trail too narrow to allow anyone to walk side by side. Waist-high grasses and bramble bushes lined the path. The bushes threatening to grab her blanket or her sleeves if she got too careless. Trees towered overhead. Muffled words and the shuffling of feet assured her they were all still there.

"We don't know how many men are left, or where they are, or when they'll get there. The plan said the next full moon but we'll be lucky to make that and ya know how fast we've been traveling." He stopped abruptly.

A hush fell over the men. The scraping of metal and creaking of leather signaled the readying of weapons.

Olando raised one hand in the air and pointed the other to the brush to their left. Sahmara got an arrow and a prayer ready, waiting for a target. When the battle cry came, she tried not to jump, but the bellow was so sudden in the absolute tense silence that it was impossible to still the reflex. Her first arrow went wild despite the Mother's help.

The second found a home in the chest of a charging man. Still, he ran towards then, grasping the arrow with one hand, his fierce cry becoming a roar of agony.

Sahmara loosed another. This time it sunk deep into his belly, dropping him into the tall grass. More men ran towards them, some leaping over the fallen man, others running directly overtop him. Sparing a glance to her right, she spotted Olando fighting off two of two large men with skin the color of his own. His face mirroring the look of concentration she'd often seen Zane wear during his practices.

Though the enemy was all around her, so were her friends Everyone was dirty and ragged, making it hard to tell one from the other except by familiar faces. She stepped up onto the remains of a fallen tree to try to get a better vantage point, but even with the Mother's help, there were no clear shots.

Roy and the others hacked at their attackers with swords and axes. The clang of steel on steel echoed in her ears.

Agis and Jon fought back to back, cutting down men and grunting with their efforts. Bart called out threats and ducked through the chaos, stabbing men in the back. Sahmara jumped off the log and slung the bow over her shoulder. She reached for her sword but her hand stilled, her gut screaming for the bow. She knew better than to argue with the Mother.

The sky darkened, and moments later, rain again began to fall. More men burst from the bushes to join the fight.

Before they could join the others, the prayers that were quickly becoming second nature came to her lips and her arrows flew. Everywhere she turned there were more men. In the rain, even familiar faces were hard to discern.

It took an arrow landing directly next to her boot to give her the position of one of their archers. Sahmara made quick work of him and the two others standing by his side near the brush where the second wave of men had come from. The path itself was impossible to find now that the brush on either side had been trampled by men intent on killing on another without regard for the thorns. The battle had expanded onto every bit of ground under the trees, giving her more room to fire through the rain running down her scalp and over her face.

A cry beside her caught her attention. Roy limped away from his attacker. Olando glanced in his direction but there were too many men around him. None of them looked familiar. Sahmara concentrated her arrows on them. Trusting that the Mother would guide her arrows true, she loosed one and after another until the quiver was empty.

The bow was of no further use, whether the Mother wished her to use it or not. She slung it over her burning shoulder and drew Yanis's sword, hoping she remembered some of what little Olando had taught her. Point and thrust were the only things that came to her mind when the first man came at her.

He raised his ax. Her eyes went wide, but she held up her sword. Her legs had a mind of their own. She jumped out of his reach. Spinning around, she landed beside him before he got the chance to raise his heavy weapon again. His belly was a big, soft target. She drove her sword up into his stomach, thrusting with all her might. He staggered forward. Sahmara staggered with him, keeping her hands firmly on the weapon she wasn't willing to lose.

When he collapsed in the wet grass, she wrenched it free. Her hands tingled as she did so. Her shoulder felt hot and wet. She glanced backward to see the dirty cloth that had been Yanis's sleeve was again crimson. She grimaced. If she wasn't careful, the Mother would be drinking her blood too.

"Spark!" Someone called out.

She raised her sword and spun to find the threat. Another man, smaller than the last, rushed toward her with blackened teeth bared in a menacing snarl. His sword was poised to strike.

"You killed my husband." The voice was decidedly female.

Would she be so enraged if someone killed Olando? Though they were far from married, he was the one true connection she'd managed to find since leaving home. Deciding that yes, she would be irate to lose him after what they had shared together, Sahmara focused her fury on the woman before her.

Her defense was a horrible mockery of what Olando had tried to teach her, but her shoulder hurt and the sword was heavy. The woman intent on killing her drove her backward with powerful blows. Sahmara's arm went from tired and hurting to numb. Her heel hit something hard. She stepped over it, retreating under the barrage of attacks.

The woman raised her sword and darted forward. And then suddenly she was face first in the mud as she tripped over the body Sahmara had stepped over.

Not wasting any time, Sahmara plunged her sword into the back of the downed woman. Getting a blood-curdling scream for her efforts, she grabbed her sword. The tingling ran up her arms. She backed away, trying to find an open space to get her bearings. The sounds around her seemed muffled in her ears, the men blurring together. She shook her head, trying to clear it. Then as quickly as it had started, the fighting ceased.

More, mite. More.

Sahmara wiped the rain from her eyes and turned in circles trying to ascertain which side had won. Bodies littered the ground. One was crawling towards her, fighting to get to his knees. It was no one she recognized. She thrust her sword into his side and pulled it out.

Where was Olando? She blinked the rain from her eyelashes as she darted from body to standing man, looking for him. Twice more she came across wounded men. Men who looked no different than those who had dragged her from her home, who had taken her freedom and crushed all hope for the perfect future she had dreamed of since she was a young girl. Now she was the one with the sword and they were the ones crawling on the ground begging for mercy. Like them, she had none to give.

Olando staggered out of the grey rain and came toward her. Blood splattered his face. His sword hung from his hand. "Spark." His voice sounded hollow to her ears. "Spark, it's over. Put down your sword."

Sounds flooded back into her head at full volume. Weeping, moaning and cries for a swift death called out from the mud and grass.

"Did we win?" She surveyed those still standing, searching for the faces she had come to know.

"Yes. I suppose you could call it that." He replied bitterly. "We lost too many. Another attack like that will do us in."

"Then let's hope there isn't another," Roy said, limping over to them. "Gather up those able to walk. Grant Hasi's mercy to the others. We best make quick work of the bodies. We need to put as much ground as we can between us and this place."

Sahmara joined in the plundering of bodies while she reclaimed her arrows. She took everything that was small enough to carry. She also added a few Atherian arrows that she pulled from the back of a body, only to discover that it was Jon when she wrenched the last one free. She took the time to take every coin he had on him as well as a ring of silver that he wore on a leather thong around his neck. Seeing no one else watching her, she spit in his dead face for good measure.

Her quiver was full as were her pockets. She'd found three more daggers and a sword in much better shape than her own.

She gave it to Olando, knowing he could make much better use of it than she would. Besides, hers had belonged to Yanis and it felt wrong to be so quick to get rid of it no matter what shape it was in. It was still sharp and that, as she discovered, was what truly mattered.

On one of the Atherians, she found a leather pack that she took for herself. It was of similar size to Olando's and she felt better for having something of her own to carry the things she was beginning to acquire in this new life. One of her new daggers was adorned with a green jewel, at least she hoped it was a jewel and not just colored glass. She didn't need anyone else trying to steal it from her. She wrapped it in a spare shirt she'd found in another man's threadbare pouch.

The shirt wasn't in any better shape than her own, else she might have been inclined to change into it. Besides the shirt, she had also found a couple mostly shriveled apples and a stick of hard meat. Those also went into her new pouch. Her last acquisition was a white fur lined helm from the woman she had killed. The coins joined the few she had found on Yanis.

Heeding Roy's call to move out, Sahmara wished for a friendly inn so that she would have cause to spend some of her newly acquired coin on a hot bath and a decent meal and perhaps even a real bed. But that night there was no inn.

Instead, she walked in the rain, her body aching and her stomach rumbling. Olando was in similar shape. Neither was in the mood to talk. She didn't dare pull out the food she had found, knowing she would be expected to share with the others. So she walked, praying for a secluded place to stop for a few hours. Sharing food with Olando was one thing, but there wasn't enough to make it worth passing to everyone else.

All told only eighteen had survived. Agis and Bart were unfortunately among the living. Sahmara found herself hoping that they were just as tired as she was because Olando was in no shape to do any defending.

CHAPTER TEN

An hour later the rain stopped and what was left of the sun went down. After two more, Roy brought their march to a halt inside a dense grove of trees. Four rabbits had been scared up in the time it took to set their things down. Someone started a fire.

"We should be safe here." A man Olando informed her was called Wendal decreed. He was an older man, thin and balding but seemingly quite able with the long staff he walked with.

It seemed everyone was hungry and impatient. The rabbits were barely cooked when her small portion landed in her hands. Sahmara didn't care. She ate it hungrily even going so far as to suck the marrow from the tiny bones as she saw others doing.

There were no forks or spoons, no fine plates. No need for table manners or being concerned about who was seated near the salt. Conversation was out of the question and the idea of dressing for dinner seemed perfectly absurd. Her life before seemed like a beautiful dream. Yet in some ways, she was freer now than she had been before.

Olando took her hand and led her to a spot of short, soft grass under the trees. Low hanging branches covered the yellowed leaves. He had spread his cloak and her blanket over the branch to help them dry faster. Sahmara ducked behind the makeshift curtain and pulled her shirt over head. She slipped into the dryer one she'd found earlier.

"Better?" he asked.

"A little. Thank you."

He nodded.

Now that she had more time, she took the helm from her bag and admired it. The fur was matted in places and dirty, but softened the hard edges when she set it on her head.

"You should have taken more armor." He chided. "Though that does suit you nicely."

"I didn't have time, and besides I have a hard enough time keeping up with all of you. Weighing myself down with armor would only make me slower."

"But it would keep you safe." He looked at her shoulder. "Let me check that for you. Here, give me your jug." He took a long drink. "Sit." He pointed at the ground, giving her a look that invited no argument.

Sahmara sat in the grass, pulling her knees to her chest. She did her best not to flinch when he pulled the wide neck of her new shirt down to expose her shoulder. "How is it?"

"I wish we had a healer, ya should have that stitched up. It's quite deep. Who bandaged it?"

"Roy."

"I see."

Sahmara was surprised by his jealous tone. "It was just a bandage, and he wasn't very nice about it. He wasn't happy that I chose to stay behind with Yanis rather than go with the rest of you."

"As ya say." He sounded somewhat satisfied. "Ya don't happen to have a needle and thread?"

"Sorry, didn't have time to grab my sewing basket when I was enslaved and hauled off to Atheria."

He raised a single brow and chuckled. "Ya should have asked to pack first."

"Before or after they put the sack over my head?"

He dabbed at the cut, making her wince. "Probably hard to understand ya with the sack."

"Right, before then. Didn't think of that. I'll try to remember next time."

"There won't be a next time," he said firmly.

"You're right. They wouldn't bother taking me anywhere

now. Serve the line until there's nothing left of me."

"Nah." He pulled the shirt back over her shoulder and rested his hand on her cheek. "You'd kill them all first."

She smiled. "I'd certainly try."

"That you would, dear lady. Just don't try for a few days unless ya have to. Ya need to let that arm rest."

The thought of drawing her bow with her other arm felt wrong and what little balance she did have with the sword would be off if she shifted to her other side. "What if I don't have a few days?"

"Just do what ya can."

"Did you have a woman of your own, you know, before all this?"

"There were a few in the city that would take my coin when I had the fortune to have some, but not many were interested in a poor man who spent his days herding sheep."

"You should have told them that you were guarding the sheep, it sounds so much more dangerous."

"That would have been rather misleading." He snickered. "But yes, you're right. Honesty was not working in my favor."

"Honesty is good too. Not many men can lay claim to that." Seeing him smile, she felt one creeping over her face as well.

"My dear lady, are you actually beginning to like me?"

Sahmara face grew warm and was grateful for the fact that only moonlight filtered through the heavy canopy of leaves overhead. "I never said I didn't." Granted he was not the sort of man she would have chosen at any other time in her life but he was here and he was kind.

"As ya say." He chuckled.

"Here." It was dark enough that she dared pull the apples from her pack. "I have a little something for the morning too. I'm so sick of being hungry."

"Clearly, ya did not have eleven brothers and sisters to share food with. I suppose you'll tell me that your every meal was like a feast to rival those in the songs of a minstrel."

"Not always. There were days when we had to get by on

four courses rather than eight." Sahmara said lightly.

Sadly that had been the truth. There was rarely ever a shortage of food but her mother was frugal with the household funds and often had to convince her food loving daughter that there was no need for putting quite so much on the table at every meal.

"Ya were very fortunate then." The humor had disappeared from his voice.

"Yes. I suppose I was." She bit into the soft apple, trying not to think about whether it might have worms or not. Though there was an edge to it, the juice was still somewhat sweet.

When the apples were gone, they lay down together. There was no longer any hesitation, Sahmara curled up next to Olando with her back against his chest, her head resting on his arm. The night was chilly and the air still moist from the earlier rain. That night there were no dreams of home.

❧☙

For the next three days, they walked. Sometimes they ran. No more attacks materialized out of the brush as the grassland turned to heavy forest. The Atherians who had come before had left a clear path through the trees, having had to make room for their siege weapons. They used the path as much as they dared, grateful to make up some of the time they had lost. On the third night, the wind brought a sour smell as they set up camp.

"What is that?" Sahmara held her hand in front of her nose and mouth.

"We are very near the town of Trentec. A day away from Antochecki."

"So we're close then?"

He nodded, staring off into the woods. The moon covered the mostly bare-branched trees in an eerie silver light.

She almost didn't want to ask, but the stench was truly awful. "What is that smell?"

"I forgot ya have not seen what they have done to the cities and towns," Olando said gravely. "It is the smell of death, my dear lady. I will speak of it no more or you'll not sleep."

Knowing from what she could see of the dismal look on his face, that he was sparing her, she nodded her acceptance of his decision.

Morning came late, the day cold and grey. The foul air made everyone uneasy. "We best pass though Trentec lest any of you forget why we're doing this," Roy announced grimly.

Their solemn nods filled Sahmara with dread.

The march was long and not especially fast since no one was in a hurry to get any closer. When the first of the bodies came into view, lying alongside the road, she couldn't help but close her eyes. But even in that brief glimpse, she'd seen enough to know what she was passing.

A young girl lay rotting on the ground. One arm was missing from what remained of the corpse. A quick glimpse as she tried to keep her place in line, revealed most of the flesh and the eyes were missing. A knotted cord with red wooden beads around her neck marked her as one of the Mother's own. They'd spared no one.

The cries of crows, angry at being interrupted from their feast, filled the air overhead. The closer they got to the gaping hole in the city walls, the more bodies they found. Some were merely jumbled piles of bone, others half-eaten and black with decay. Some were fresher and wore mismatched armor. The stench coming from them made Sahmara's eyes water.

"There are some who will not be joining us in Antochecki," Olando muttered.

Inside the walls, the destruction was far worse than Sahmara could have imagined. Buildings burnt to the ground. The larger structures, skeletons of charred timbers that looked ready to collapse on anyone that dared to get too close. With the absence of foot traffic, weeds had begun to take hold in the bare earth. All that remained of order in the town were the cobbled main streets, though they were littered with debris and bodies.

Feeling her boot catch, Sahmara looked away from the devastation to find she'd almost stepped on what appeared to be a crushed head. What was left of the hair was long and blonde on the flattened skull. It took someone bumping into her from behind to tear her horrified gaze away.

"Why would they do this?" she asked Olando.

"To dissuade people like us from doing what we're doing. If we peacefully become slaves, it would save them much time in taking Revochek. I do not wish to be anyone's slave."

"Nor do I."

Olando spared her a small smile. "I will not let you become anyone's slave."

Reaching out to take his arm, she walked beside him rather than behind him, glad for the comfort he offered. Her presence also seemed to have a positive effect on him, restoring some of the life to eyes that had been filled with sorrow since they had entered the city.

"Why has no one come to take care of these people?" she asked.

"Who would come for them? Everyone here is dead. Anyone left alive is hiding, in the hills, in the forests, or the lucky ones, in their homes."

As if reading her mind, Roy called a halt to their dismal march in what looked to be the marketplace. Overturned carts and the skeletal remains of three horses littered the mostly open space. "We will pray." He declared, his low clear voice carrying in the crisp air. Raising his hands to the foul winds, Roy intoned the prayer for the dead. Bowing their heads, Sahmara and the rest whispered the all too familiar words along with him.

They resumed their walk, some looking side to side and others refusing to look up from their feet. She wondered if any of the men had called Trentec home, but she didn't dare ask.

An hour later, they stood outside the far gate of the ruined city, gathering up their wits and loudly declaring their need for vengeance. Olando merely put his hand on hers and stood silently with his eyes closed for a good while until they were ready to move on.

As they walked onward, Sahmara found the hastily spoken threats of revenge absurd. They were only a few men, mostly wounded, hungry, and all of them exhausted. How could they hope to turn out the Atherians in any manner, let alone bring about the elaborate deaths the men muttered about?

But these people had caused so much death and destruction, they deserved such fates. Didn't they? Wouldn't the gods see the Atherians put in their place? Yet, her people kept losing and the Atherians kept winning and soon there would be nothing left of Revochek.

Surely the Mother wanted revenge too. The young acolyte couldn't be the only one of the Mother's servants to suffer at the Atherian's hands. And how many of Hasi's men had given their lives?

"Too many, mite. We need more."

Sahmara started. *"Get out of my head."*

The Mother merely chuckled but her presence faded, leaving Sahmara feeling empty. She hadn't realized how much the Mother filled and soothed her until she was gone.

More blood would bring her back. More blood would allow them all the revenge they sought, both gods and men. She ran her fingers over the carvings on the bow and then pulled it off her back to examine it while they walked. Something red near the center caught her attention. Probably spatter of blood, but when she searched for it in order to clean it off, she couldn't find it. Her eyes refused to focus on the pattern, but she knew deep inside that it was beautiful.

The quiver weighed heavy on her sore shoulder. She slung the bow across her back and marched with the others toward Antocheck. *Tomorrow we will both have more.*

CHAPTER ELEVEN

"Spark?" Olando whispered in her ear shortly after they had lain down together.

Sahmara turned so that she could see his face in the moonlight. "What?"

He turned his face up to the stars shining brightly in the clear cold night. "Do ya think Antochecki is still standing?"

It was the first time that she had heard him sound uncertain. His breath floated like steam into the night.

"I suppose we'll find out in the morning."

"I suppose we will." He wrapped his arm around her.

The steady sound of his breathing lulled her to sleep.

The horrific images of what she had seen floated through her dreams. The dead girl from the roadside walked toward her with lurching steps. Two crows rode on her shoulders, picking the flesh from her face. Her lipless jaws moved, but the wind was howling, louder and louder, drowning out whatever it was that she was trying to say. The Mother's acolyte raised one arm, pointing one of the three remaining fingers at Sahmara.

Sahmara's eyes flew open. She gasped for breath, her body covered in sweat. Sliding out from beside Olando, she got to her feet to try and walk the dream off. Everyone appeared to be sound asleep, though from the tossing and occasional groan, she gathered that she wasn't the only one that was plagued by nightmares. A stick cracked far off in the woods. It was faint but it had been there. She listened harder, pushing the sounds of the sleeping men out of her head. A cough. A man's cough muffled but certainly there. As quietly as she could, Sahmara darted back to Olando.

She shook his shoulder. "I heard someone."

Half asleep, his bleary eyes fought to focus on her. "What?"

"In the woods, there's someone out there."

He came awake and pulled his sword from its sheath. "Are you sure it's not just someone off having a piss?"

"It was far away. At least I think it was far away." She pointed to where she'd heard the cough and the crack. Doubt crept into her mind. Dealing with men out in the wilds wasn't something she'd had much practice with until lately.

He got to his feet, listening. "Wake the others. Quickly."

Sahmara took a deep breath to still her pounding heart before running to the nearest sleeping form and on to the next.

A stick snapped, grabbing the attention of every man on his feet. "Ya be men of Captain Yanis?" A raspy voice called out.

"Crag, you're still alive?" Roy called out.

"It would seem so." A grinning, white-haired, one-eyed man stepped out of the shadows. "Where's the Captain?"

"Sitting alongside Hasi trading tales of battle, I'd guess."

"That's a damn shame." Crag's face seemed to fall. "He was a great man."

"That he was." Roy nodded, leading Crag into the camp. "How many do you have with you?"

"Nearly a hundred. Me and couple scouts were having a look around. Glad we found ya. Or what's left of ya." Crag surveyed the men before him with a sorrowful shake of his head. "Damned Atherians."

"If anyone should be damned it's those scouts that mislead us. Had we known what we were truly up against, I'm sure the Captain would have done things much differently."

"Of that, I have no doubt." Crag agreed. "I hope you're taking good care of his horse. Yanis is like to come back and haunt us all if she's not cared for just right. Mila was as much his wife as any woman could be."

She bowed her head and stood closer to Olando now that it was clear there was no danger to be had.

"So ya did care for him?" he asked.

"I barely knew him." Sahmara squeezed his hand, then left Olando with the men to talk of the others they had lost.

She sat within view of the others, watching and listening as they mourned the loss of friends and brothers. She was not the only one who had lost everything. It was little wonder that Yanis had been a sullen, angry man of few words. If she ever made it to a shrine, she'd vowed to make a suitable offering in his honor.

More men filtered through the trees, joining those she knew. Someone stoked the fire. Backs were slapped and welcomes exchanged. Their hushed voices blurred into a drone that coaxed her eyelids to slip closed.

This time she dreamed of Yanis. Like the acolyte, he also seemed to be trying to talk to her, but no sound came from his sand-covered lips. She took comfort that no birds were feasting upon him, and other than being pale and covered with a fine dusting of sand, he could have been alive.

When she woke, Sahmara found that she held Yanis' sword pressed against her chest. She stretched her cramped arms and put the sword away. Olando made a much better bedmate than the sword did, but he was still missing from her side.

The conversation by the fire was still going strong. Sahmara sighed. Since sleep wasn't her friend, she decided to hunt Olando down and see what she could learn about Crag's plans to retake their homeland.

Making her way to the fire proved treacherous. Sleeping bodies lay underfoot everywhere. The flickering flames ahead made it harder to see in the dark. By the time the warmth of the fire kissed her skin, she'd spotted Olando sitting next to Roy and Crag and several others. She wriggled her way in closer and slid to the ground next to him.

Crag's heavily lined face frowned with disapproval. "Ya got a woman with ya?"

"We found her wandering in Atheria," Roy said. "We couldn't just leave her there. Besides, Yanis claimed her and no one was going to argue with that."

"Taking the Captain's leaving are ya?" Crag looked to

Olando with a raised bushy white eyebrow. "One of the guard? I don't recognize ya."

"No, Sir." Olando took a deep breath, clearly not willing to elaborate.

"He was a sheepherder out of Antochek," Roy said, clearly having no qualms about laying out the bare truth.

Olando scowled, his body stiffening. Sahmara considered glaring at Roy, but he wasn't paying her any attention. She rested her hand on Olando's arm.

Crag shook his head, a smirk on his lips. "Couldn't leave him behind either?"

"Actually, he's the best sword we have left."

Whether Roy's acknowledgment of his skill or appreciation of her support, he relaxed slightly and slipped his other hand over hers.

"Good thing I found ya sheep when I did then, eh?"

"We're not sheep." Roy glared at Crag. "Olando is good with his sword and has been since the day we took him on. Yanis spoke nothing but praise for the man. You might want to consider that before saying anything further."

If Roy meant what he said, he must never have voiced his appreciation before because Olando's brows rose and his mouth gaped a bit. Sahmara squeezed his arm. She'd known he was competent with a sword and he'd told her he was the best among them with Yanis gone, but she'd assumed he was bragging, at least to some degree. It would seem not.

Crag turned toward Olando. "Well then, boy, if Yanis spoke for ya I guess ya must be all right. What use is the woman, other than for bedding, I mean?"

"She's good with a bow. The only archer we've got at the moment." Olando said.

He gripped her hand tightly. She made no mistake that it was not in support but a warning to keep her temper under control. She swallowed her annoyance down, but she wasn't happy about it.

"Well, I suppose that is useful." He conceded, turning his attention back to Roy.

"Actually," Olando said, "She hurt her shoulder pretty bad. You wouldn't happen to have a healer among you?"

"Have you seen my men? No, sheepherder, we don't have a healer among us."

His nostrils flared but he kept his voice level. "Do you have archers then? She really shouldn't be drawing that bow until it heals."

Roy looked between Crag and Olando and then settled his glare on Sahmara. " We'll be in Antochecki tomorrow. Hurt or not, I expect a bow in your hands at the first sign of trouble, woman. You understand?"

Sahmara nodded.

"Good. Olando, you better see that she does, or we'll all be the worse for it." Roy dismissed them with a nod. "Now get some rest."

Olando led her away to where they had left their belongings. "Can't say as I like him," she said under her breath.

"You're not alone, but we need his men." He sighed. "We'll be moving out soon I'd guess. Might as well let your shoulder rest while we can." He gestured to the blanket. "Unless you need to…"

"Piss?"

He snickered. "I've never known a lady to say piss."

Sahmara chuckled. "You haven't known any ladies but me. How would you really know?"

He laughed. "As ya say. Yet it sounds funny coming from your lips. They were not made for saying such things."

"Now you sound like my mother." She slapped him lightly on the arm. "I can go on my own, thank you very much."

"There are too many men here now and most of them don't know you. Don't go anywhere alone. Stick by me or Roy."

"I take it Crag's men aren't anymore well-mannered than Bart and Agis?"

He peered off into the snore-filled darkness. "None of us are."

"I wouldn't say that." She kissed his cheek.

Olando smiled and pointed again at the blanket.. "Get some sleep, dear lady, before I have a mind to prove ya wrong."

Sahmara settled onto the blanket, making sure her sword was within reach. Olando lay down next to her, stroking her head with his fingertips.

"Your hair, it's beginning to grow."

"Really?" She ran her fingers over the light fuzz.

"Your head has been bare since you came to be with us. How is it that it is suddenly growing?"

"I don't know."

Olando kissed the back of her neck. "Perhaps this day is not entirely bad after all."

"You might be right." She only hoped that it kept growing. To have her hair back would go a long way toward making her feel herself again.

"Spark, can I ask ya something?"

"Yes, of course."

"The jug. How is it that it is full every morning yet I never see you fill it?"

Sahmara pinched her eyes shut and wished the question away, yet it hung between them. She sighed. "It's enchanted I guess you could say."

"Where did ya get it?"

"On the beach near where Yanis found me. It was a gift from an old woman. She also gave me the bow and arrows. I had nothing when she found me. Not even these clothes. They came from her as well."

"The other things, are they enchanted?"

"The clothes, no. The bow… Perhaps," she said reluctantly.

"Did this old woman touch you?" He asked just as reluctantly.

"Touch me?" Sahmara carefully shifted onto her back so she could look at him.

"Spark, there is an old story that my mother told us as children. A story passed from her mother and such. It is the tale of an old hermit woman who lives on the beach and every night at sunset she comes out from her house to search for those who have lost their way. She can never leave the beach but helps those who wander to it. In return, she takes their blood so that she can live long enough to help the next lost soul." He shook his head. "I always thought she just told us stories like that so we wouldn't wander off."

"It wasn't just a story." She rested her head on his shoulder, praying he wouldn't pull away. "Yes, she touched me."

He didn't move. "Does that make you blessed or cursed?"

Having no answer, Sahmara let silence fall upon them.

CHAPTER TWELVE

They woke to the mouth-watering aroma of a stew that had simmered for a few hours. After waiting their turn in line, they gratefully slurped down their cup-full. The arrival of Crag's men had its benefits, one of which was more men able to hunt and the other was one man who'd declared himself the camp cook. Given the luxury of a fully-cooked meal, even if the portion was small, went a good way to restoring their spirits. Sahmara hoped to never be subjected to moldy biscuits or half-cooked meat again.

Roy and Crag pulled several other men she didn't know aside and sunk into a hushed discussion. The rest of the men gave them a wide berth, seeming to relish the time to rest and tend to their weapons and well-worn armor. Olando put the cup they'd shared away in his pack and set to sharpening his sword before going to work on hers.

"This was his father's sword," Olando said as he tried to clean some of the rust away from the blade that had belonged to Yanis. "He was just as crazy about it as he was about Mila. They were the only two things that mattered to him. But after we were divided and Mila was put down, he stopped caring for it. Used to be, you could see your reflection in the blade." He drew his stone over it with well-practiced strokes. "He lost the scabbard in that first fight. We should look for a better one so it's easier for you to wear."

She watched him in case she should need to care for the sword on her own. "When we get to Antochecki?"

"Perhaps. Crag wants to set out before midday. They're just

clearing up the details now. Ya need to stay still until we do. We need your shoulder rested."

Sahmara settled herself on the blanket next to him and listened to the rasp of the stone on steel. Echoes of similar sounds rippled through camp. She wondered what Zane was doing. Would he be sharpening his sword too, maybe staring at the same grey sky? Her thoughts drifted to her parents. She'd not seen them in any dream or vision. She prayed that Sloveski hadn't suffered the same fate as Trentec.

Murmurs spread throughout camp, the men passing word from one to the next. Within minutes, everyone had packed up and was ready to move out.

Crag stood on a log and addressed the milling men. "I want the swordsmen of Yanis at the front. Keep your archer with you. The rest stay close behind. You've got your groups. We'll spread out once we enter the city to avoid detection.

"We've word Antochecki has been hit hard. There'll be no looting, ya hear? We're here to find any of our men who may have lived to meet us and that's it. If you see an Atherian, kill him. If you see many Atherians, fall back. We can't afford to lose the lot of you. Now, move out."

Sahmara stuck close to Olando and the few men she knew. Crag's fifteen archers traveled near the rear. Her pounding heart wanted her to be with them.

"When we get closer," Olando said, "I want you behind Roy. In fact, work your way back as far as you can. I don't want you up front if there's any trouble."

"I have a sword too."

"You're far better with your bow."

She nodded, not truly wanting to argue, but not wanting to look a coward either. "I will."

Crag's men traveled with determination, driving Sahmara and the others ahead of them. Weary men jogged and sweated beside her. The stink of them encouraged her to breathe the chilled fall air through her mouth as she did her best to keep up. Yet, for all she tried, Olando slowly pulled ahead of her and then Roy was beside her. Then his broad back filled her view. Soon strangers surrounded her. She hadn't meant to fall back yet, but her legs made that decision for her.

"Where ya from?" asked the man beside her now.

"Sloveski."

He nodded. "Hagenton."

"On the coast, right?" She remembered seeing that name on her father's map. He'd docked trading ships there.

"Ya been there?"

"No, just heard of it." She was about gasping for breath with trying to keep up and talking at the same time. Sahmara slowed half a step and let him drift ahead of her.

Twice she spotted Olando and Roy up ahead. She missed the relative safety of their presence. Crag's men didn't know her. Most didn't know she *was* a her, and she wanted to keep it that way. Sahmara pulled her helm down on her fuzzy scalp. The fur edging tickled the tops of her ears.

Within a short while, the helm lining was soaked with sweat. She wanted to rip it off. Men bumped against her, their faceless forms drifting ahead one by one as she fell further back within their ranks.

As the city walls rose over the trees, they broke away from the trails they'd been using to reach Antochecki. At least the walls were still standing.

One guard atop the wall, frozen in place. Within minutes, six more men stood beside him.

The man beside her pulled a bow from his back. Had she really fallen back that far? She glanced around and found that she had. At least Olando would be happy. But her bow wouldn't be at the front to protect them like Roy and Crag had wanted. She prayed to the Mother that they would be safe.

The goddess didn't answer.

Sahmara followed the lead of the other archers and readied her bow. When she put an arrow to her string, the man beside her scowled. "Don't shoot until Holms gives us a target." He nodded toward a thickset man in a ragged uniform who stood a few rows in front of them.

She never had to wait for someone to choose her target

before. The longer she stood there watching the men atop the wall, the more it chaffed at her. What were Holms and Crag waiting for?

The men atop the wall converged on one of their number. A single body tumbled over the edge. It landed in a mass of sharpened sticks below, arms hanging wide open as if inviting an embrace from the sky above. The body settled there limp and still. Another followed a second later. The men around her cheered quietly.

"What just happened?" she asked the archer beside her.

His squinty gaze gave her a once over. "Ya must be new."

She nodded.

"We had a message that some of our men had infiltrated their ranks. Seems they outnumbered the others on the wall. We heard the Atherians have moved their main force onto the next city. After that big mess though, Crag don't trust nobody. He's a cautious man, and I'm still alive. Can't argue with that."

"I suppose not," she said.

The gates began to close, their chains creaking.

Holms pointed to the men just inside the quickly closing gates. "Now!"

Sahmara loosed her arrow and several more after that, only halting when the signal was given to stop. The gates were nearly closed as the front line of men reached them with swords in hand and battle cries on their lips.

More men crowded the tops of the walls. Arrows fell upon the men approaching the gate.

"Aim for anyone on the walls!" Holms shouted.

A volley of arrows rained down, downing several of the city's archers. Sahmara found herself praying not only that her arrows found a home in the enemy but that they didn't stray into those, that for the time being, she was loosely calling friend.

Another wave of men rushed past to join those already making headway at the gate that had never quite closed. Men poured into the narrow opening, leaping over the bodies of the fallen that had caused the jam.

The clang of steel and battle cries of men filled the air. Her quiver near empty, and all but a few of Crag's swordsmen left on the outside of the gates, Sahmara allowed herself a few seconds to glance over the bodies littering the trampled ground. Olando wasn't one of them.

Holms beckoned the archers to follow the remaining men into the city. Sahmara put the bow over her shoulder and drew her sword. She stumbled over bodies as the push of men shoved her through the gates.

A thickset man with an angry snarl and bloody side charged at her. Leaping aside, Sahmara swung her sword but missed. He charged again, grazing her thigh with his blade as she retreated further. All around her chaos ensued. Men grunted, screamed and yelled as they exchanged blows with all manner of weapons. Swords sliced through the air. Arrows pierced men. The more she moved blindly, the more likely she'd end up the victim of either.

Sahmara clenched her teeth, uttered a prayer, and held her sword firmly. When he charged again, she held her ground. She thrust deep into his already wounded ribs. The man fell, taking her sword with him.

The glimpse of a sword flashing through the air toward her head was all she saw as she spun aside to evade the deadly blow. She fumbled to grab her dagger from her belt but managed to finally get it in hand and twisted away from the next downward swing.

Sahmara darted back to buy herself some space. He came at her again. While his hands were busy raising his sword, she raced at him with speed she hadn't known her weary body yet possessed and plunged the dagger into his shoulder. He glanced at the offending blade. A tingle ran up her arm, making her almost giddy with an energy she'd never felt before.

She wrenched her sword free from the dead man and brought it up just in time to block the next attack. Before he could swing again, an arrow plunged through his chest, dropping him to the dirt. A friendly archer nodded in her direction before turning the bow for his next shot.

Breathing heavily and heart racing, Sahmara followed what remained of Crag's men as they moved further into the city. Citizens joined them along the way, armed with whatever they had grabbed before dashing out of their homes. A girl, likely no older than herself, fell into step beside her, wielding a worn and nicked short sword. Her green eyes narrowed in anger as she searched for a target for her rage. Feeling a kindred spirit, Sahmara stuck by her side.

They worked well together, the girl distracting their target while Sahmara attacked with her sword from behind. They were able to take out four men before breaking into a large courtyard filled with men fighting for their lives. The rush of energy waned, unable to mask the pain in her shoulder any longer. Each time the tingle came it left her feeling raw and a few inches further outside her body. Her sword arm shook with exertion. She needed to find a safe place to sit down for a few minutes. Pulling the girl behind her, she ducked back around a corner, sinking into the afternoon shadows.

"I'll use my bow, watch my back," she ordered, wondering where the sudden authority in her voice came from.

The girl, her face spattered with blood, merely nodded.

With only a handful of arrows left, she had to make every one of them count. She picked out her target on the edge of the fray, waiting for just the moment when he would turn his back on her so that she had the widest target available. With a prayer, she launched her arrow with deadly purpose. When he fell, she found a second target and then a third.

"Watch out!" The girl screamed.

Sahmara's concentration shattered, sending her last arrow wild into the crowd. She spun around, dropping the bow and drawing her sword. The girl tried to stab at their attacker once but he knocked her aside with a heavy blow to her face. The sword shook in Sahmara's hand as she held it up to guard herself.

He grabbed her wrist before she could jab at him. His grip crushed her wrist until she let the blade drop. Somewhere, seemingly far away, the sword clattered on the cobbles.

Though the world around her took on a distant blur, fetid breath wafted into her face with a sense of unwelcome clarity.

He shoved her hard against the wall. His large hand wrapped around her throat.

His intense grip made it impossible to draw another breath. Spots floated before her eyes. Then suddenly the pressure eased and his hand was gone. Her legs shook beneath her and if it hadn't been for the wall, she would have fallen into the dirt.

The man dropped to the ground on his belly, vainly trying to reach the middle of his back where the hilt of a worn short sword protruded.

The look on the girl's face was so familiar, that Sahmara took her in her arms and held her close. The horrific realization of killing someone was something she understood well.

"It will be all right," she whispered over and over to the trembling girl while still trying to keep an eye out for anyone coming up behind them. The worst of the fighting seemed to be beyond them, having moved mostly through the courtyard. Her own head spun and her shoulder burned. "We need to get out of the street. Is there somewhere safe close by?"

The girl nodded numbly, pulling out of Sahmara's arms but then taking her hand in a death grip. She picked up the fallen bow with the other, peering at the carvings a moment and then handing it to Sahmara. She slung it over her shoulder and retrieved her sword.

Sahmara followed as the girl led them through the maze of buildings, back the way they had come. Here and there small pockets of men did their best to kill one another, the noise of their efforts stark against the moaning of the not quite dead on the streets.

"My home." She pointed to a stone building with a narrow garden lining the walk.

Joining the girl inside, Sahmara found nothing but the expected common household items inside the tidy two-room house. Two beds stood along the wall opposite from the one she leaned against. "Where's your family?"

"The soldiers killed my father for not allowing them to take me and my mother. Then they took her and my brother away. I buried my father, and I haven't seen my mother or brother since. The soldiers…they come to *visit*." She looked at the floor.

"They won't be visiting anymore. You've seen what is happening to them out there. You're free now."

The girl sobbed and drew Sahmara into a tight hug. She jerked backward and raised her brows. "You're a woman!"

"Yes?" Sahmara shrugged, wondering what difference that made.

Determination dried her moist eyes. "Take me with you. They need to pay for what they've done."

Sahmara made her way to the bench beside the table and considered the request. It would be nice to have another woman around, someone who understood what she'd gone through, to have someone to talk to. Would the others allow it? She'd just gotten her place mostly settled, and now they had all of Crag's men to deal with. Did she want to have another woman around to cause the same problems? This one didn't even have an enchanted bow to help her gain respect. All she had was the short sword that, though she could use it, had also clearly only used it once.

It wouldn't hurt to ask, would it? "I'll talk to the others." She'd at least ask Olando about it, but she didn't want to crush the hopeful look in the girl's eyes just then by pointing out her lack of clout with the men.

"Would you? Please? I can't stay here." She motioned around the room. "Not after what they did to my father, to me in this place."

Would she agree so quickly if she realized she would only be exchanging the needs of many soldiers for the needs of one? Who could she trust to treat this girl well? Maybe one amongst Crag's men was like Olando. Maybe. Certainly none of Roy's men. She would be sentencing this poor girl to be shared around the fire if she chose unwisely. She'd heard their hopeful stories at night, thinking that Olando might be swayed by their words. Thankfully he hadn't. She didn't think she could bear that. She'd take as many of them out as she could before they killed her because there was no way she was going to lay there and take what they wanted to give.

"What is your name?" she asked the girl.

"Sara." Her wide green eyes looked up at Sahmara, so filled with hope that it near broke Sahmara's heart.

"Have you ever used anything but that short sword? A dagger, a bow?"

Sara shook her head. "I didn't dare get my father's sword out until this morning. They would have taken it if they'd known I had it. I only got it out when I heard the soldiers shouting that we were being attacked. Even then, I wasn't sure which bodies to try to stick it into. It wasn't until I saw you that I found courage enough to use the sword." She dropped her gaze to the floor. Long dark curls slipped over her face.

"You would need to learn."

"I can do whatever you want me to do. Please, just take me with you."

Could she take Sara with her right now? "The men I'm with are little better than the ones here. I don't know if you understand what you are asking."

"Surely they don't force you to…" Her face flushed. "You're one of them. I saw you kill many men today. No man could make you serve his wishes, not when you are a soldier too."

Sahmara wished that very thing were true. "I'm only a woman. Just like you. Very like you, actually." She smiled weakly. "I am claimed by one man. A good one. He treats me well and has been teaching me how to use my sword. Being a woman among these men is little different than what you have here. I have an honorable man." She faltered, wondering where he was just then. "At least I hope I do. I haven't seen him since we charged the city walls."

If he were gone, would she be stuck with another, having to pick the lesser of evils? Would Agis and Bart try to claim her for themselves? Her mouth went dry. She had to find Olando. He had to be safe.

Sara put a hand on her arm, rubbing it gently. "You will see him again." She smiled, her white teeth shining radiantly in the sunlight that shown through the one window.

Sahmara forced a smile. "What I'm trying to say is, I don't know that you'll get a good man like I did. You'll be taking your chances. They may use you until there is nothing left and toss you aside for all I know. Crag, he's the one in charge," she explained. "He doesn't seem to like the men being distracted by having a woman along. Even one who can fight beside them."

The hoped dimmed in Sara's eyes. "But you're one of them." Her lower lip began to tremble.

Her words swirled in Sahmara's mind, giving her inspiration. "Perhaps I am just that." She grinned. "You will have to do everything I say without question. Can you do that?"

Sara nodded. "I will. I promise."

"You may be asked to do things you find distasteful, but they must be done or another will try to claim you."

"Nothing can be worse." She shook her head. "To have a chance to get back at them...I'll do whatever it takes."

Sahmara was heartened to see so much conviction on Sara's beautiful face. That fact alone was going to make what she was going to do even harder. "Then I claim you, Sarah. You can call me Spark."

Sara grinned and embraced her tightly. "Oh thank you, thank you." She kissed Sahmara lightly on the cheek. Then she pulled back. "But you're a woman. Can you do that?"

"We'll find out."

"But you're claimed by a man. Would I belong to both of you?"

"We could make that work. Or you could stay here. You haven't left your house yet. You can still change your mind."

"No," Sara said firmly. "Let me get my things."

"Take only what you can carry. We do a lot of walking."

Just thinking about the trek she'd been on, made her body ache and her eyes begged to close. "Go ahead and pack, I'll just rest here a minute." She took off her helm and rested her head on one arm, letting the wounded one hang by her side.

Sara dashed around the house, gathering up bottles, clothing, a sewing kit, and a multitude of other things into a large pack.

"Make sure you keep it light."

"I have food. How much should I bring?"

Real food. Sahmara's mouth watered. "Bring anything that will last. I can carry some as well." She regretted that her pack was back at the camp.

Sara handed her a wheel of cheese wrapped in cloth and several wide strips of dried meat. She put a good deal of fruit at the top of her own pack.

Sahmara waved at her dress. "You'll want to change. Men's clothes work best." Looking like she did now, young and pretty, was only asking for trouble.

"Yes, of course." With only slight hesitation, Sara slipped out of the blood-spattered simple dress that she had worn on their run through town. She turned her back to Sahmara as she pulled her shift over her head, leaving her naked as she reached into a trunk at the end of the bed on the far end of the room. After fumbling around for a few seconds, she crouched down to root through the contents.

Sahmara couldn't help but look at the young woman. Her skin was fair, marred only by a few fading bruises on her back. She did not appear to bear any of the scars Sahmara did. A healthy glow proved she had worked outside a good deal, but she was also well fed and certainly well formed. For this one moment, she was glad her parents were far away so she could enjoy the view without any guilt.

Sahmara cleared her throat. "Something baggy would be good."

While Sara dressed in what could only be her father's clothing, doubts ate at Sahmara. Sara was beautiful, much more so than herself. Her charming spirit shown through her big eyes and full lips. Would Olando prefer Sara? She could hardly blame him if he did. But could she risk losing him? If he tossed her aside, Agis and Bart wouldn't hesitate to finish what they'd started. They'd make her pay for every word and gesture.

She was just about to revoke her claim and head back out into the streets to find Olando when Sara turned around. Her shining smile melted Sahmara's heart. She couldn't leave her behind. Nor did she really want to.

Sara walked over and knelt in front of her, resting her head on Sahmara's lap. "I will do whatever you ask. Thank you."

Brushing the hair from Sara's face, she admired the thick silky curls against her fingertips. Would her own ever feel that away again?

Sara sighed wistfully and turned around to face her. A slight scowl touched her lips. "You're hurt," she said as if she'd just taken the time to notice the layers of dried blood on Sahmara's shoulder. "I have some ointment for that."

She leaped to her feet, rummaging through the jars she'd left on a shelf on the kitchen wall. She returned with a small brown clay jar and gently pulled the bandage from Sahmara's shoulder. She hissed. "That needs stitches." She dug through her pack and pulled out the sewing kit.

Sara buzzed about the kitchen, getting a bowl of water and dabbing a clean strip of cloth into it and then onto Sahmara's shoulder. Sahmara winced.

"Sorry, this is going to hurt, but you can't keep tearing that open or it will never heal right. It's going to scar anyway, but at least we can make it start healing properly."

"You're a healer?" She asked trying to take her mind off the pain.

"My mother dabbled. The neighbors trusted her as a midwife. The rest rather came along with that as needed. I helped when she required it." She cleaned the cut on Sahmara's leg as well. Then she pulled out a needle and a length of thread. "This will hurt."

Sahmara had pricked herself with a needle enough to know the pain they caused, but the thought of being the cloth, of the thread dragging through her skin made her break out in a cold sweat.

"I don't know if I can do this," Sahmara whispered.

"Sure you can. Just watch out the window. Let me know if anyone is coming."

"What if someone does come?" She'd be no help with a sword if Sara was busy sewing up her shoulder when a soldier barged in.

"We'll deal with that if we need to. For now, just yell."

The needle jabbed into her flesh. Sahmara cried out.

"Quiet now, we don't want to attract attention."

"I know. It's just…" The thread tugged through her skin and then another jab. She gritted her teeth, trying to keep her screams inside.

"Hush now. Don't squirm. You'll only make this take longer," Sara said as if she was talking to a child with a skinned knee. "We're almost done here. Just a couple more."

By the time Sara finished, Sahmara was feeling dizzy again. As much as she wanted to go find Olando, flopping onto the floor like a fish wasn't impression she wanted to make on Sara. She breathed deep through her nose and out through her mouth until the hollow thrumming in her ears faded. Sara rifled through a basket and pulled out two long clean strips of cloth.

"Now that your wounds are clean, let's keep them that way." She opened the clay pot and dabbed yellow paste on the wounds then wrapped her shoulder and leg with the cloth. "Good as new. As long as you can rest for a bit, that is."

"The chances of that happening aren't very likely."

"Then at least take it easy when you can."

"Not much time for that either."

Sahmara wondered if Sara would be cut out for this. Sure the soldiers came to her home, but they left her there, surrounded by food and comforts with maybe a guard at her door. She wasn't walking through sand, grasslands, or ruined cities on an empty stomach all day. How long would she retain her beauty and youth with arrows and swords and rough men all around her?

She eyed the bed by the trunk, covered with quilts. It looked so warm and soft. She wanted nothing more than to crawl into it and sleep for days. And maybe a bath, and a full meal. And clean clothes. And to feel as good as Sara looked. She sighed.

"You won't get any beds on the march."

Sara's face crinkled. "That bed? I'd rather burn it than sleep in it again."

"Are you really sure you want to come along?"

"Yes, and not another word about it."

Sara knew healing and that was something all of them would value. Maybe that would be enough to grant her safety.

"You're good with the needle and thread, what else do you know of healing?"

"Mother didn't like me around the men who came for help, so I mostly helped with the women and children. Most of it was setting bones or birthing when she needed an extra set of hands. I do know some plants. She had me gather what she needed when she was busy with my brother."

"Good. If anyone questions you being with me, you're a healer. Got it?"

"But, I don't know how…"

"We've had nothing. You're what we have now. What you don't know, do the best you can."

Sara nodded.

Sahmara eyed the chest. "Do you perhaps have an extra shirt? Mine is rather bloody and cut."

"Yes. There is one more." Sara went to the chest and pulled out a faded blue homespun shirt. She shook it out and handed it to Sahmara. "It was too small for my father. He wore it when he was younger. We were saving it for my brother. I can wash your other one and sew it up for you."

"I don't know as we'll have time for that. Clean clothes are a luxury of the past."

"At some time then. Wear this one for now." Sara glanced back at the chest. "Do you have a cloak?"

"No." Though she'd planned to relieve one of many dead bodies of one before they left the city. The days were growing colder, the mornings especially.

"You're tall enough. My father's shouldn't drag too much on you." She took a folded bundle from the chest and set it on the table beside Sahmara.

Sahmara started to take off her shirt, but the fresh stitches on her shoulder stung. Sara set the shirt beside the cloak and helped her. Sahmara felt her hands falter.

"Did they do that to you?"

"Yes. I wasn't very cooperative at first."

Sara's soft hands ran over her back. "I'm sorry I can't take those away for you."

"That's all right. I'm working on it."

Sara slipped the clean shirt over her hand and helped her get her arms through. She came around to stand in front of Sahmara. "And I will help you with that too."

Sahmara grinned as Sara spread the cloak over her shoulders. A comforting warmth settled upon her.

"Let's go find Olando." She reached for the cheese and dried meat, but Sara batted her away. You're not carrying anything extra right now. You're resting, remember?"

"I'll have to carry my things when we get back to camp. You can't do that too. And your pack will get heavy, you aren't used to carrying it all day."

"Then you will carry your pack when we get back to camp, but until then, you rest."

"All right, all right. I'll rest."

"Good." Sara gathered up her things and slipped the food into a second long-strapped sack that she slung over her other shoulder. She tucked her father's short sword through her belt. "Let's go."

Leaving Sara's house behind, they set off to learn who controlled the city.

CHAPTER THIRTEEN

Bodies lay in the streets. Sahmara and Sara avoided them, never trusting the dead to be fully dead. Sara stayed right by her side.

"You need more arrows," Sara said.

"There should be a lot of them by the gate." Sahmara led the way there. She too would feel safer once her quiver was again full.

Bodies lay piled on top of each other, the mad rush to get into the city through the closing gates plain as day. Many of them sported arrows.

"Wait here," she told Sara. Sahmara drew her sword and approached the nearest body. She kicked him first. He didn't move, grunt, or even flutter an eyelid. She yanked the arrow from his chest. Her finger tingled.

There were enough arrows here to fill several quivers. Had any of the other archers made it into the city? It didn't look as though anyone had come through yet to plunder the dead. She worked her way through the bodies quickly, harvesting arrows and ending a few lives while she was at it. She lost track of how long her finger tingled. The Mother was getting her fill today.

By the time she was done, Sara's nerves looked ready to shatter. Sahmara slung her full quiver over her good shoulder and gathered up the rest of the arrows in her arms. It was a light but bloody load. The other archers, if there were any left, could clean them later.

Sahmara led them back along the streets, following the thickest trail of bodies. Now and then she'd glimpse a living person between the buildings or on the other side of the street, but they left her and Sara alone. Most seemed more intent on plundering the dead than attacking anyone.

The buildings crowded inward the closer they got to the center of the city. The narrow road made the dodging of bodies near impossible. Some looked like they'd been in the streets long before Crag had led the charge on the city.

"Doesn't anyone care for the dead anymore?" Sahmara muttered.

"They wouldn't let us. I managed to bury my father behind our house, but the ones in the streets, they declared would serve as a warning," Sara said in a tense whisper, her gaze darting to every shadow and moving form. "They burned piles of them every few days. I saw the smoke. Must be they didn't get to this street yet."

"I see." Sahmara stumbled over an outstretched arm. Looking down, she was dismayed to find it was the friendly archer from the coastal town. Half of his face was missing.

She took a deep breath and crouched. After setting the extra arrows down, she pulled his quiver from around his limp body. With his bloodstained quiver filled, she slung it over her shoulder beside her own. She felt better, knowing she could grab her sword if she needed to without having to drop all the arrows first.

A ragged voice halted their progress through the streets. "Where ya off to?"

Her pulse raced for a second until she recognized him as one of Crag's men. "We're looking for the others. Are they up ahead?"

The man glared at her. "You'd know where they are if you'd have stuck with them instead of running off."

She glared right back. "Hardly. We got separated. That's all."

"Tell your tale to Crag. Don't matter none to me. Off with ya boy." He waved them toward a long sprawling building that looked to have many additions in whatever style was popular at the time.

Entering the building, they found an open hall full of milling soldiers seeing to each other's wounds, comparing accounts and some staring numbly at the wooden floor. Sahmara scanned their faces for Olando. Everything depended on his being alive and well. With Sara right behind her, she worked her way around the hall. She spotted Roy bandaging a wounded man who was sitting on a bench. Other men crowded around him, likely waiting their turn. She didn't want to draw too much attention to herself or Sara so she stood nearby and waited for him to notice her.

Roy finished with the man on the bench and looked up for his next patient. He spotted Sahmara. "Ah, Spark, there you are. I was beginning to think we lost you."

"No such luck." She forced a smile, making sure to keep Sara behind her.

"Olando's been looking for you. Likely losing his mind by now." He pointed around what she thought was the back wall, only to discover it was a passageway.

She dodged a crowd of men and made her way around the corner. Men sat against the walls on the floor, their legs further obstacles to keep her from her goal. One particularly grim-faced one, leaped to his feet when she drew near.

Suddenly grinning from ear to ear, Olando raced towards her. He grabbed her arm, pulling her down the hallway to a second room where far fewer men milled about. He pulled her into a nearly bone-breaking embrace.

"Where have ya been? I've been so worried." He held her at arm's length, looking her up and down. "No one remembered seeing ya after the rush on the courtyard. Are ya hurt?" He took in her fresh bandages with a questioning glance.

Sahmara pulled herself back against his solid, whole and comforting chest, relishing the sound of his beating heart. "I'll be fine."

He held her there a moment before letting his arms fall to his sides. "Ya were hurt. What happened?"

"That's all taken care of now."

A slight scowl replaced his relief. "How long have ya been

here? Why did no one get me? I left word with everyone I could think of that might recognize ya."

"I just got here. Roy told me where you were. It was Sara who saw to me." She gestured for Sara to come forward. Olando's dark eyes took in Sarah, detail by detail, and certainly in no particular hurry.

Jealousy burned through Sahmara's veins. She cleared her throat loudly. He pulled his gaze away but seemed to have lost his tongue. She leaned in close. "That's quite enough of that."

"Spark, I…" His gaze drifted from her to Sara and back again.

She thrust her fist onto her hip and gave him a challenging glare. "She's mine, so don't get any ideas."

"Yours?" He asked as though she was speaking in a foreign tongue.

"Mine. I killed just as many men back there as everyone else." She waited for him to contradict her, but he merely nodded.

"So I heard. Ya did well. I'm very proud of ya." He rested his hand on her good shoulder and squeezed it lightly.

She found herself smiling even though she was trying to be firm about Sara's position with them. Her heart swelled from his words. Her throat threatened to silence her voice but she swallowed the warmth and brought back her father's no-nonsense tone. "So you understand that Sara is mine then."

"What do ya want with a woman?"

"Perhaps I'd like to indulge my unmarriageable tendencies." She answered through a brash smirk. "She also has some training as a healer. I thought she might be useful."

He seemed to be waiting to see if she was joking, but when she didn't say more, he shook his head. "You're are full of surprises, Spark. As you will then." He grinned. "Crag isn't going to like this one bit."

"I don't really care." She took Sara's hand in her own.

He snickered. "Truthfully, neither do I."

He brought them to Roy first. Hearing that Sara was a healer, however unaccomplished, was all Roy needed. "I'm trusting that the two of you will keep her safe from the others? Do what you will with her, but if she stays, you best be sure she's able to do her part."

"Yes, sir." Olando and Sahmara answered in unison. Sara stood mutely behind them as they decided her future.

"I'd like you to stick by me, both of you. The three of you, I suppose it will be now," he amended. "Crag is going to stay on here for a few days to get the city back in order. We met with Roger and learned that several of the city council had to be disposed of due to their recent change in allegiance. It will take awhile to get things settled. In the meantime, we're to take those who are able back to camp to gather our things.

"Are we to stay in the city?" Olando asked.

"No. There's enough trouble to deal with here without women-craving soldiers climbing into their wine cups. We'll be setting up camp outside the walls. There's plenty of game about this time of year. We'll eat well, likely better than those that are stuck behind the walls with Crag and Roger."

"Be nice to have a roof over our heads," Sahmara muttered as they went outside to wait for Roy. "Maybe Roger hasn't noticed that it's getting damn cold at night."

"At least we have an extra body to help us stay warm," Olando said.

Sara smiled nervously. Sahmara took her hand and held it tight. "Give one of those packs to Olando. You don't need to carry both."

He took it, hefting the weight over his shoulder. "What do you have in here?"

"Food."

"Oh. Then I'll gladly carry it."

"It will only get lighter," Sahmara said.

"If only it were like your water jug."

Sahmara laughed. "Now *that* would be really useful." But she was grateful it wasn't also enchanted. Only the Mother knew what sort of payment would be required for that favor.

Roy joined them shortly, along with a trail of men who flowed from the hall. The trip back to the camp was filled with conversation since no one was concerned with an Atherian attack at any given moment. Those within the city that had survived the initial attack had been put to the sword. No mercy for the merciless.

Sahmara hoped it would be a good while before the Atherians learned of their loss of Antochecki. She looked forward to a few days in one spot. Maybe she would finally get the rest that Olando and Sara kept telling her that she needed.

They left Roger's men just outside the wall and went on with Roy and Crag's men to where they had left their things in the woods. She was relieved to see that everything was just as they'd left it. Even though she had little in the way of belongings, the thought of losing what she did have was terrifying.

Sahmara picked up the water jug and shared it with Olando and Sara. Nearby, three men decreed they were forming a hunting party. One of them was an archer. The other two carried swords. She didn't know what they were setting off after, but she hoped they brought it back quickly. Men with full bellies were much more likely to go to bed after a hard day without causing trouble.

She and Olando gathered up her blanket, his cloak, both of their bags and the water jug. At an urging look from Sara, Olando took everything but Sahmara's small bag. They made their way back to the camp now being set up just outside the walls.

Fires had been started. Men sat around them. Tents were being set up. Those must have been Roger's men. Crag's men hadn't used tents the night before. Had they had them at one time and lost them? Or had Roger's men gained them along the way? Sahmara longed for a tent. Anything to keep away the sensation of bugs crawling on her as she slept. Usually, she was too exhausted to even think about that until morning when she was lying under the cloak with Olando, warm and cozy and not wanting to rise.

They claimed a grassy spot under a tree. Sahmara had just wrapped her blanket around Sara in the hopes of further masking her from hungry eyes when she saw the hunting party returning with two deer. They didn't appear to be very large, but it would at least offer everyone something to eat. She rifled through the bag of food Olando had carried for her and pulled out a strip of the dried meat. She took a bite and passed it to Sara. "It will be a good while before the meat is cooked. This will tide us over until then."

Sara took a big bite and then passed it to Olando with a shaking hand. He took it gently from her fingers and chewed slowly on the tough meat. Sahmara settled herself between the two of them and removed her helm. She rested her head on Olando's shoulder.

"We may as well get some rest while the meal is roasting," she said. "Don't worry Sara, we'll keep watch over you. You'll be safe here."

Sara pulled the blanket tighter and curled up against Sahmara, using her lap as a pillow. Sara's warmth made her drowsy, but she didn't allow herself to sleep just yet. After awhile Sara breathed softly, letting them both know she was asleep.

"Ya claimed a very nice one," he whispered.

"It was more that she claimed me, but yes, she is very pretty, isn't she?" She was tempted to touch Sara's soft curls again but didn't dare for fear she'd wake her.

His tone turned serious. "Spark, can I ask you something?"

"Of course."

"Did ya claim her because she's pretty or because she's like ya?"

She looked down at the girl in her lap. "Yes."

"You didn't-"

"I won't have her further mistreated by anyone," she said more vehemently than she intended. Olando hadn't been the one to hurt either of them. She snuggled against him, hoping to soften her words. "She reminds me of all I've lost."

"You're beautiful, Spark."

"Not like her."

He kissed her forehead. "No, but like *ya are*."

She had to admit, she loved him just a little bit just then. His words were sweet like Zane's, but they were also honest. Looking back now, did all of Zane's pretty words mean anything, or was he merely enjoying liberties with his sworn charge that he should have never taken? Then again, she'd let herself be taken. She'd been curious, and he'd been everything she'd dreamed of.

Olando's words ate at her devotion. Had Zane allowed her to be taken? It was a betrayal she didn't want to consider.

Zane loved her. He'd told her so many times. They were to always be together, even after she was married off. He would always be by her side. But he wasn't here now. Nor had he been when she was bound and dragged from her home. He had to have been gravely injured or overpowered.

She recalled her dream. He'd looked healthy enough. Surely if he'd been badly injured the Atherians would have put him to the sword rather than enslaving him. So he was overpowered then. One man against many. She'd seen him practice each morning, watched and ogled his muscled form as it went through the motions he'd been taught since childhood. He was so graceful, flowing across the yard with his sword flashing in the morning sun. He looked up at her bedroom balcony as if he knew she was watching and smiled, his blue eyes twinkling.

"Spark, wake up. The meat is done."

She jerked awake, startling Sara in her lap.

"Stay here with her. I'll bring back our portion."

The venison was cooked to perfection. Even better, Roger had sent out a wagon from the city filled with bread, squash and two barrels of wine. Soldiers could be heard making loud toasts throughout the camp. It had been a long time since Sahmara had tasted wine. Even with her belly full of food for once, it didn't take long before the warm, hazy feeling filled her head and body.

Sara grinned, rosy-cheeked and eyes glittering in the firelight. Both of them turned to Olando and asked for more.

"Careful my ladies. I'll not have ya retching on the blankets."

"Shut up and get us more wine." Sahmara grinned and waved him off.

He laughed, taking their cups over to the wagon where the barrels waited beyond a line of men.

Sara giggled as she watched him walk away. "He is a good man."

"Yes, he is." Sahmara spotted him in line, talking to the other men. There seemed to be a good many gazes darting in their direction, and not only from the men in line. A few obscene gestures were also aimed her way now that Olando wasn't at her side.

Emboldened by the wine, she picked up her helm and her sword and got to her feet. It wasn't just about her anymore. She had Sara to protect. "Stay here, and if trouble breaks out, run for Olando."

"What are you going to do?"

"Put an end to this. Hopefully." She'd killed men with her sword now. She was one of them. She headed for a group of Crag's men who had been the first to jeer her.

She put a hand on the sword at her side and addressed the one who had made the gesture. "Would you care to repeat that?"

He stared at her uncertainly. The three others looked at her in surprise. Sharing a questioning look among them, the offender said, "We were just having fun is all."

"I don't like your idea of fun." She didn't move other than to grip the hilt of her sword a bit tighter. She prayed that she wouldn't embarrass herself.

"I see," He said tightly, reaching for his own sword.

A calm came over Sahmara, filling her with unexpected strength. Yanis's sword rested in her hand as if they were old friends.

Every nerve tingled as she watched him get to his feet. She gauged his every move from which hand he pushed himself up with to how he staggered a little as he found his footing and drew his sword.

He lunged first. His sword flashed bright, catching the light of the fire. She countered his moves, pushing him back into his friends, who emitted loud protests about the possibility of spilling their wine.

Voices approaching announced the beginnings of a crowd gathering. Loud boasts and frantic betting filled the air. Sahmara stopped listening to them after a moment, blocking them all out in favor of trying her best not to lose this fight. If she did, she'd be nothing in all of their eyes. She couldn't let that happen. He'd clearly had more wine than she had, stumbling here and there as she pressed her attack. Her shoulder started to burn. She couldn't allow this to go on much longer or all of Sara's work would be undone. She pressed harder. His attack became solely a defense.

She noticed his gaze darting to the crowd behind her and then snapping back to her sword at the last moment, only barely keeping his footing as he retreated further into the ring that remained around them no matter how many steps she took.

Sahmara knocked his sword aside. He dropped to his knees, scrambling for his weapon. She reached it first and kicked it into the ring of boots.

"Call her off, damn ya."

Olando's calm voice penetrated the raging pulse in her ears. "Spark, enough."

She was no dog to be called to heel. "Are you sure?" She glared at the man on his knees before her. "I better hear no more out of you." She spun around, sword still in hand. "From any of you. You hear?"

The crowd broke out into nervous laughter and began to disperse. She spotted Roy among them. He caught her gaze and shook his head before melting into the darkness.

Olando met her gaze with a proud grin. He called out to the departing men, "Best watch yourselves. Ya touched off Spark. Next time I might not be here to put her out."

Grumbling came from her victim and his friends, but no one else rose up to challenge her. Which was good, because her arms shook with exhaustion. The fight was far different than the calm morning practices she shared with Olando or the plunging steel into attacking enemies. The calm strength she'd felt at the beginning of the fight had vanished.

Chilled evening air settled on the wet sheen of sweat on her face and neck, leaving her with an uncomfortable tight feeling like that of dried blood on flesh. Had this been her own bravado or the Mother speaking out through her, venting her godly frustration?

She followed Olando back over to Sara who regarded her with open awe. Sahmara settled on the blankets beside her.

Olando held out the filled cups, offering one to her. "I got ya more wine," he said as though nothing had happened.

Sahmara took a long draw. A velvety warmth raced through her body.

Sara watched Sahmara over the rim of her cup. "Thank you both."

"You're welcome," Sahmara said.

Olando held up his cup. "That was quite amazing, my lady."

"I had a great teacher." She met his cup with her own.

"Yes, that was marvelous." Sara's cheeks were rosy with wine. "I mean, when I saw you in the city, I thought you were wonderful, but this… I was right to come with you." She leaned forward and planted a wine-flavored kiss on Sahmara's lips.

With the rush of the fight, their praise and the wine, Sahmara found she was quite enjoying herself. Sara's thin delicate fingers intertwined with her own. The sound of Olando choking broke them apart at last.

Sahmara grabbed the cup from his hand and patted his back. "Are you all right?"

It took him a minute to get his breath back. "I assure you ladies, I am quite fine. It was just that I… I was… I seem to have swallowed my wine wrong. That's all. Please, continue." He urged them on with a wave.

Sara giggled, a sound Sahmara found quite charming.

She chuckled too. "I think that perhaps we should all get

some sleep. Who knows what tomorrow will bring."

"That's for sure. However, I'm not sure that I could sleep right at the moment." He winked at her.

"Oh, is that right?" she said innocently. "I suppose you need some help relaxing after that long, hard day then?"

"That would be most appreciated." He grinned and pulled off his shirt. He went to work on his laces.

"Spark?" Sara whispered.

She went to work on her own shirt and leaned in to see what Sara needed.

"Is this what you meant?" Her curious face was lit by the soft glow of the distant fires.

"Yes." She pulled the helm from her head. It had become so much a part of her that she forgot she was wearing it. She loosened the laces and slipped out of her clothes safe between the blanket and Olando's cloak. Her hand discovered he was waiting anxiously for her. His skin was warm, despite the cool evening air. He sought her out, pulling her closer and squeezing her breasts. Seconds later his tongue dove deep into her mouth. Feeling that she was ready for him as well, he slid inside her.

They were both surprised when the blankets lifted and another warm body joined them. Slipping in behind Sahmara, Sara continued the kiss they had begun earlier.

CHAPTER FOURTEEN

The next morning found them all with dry mouths. Sahmara passed her jug around. Sara blushed prettily when she took the jug from Sahmara's hand. Olando didn't seem able to stifle his grin long enough to take a drink. Water dribbled down his chin. He wiped it away on his shirt and before pulling it over his head. He slung his cloak over his shoulders and went to work on folding the blankets, making a nice shield from the others while Sahmara and Sara donned the rest of their clothes. Sahmara was just getting her helm in place when he stopped airing the last blanket and got it rolled up. He gathered the blanket rolls and handed one to each of them. "Good morning, ladies."

"Indeed." Sated in so many ways, Sahmara hoped they weren't going anywhere today. She wanted nothing more than to rest her currently very relaxed muscles. Her shoulder was sore, but it didn't burn like it had before Sara had stitched it shut.

Sara stayed close to her, just as she had done the night before. While she had ventured over to kiss Olando, she'd lavished most of her attention on Sahmara. She'd felt Olando watching them avidly. He hadn't seemed to mind being on the outside of most of their activities, and she had done her best to include him when she was able. She watched Sara adjust the straps of her bags which fell right between her breasts. Sahmara grinned, remembering the silken feel of Sara's fingers on her skin. All over her body. Her face grew warm.

Roy approached Olando. "We will be staying here for three

days. We need to make sure we got them all. After Roger is satisfied, we'll take some of Crag's men and head to Omasii. He's had a report that there is only a small force there." He glanced up at the grey morning sky. "We should be able to take them and settle in for ourselves before winter hits."

"Sounds good. None of us wants to spend a winter night outside," said Olando.

"At least you have something to keep you warm." Roy nodded toward Sahmara and Sara.

Sahmara scowled. "We're right here."

Roy's jaw tightened. "I'm well aware of that."

"Maybe you'll find warmth in Omassi," Olando said.

"I hope to Hasi that you are right." Roger clapped him on the back. "We could all use a little warmth."

Olando nodded.

"The Atherians took what they wanted. Crag and Roger want to make sure these men don't do the same. We can't have our people thinking us no better than our enemies. That's why we're out here."

"I could have stayed in the city." He waved to Sahmara and Sara. "A roof would have been nice."

"You're here for your own good. Crag doesn't like you, and that woman of yours even less. You'll be happier in Omassi with the rest of us."

"We're not real fond of him either," Sahmara said. "Omasii it is."

Roy nodded to them both and went on to talk to some of the others.

The morning passed with food from the city, mostly apples and warm bread with a little cheese added from Sara's supplies. The wine was long gone so it was fresh water for everyone. At least Sahmara didn't have to make the trek to the nearest stream to get it. The jug provided plenty for all three of them.

One of the soldiers approached them. "We're to go into the city and retrieve some supplies to carry us over on our travel to Omasii. No weapons."

Sahmara left her arrows and sword behind but took her

bow with her. There was no way she was leaving her most precious procession in a camp half-filled with men she didn't know. She took the water jug too. They, along with seven others, filed back through the city gates.

Someone had been busy cleaning up the dead. A pyre burned in the midst of the courtyard, stacked high with bodies. More waited where they'd fallen. The smell was enough to make her gag. She covered her nose and mouth with her sleeve. Sara did the same. They followed the others as quickly as possible to put distance between them and the stink of the fire.

Roger met them outside the hall where she had found Olando the day before.

His rough face was similar to Roy's in the square nose and jawline, but his eyes were deeper and harder, brows bushy, and several days of graying stubble on his cheeks. His greeted them with a scowl.

"Why did you bring her?" He pointed directly at Sara.

Sahmara stepped forward. "She lived here. She can tell us what things won't be missed."

Roger seemed to consider that for a second and then nodded. "All right then. Keep her close. We don't need any more casualties."

Olando said, "Then why don't we have weapons?"

"I'll send three of my own men with you. They know well enough what to look for as far as enemy forces. The ten of you will concentrate on locating two wagons and filling them with supplies. Take nothing from the living. Use your woman, but don't let me catch word of any trouble. I won't hesitate to make examples of any one of you."

He turned on his heel and strode inside. Three soldiers with swords came out to join them shortly thereafter. They spent the afternoon locating four horses. That in itself was a challenge as the enemy had used many of the horses that the forces from Antochecki hadn't taken with them the first time around. They took the horses with them and returned to the hall to get some dinner before setting out for the last few hours of daylight.

The evening brought two Atherians to the sword and a single wagon. It seemed the enemy forces had taken most of those too.

They returned to camp. With no wine to ease the nerves, the night passed with Sahmara in the middle and a warm body on either side. She felt safe, rather needed by both of them in their own ways, and for once in her life, in control of herself for better or worse.

The next morning the three of them lagged behind as their assigned mates funneled into the city. Olando paused outside the gates. "I'd like to take a little detour this morning if you ladies wouldn't mind?"

Sahmara wished she'd brought her arrows and Olando his sword, but their weapons rested atop their blankets and bags. "Are you sure that's a good idea?"

"It's not that far from the city."

"What isn't?" asked Sara.

"My home," said Olando.

"Will there be Atherian's there?" Sara asked.

"Hard to say where they will and won't be. I did bring my dagger just in case." Olando pulled up his shirt to reveal the dagger tucked into his belt.

"Not much good that will do the rest of us," said Sahmara.

He bowed his head a little. "I'm sorry. I should have said something before we left camp."

"If there were any Atherians still lurking about, I suppose they would have shown themselves by now." Sahmara took his hand. "Lead on, but make it quick. Roger will want us to check in before long."

"Too bad for Roger. It's a bit of a walk." He set off at a brisk pace.

Sara's shorter legs left her at a half-jog to keep up. "Did you leave any supplies behind? That would explain why we were out here."

He shook his head. Sahmara recalled his nightmarish tale of losing everything. There would be nothing there to recover, but perhaps he would find a little peace. She couldn't begrudge him that.

They left the main road once the city had shrunk to half-size behind them. What appeared to be a game trail led them into the trees and then over a meadow filled with birdsong and sweet grasses. Sahmara breathed deep. It smelled so clean here. Other than the stink of their own unwashed bodies, it was if the war hadn't happened.

Olando's fingers were still intertwined with hers as if he were afraid to let go. His hand was clammy and his step determined.

She couldn't imagine growing up here, so far from other families, from the streets full of vendors and shops, the smells of fresh bread baking, the titter of shared gossip around the fountains, the colorful dresses of the season swishing into coaches.

The meadow gave way to more trees decorated here and there with the gold and red of fall. Crickets and birds chittered around them. As they walked she picked up the gurgle of a brook and then a clearing opened. A few orange wildflowers peeked out from behind stones that lined a path to a tumble of rock and charred wood. His home.

Olando came to a halt with a choking sound. His hand hung limply in hers. Sara came up behind them and gave her a questioning look. Sahmara waved her off.

She didn't know what to say so she wrapped her arms around him and held him tight. His cheek rested on her forehead. Dampness quickly followed.

She watched Sara pick through what must have been the house garden, rubbing leaves and stems and sniffing her fingers. She picked a few things here and there while keeping a wary eye on the edges of the clearing.

A row of mounds lay beside the house, stones marking the outlines of each one. Olando pulled away from her to walk toward them. She stayed a few paces back to give him some space. He went to each mound in turn.

A chilled breeze picked up, tossing leaves around their feet and carrying his soft prayers to her ears. She hoped the gods heard them as well as she did.

A branch snapped. Sahmara reached for her bow, only to remember she had no arrows and then for her sword, only to recall it wasn't at her side. Sara had heard it too, staring into the trees with wide eyes.

"Olando," Sahmara hissed.

He picked up his head to look at her with red-rimmed eyes. Tears had left clean tracks down his cheeks.

"There's something out there." She pointed to where she'd heard the snap. Footsteps, several of them sounded seconds later.

He wiped his sleeve over his face and pulled the dagger from his belt. "Get Sara inside."

There wasn't enough of what was still standing to call it a house and she certainly wasn't going inside. One step could bring the whole precarious mess down. She gestured Sara to her side. They waited anxiously while Olando stalked toward the footsteps. There had to be something she could use for a weapon, but the only thing she spotted were rocks. They would have to do. She grabbed one with a jagged point at one end. Sara scooped one up as well.

A flash of someone hunched low in a dirty white cloak moving through the underbrush caught her eye. Then another. She readied the stone in her hand, waiting to see if she should throw it or keep it for smashing against a skull.

Olando dropped to his knees with the dagger still in his hands. She left Sara there and ran toward him, looking for where an arrow must have struck him. But there was no sign of one. A gurgling noise came from him. His back shook and he dropped the dagger, bowing his head.

She grabbed it in her empty hand and picked up speed, dashing into the woods to strike down the enemy. Two sheep stood before her. They bleated loudly and scattered. But if it had only been sheep... she dropped the rock, spun around and dashed back into the clearing.

Sara stood at Olando's side, who was now back on his feet,

though still shaking. With laughter—she discovered as she came closer and caught the gurgling noises for the silent laughter that they were. She punched him in the arm.

"Ouww." He rubbed his arm and pulled her in for a quick squeeze. "Thank you for rushing headlong into danger to save me from the sheep."

She considered punching him again until she saw Sara laughing too. A giggle bubbled up from deep inside her.

"Do you think they went far?" she got herself under control enough to ask.

"Probably not."

"Then I'm thinking mutton over the fire tonight." She tugged him forward and put the dagger in his hand. "Go on. You owe me for scaring me half to death."

His warm smile made her heart miss a beat and then plunge into double time. She forgave him instantly, but he wasn't getting off that easy. "Go." She pointed to the woods and crossed her arms over her chest, waiting.

"Yes, my dear lady." He slipped into the woods without a sound.

The moment he hit the tree line Sara laughed out loud.

"Shush. No need to call attention to ourselves," Sahmara half-heartedly scolded.

Sara took a deep breath and Sahmara's arm. "You two...are you sure he doesn't mind me tagging along?"

"Has he said he minds?"

"Well no."

"He hasn't said as much to me either so, no, I don't think he minds in the least. He's the envy of many. I just hope it doesn't go to his head."

Sara flashed a radiant smile. "The way he looked at you back there? I rather doubt he'd do anything to jeopardize the two of you."

"Well, I had just saved him from the sheep."

Sara giggled again. "Come on, if you're not going to allow me a good laugh, then help me gather up some more herbs so we can have flavorful mutton tonight."

Olando called out, "A little help here?"

Sahmara went to help him carry one of the sheep and they returned to the camp as heroes for the morning. After extracting promises of a meal saved for them when they returned, the three of them made their much-belated way into the city to locate a second wagon and supplies to fill it.

Once their mission was complete, Olando spent the next two days working with a team of soldiers to repair some of the damage the Atherians had wrought upon the city. Roy borrowed Sara to help attend to the wounded. Sahmara went with her, standing guard over the young woman while she did her work and glaring at anyone who looked at her with lusting eyes.

When the day came to leave, Roy gathered everyone up and went to meet with Crag and Roger. Crag assigned twenty of his men to Roy with the promise to send more in a few days once more work was done in Antochecki. He bid Roy farewell and excused himself to return to overseeing the city.

Roger made to leave, but Roy stopped him. "We need the men now."

"Establish a camp near Omasii, evaluate the situation. They'll be along in plenty of time to help take the city so that you will be more comfortable."

"I'm not worried about comfort." Roy's face grew red. "I'm worried about the Atherians noticing our men outside their walls and doing something about it."

Roger glared at him. "Well then, the solution is pretty simple. Don't get noticed."

Roy stared at his brother as if waiting for him to change his mind, but the older man remained silent. "Send them quickly or we may not be there."

"Is that a threat?"

"No, dear brother, that is a fact. The Atherians aren't stupid. They will have patrols, and they will notice us in time. Your men will cling to the city and comfort as long as you will let them. You'll spoil them after their long trek in hardship. Send them now before they grow tainted by warmth and women."

Roger's face grew as red as Roy's and his lips pinched into a tight line. "I'm the captain here, priest. Don't you think to tell me how to run a war. Now run off a pray that Hasi will keep you safe until we have need for you again."

It seemed Roy's men weren't the only ones to lose a little reverence for their god. Sahmara felt bad for him for a moment, but then Roy turned to them and marched them off as if he and his god hadn't just been insulted by his own brother. If Hasi's own priest demanded no respect, it was little wonder that the god had grown weak. Would she stand up for the Mother if insulted in such a direct manner? A burning sensation flared in her fingertip. Sahmara glared at the sky and wished the goddess out of her thoughts.

They marched straight down the street and out the gate and set to breaking down the camp in short order. The wagons were already loaded with supplies. The men drew sticks for who would drive them.

"If ya want, Spark, the healer can ride with me," offered the man holding the longest twig.

Sahmara looked to Sara. "It's up to you. I'll be right beside you."

Sara shook her head. "I'll stay with you."

"It will be a long walk."

"I'll walk." She fell into a determined step alongside Sahmara.

Was she that scared of the man or that eager to be like her? Either way, Sahmara rather wished Sara would take the offer and save herself from sore muscles and an aching back. She liked her as she was now, soft and womanly. Even though Sara wore men's clothing it was plain to anyone with a speck of sight that she was a woman. One of them looking questionably like man was plenty. Hopefully, one day of walking would change Sara's mind.

The march eastward began. The rutted road offered a clear path and the wagons made good time. Sara stayed in pace with the others, looking straight ahead.

Sahmara's thoughts wandered to her mother's voice. Every memory was of a shrill disappointed tone. The voice told her to stop eating so much, to cinch her underclothes tighter, stand straighter, smile more and to pay closer attention to her stitches. She was sure there had been loving words between them, but she couldn't recall those no matter how hard she tried. Her mother would have been thrilled with a daughter like Sara.

Sahmara imagined that she rode atop her fine horse with Sara tucked right behind her in the saddle. Her arms held Sahmara tight about her waist, her breasts pressed against her back. Sara nuzzled her neck as they rode, whispering sweet words that the wind took away before she could fully understand them.

As they rode, she spotted something alongside the road. She slowed and drew her sword. Yanis stood next to an eyeless girl. They waved at her, pointing her down the road, urging her to go faster.

The clang of an arrow bouncing off metal armor snapped Sahmara out of her daydream.

"Kill them all," yelled Roy.

Sahmara slid the bow from her back and an arrow from her quiver. When the second arrow was fired, she spotted the archer. She said a prayer and let loose her own arrow. The man fell to the ground.

Beside her, swords and daggers were drawn. Men charged past her, running for the trees and the men emerging from them. Another arrow arched toward her people. Sahmara sought out the second archer, but it wasn't until an arrow struck a nearby man in the shoulder that she spotted him. She said a prayer and sent an arrow in his direction. He crumpled to his knees and fell over.

The clang of swords clashing filled the mid-morning air. Men grunted and swore at one another, uttering curses at the living and the fallen. The Atherians were outnumbered and Roy's command was followed to the word before the sun had a chance to rise much higher.

It wasn't until the swords went silent that Sahmara gave thought to Sara. She threw the bow over her shoulder and spun around, searching wildly. Sara had crawled up into the wagon and sat huddled there between two barrels with her short sword drawn. Sahmara went to her and held out her hand. Sara grabbed it and held on tight.

"They're taken care of."

"You're sure?"

She nodded. "Come. They're almost done with the bodies. They're moving them away from the road so any other patrols don't see them right away."

Sara stayed put. "I think I'll ride here for a little while if that would be all right?"

"Yes." Sahmara squeezed her hand. "That will be just fine."

Sara nodded and wedged herself between the barrels a little more.

"I'm going to check on Olando. We'll be close by."

Sara's gaze darted to the trees around them. "Don't be long."

"We won't." She let go of Sara's hand and sought out the rest of the men.

Olando spotted her and jogged to her side, two arrows in his hand. He handed them to her.

Did the Mother get her fill if someone else removed the arrows? Her finger didn't answer one way or the other when she took the arrows from him and put them back home with the others.

"They've piled the bodies in a ravine and covered them with branches. We can hope that was the only patrol between here and Omasii."

Sahmara raised a brow. "You really think we'll be that lucky? This is a main road."

"I know. Ya can't blame a man for wishful thinking."

"That I cannot." She adjusted her bow and went to retrieve her belongings where they'd been dropped when the attack had begun. Olando followed, gathering up his things and those that Sara had left. He looked around.

"She's decided to take up the offer of riding on the wagon for a while."

"Ah." Olando went over to the wagon, making sure to stay in plain sight to as not to startle Sara. He held out her bags. "No reason these can't ride with you."

"Thanks." She tucked her belongings in around her and went back to scanning their surroundings.

Olando returned to Sahmara's side. "Think she'll be all right out here?"

"Time will tell."

"That it will. Shall we?" He nodded to the others who were forming up beside the wagons. The horses seemed anxious to be on their way. There was blood in the air.

CHAPTER FIFTEEN

The second attack on the way to Omasii yielded two horses in return for a life and four wounded. There had only been seven Atherians, but they were vicious and they'd been lying wait. The men had grown careless with their talking and one had even broken out in song. He was dead now, an arrow through his throat.

Two of the wounded sat upon the horses. The others lay in the wagons, Sara tending to them as best she could. Her eyes were wary and her hands shook. Sahmara had been able to do little to calm her, but at least she did not cry or complain. She did her duty.

Olando stayed close to the wagons and Sahmara close to him as they again set out after removing the dead from the roadside. This lot had also yielded a good many coins, which the men split among them.

Roy set those on the horses to watch carefully and ordered them all to remain silent. The rest of that day and the next passed without further hardship. Morning brought them within a day's march of Omasii.

They stopped at midday, Roy willing to get no closer without more men. They veered from the road, driving deep into the countryside until the wagons could travel no further. Roy dispatched three men and Sahmara to travel back to the road to cover their trail.

"Stay close to Sara," Sahmara told Olando.

"She'd rather stay close to ya, I'm sure."

"The men need my bow. Sara will need to make do with you for now."

He scoffed and put his hand to his chest. "Make do?"

She pushed him playfully. "Just go keep her company. I learned to like you, maybe she will too."

"She seemed to not mind me the other night."

"Exactly. Now go."

"Yes, my lady." He bowed.

"And quit calling me that." She shook her head and went to find the men Roy had assigned her to.

Bart and two others stood waiting for her. Had Roy done this on purpose or had his mind been scattered by the last few days? She cursed him under her breath.

The other two men didn't look familiar. They must have been Crag's.

"So you're the woman who likes women, eh?" asked one of them while elbowing the man next to him. "I saw these two women in the tavern back in Jerhastenev. They were all sorts of interested in each other. Didn't mind a bit that most of us were watching either. Was quite a show I tell ya." He winked at Sahmara. "You and that pretty little healer gonna give us a show, Spark?"

"No. Let's get moving."

Bart sneered. "Oh I don't know, there's three of us, maybe we demand one."

The other two men paused and looked from her to Bart. "Maybe you missed the show she *did* give us the other night. Come on, Spark. Keep your eyes out for them evil bastards while we cover the wagon tracks."

Bart glared at her. She glared right back and kept her hand on her sword. The other two had gotten a good way ahead before he gave up and followed them. Sahmara let out the breath she'd been holding and slipped her bow off her shoulder. With an arrow at the ready, she scanned their surroundings. The three men gathered branches from the trees and wiped away their tracks as much as possible. Then they set about using the branches to straighten the trampled grass.

They walked all the way back to the main road. Her shoulder started to hurt from holding the bow and doing nothing with it.

She wondered how Sara was faring back at the camp. Olando wouldn't let anything happen to her. But she would feel better when she was back beside both of them. It struck her odd that she was the link between two people. They had a little family of sorts, out here, far from walls and comforts. Yet, they were her comfort and she theirs.

A movement in the distance caught her attention.

"Get down," she hissed. She dropped to her knees, peering above the grass. The others had disappeared within it.

Moments later, the glimpses of movement became a group of twenty men coming toward them. Some wore scant armor, but she saw no markings on any of them. How many could she pick off before they got too close or scattered?

They stuck to the road, though two men walked along the edges, studying the grass. They were looking for them. How did they know they had even passed this way? Had they found the bodies? Her heart pounded. She pulled the string back and took aim.

The men froze, staring further down the road, beyond where Sahmara's people had turned off.

A wagon came into view, flanked by twenty men on each side, all wearing armor. Atherian armor. Sahmara's stomach dropped to the ground. She scuttled over to where she'd last seen Crag's men and stumbled upon Bart.

"Go. Run back to camp and warn them. Now."

"Why don't you run?"

She aimed the arrow she'd be holding at his chest. "I said, now."

"Sure, I'll lead the others to your corpses. And I'll have your pretty girl all to myself." He hunched over and darted through the grass toward their camp.

She popped her head back above the grass and saw one of the men in the first group noticing Bart. She glanced back to see that he was standing upright at a full run from the road. By the time she'd turned back to the road, the ones with the wagon had noticed him too.

Sweat trickled her face, the fur on her helm moist and itchy. The two men she had left had worked their way back until they nearly bumped into her.

"What should we do?" whispered one of them.

"I don't know." Sahmara didn't dare look up again, for fear they'd spot her, too. An arrow sang overhead. Bart swore. His retreat got much louder, crashing through branches and cursing.

"It was nice knowing the two of you. Not so much with that one," said the one who had called Bart off earlier. "I suppose we should get to causing as much damage as we can so the rest have a fighting chance."

A battle cry rang through the air and seconds later swords clashed between the two groups of men on the road.

"Or." He rocked back on his heels "We could hang out here for a little bit and let them sort each other out."

"We could," Sahmara said. "Or we could help." She shot to her feet and said a prayer, hoping she wasn't being foolish. She launched an arrow at the bare neck of one of the armored men. He fell. Then another and another. The men who'd come from the direction of Antochecki didn't look familiar but then she hadn't fought alongside Roger's men or many of Crag's.

Had Roger rethought his plan of not sending more men right away? Whoever they were, they were doing their damnedest to kill the Atherians in front of them. That made them friends for now.

"Get up and go help them." She kicked at the two men still by her feet.

They scrambled to their feet and ran at the nearest Atherian. He spun around just in time to keep one of their swords from slipping in under his arm while he attacked another man in front of him. The two of them made quick work of the befuddled Atherian and moved on to another. Sahmara launched arrow after arrow until her quiver came up empty.

Soldiers kept coming. She slung her bow over her back and pulled out her sword. Nothing to be gained by standing on the edges. She dove into the fray.

Her shoulder throbbed from using her bow and now large men were swatting her sword aside as if she had no muscles left at all. She didn't want to die here.

She prayed for the safety of Sara and Olando, and for the enemy to drop dead before more of those on her side perished.

They enemy didn't die immediately, but she did feel strength welling within her. It wasn't the same as when her finger tingled. This reminded her of the wine-laden night she'd drawn her sword and bested the drunk soldier. But now the flow of strength became a flood that was far more raw, burning through her like a hand held too close to a flame. She swung hard, left and right, hitting sword and armor alike. Nothing seemed to slow her attack. Like when she loosed her arrows and the Mother guided them, her sword and muscles knew where to go, how to move. Men grunted when she hit them, they fell back, some fell down and didn't get back up. She pressed them hard, back against the wagon they'd brought with them. Around her, the other men pushed along with her until only six armored men remained. Their backs hit the wood. Still, Sahmara swung, thrusting her blade into any sliver of flesh that she saw in front of her. Two more dropped. The men around her trampled the fallen in a rush to get to the three that remained.

The last men fell quickly, overwhelmed and disheartened. Without a target, Sahmara's arms fell to her sides. Her sword hung in the road, dripping blood into the dirt.

"Spark," someone said from a distance. She tried to focus on his face.

"Hey, it's over. We did well." It was one of the two men she'd sent into the fray ahead of her.

The men around her blurred. Someone grabbed her arm. She tried to shake him off but her legs gave out under her. She dropped to her knees, the bow holding her upright a moment before she pitched forward. Someone called her name and then she knew nothing.

෨෬

A soft voice sounded rather insistent close to her ear. "Spark, please, wake up."

Sahmara cracked open one eye. It was light. Her mouth was dry and her head throbbed. In fact, when she tried to move, she hurt all over. She gave up and lay still.

"She's awake!" Sara squealed gleefully.

Olando loomed over her seconds later. "How are you feeling?" He took her hand in his.

"I hurt. Everywhere."

"Not surprising from what I heard."

Sara nudged him aside. "Did you get hit on the head? You were out a long time."

"I don't think so."

"You weren't cut anywhere. Well, some cuts, but nothing big enough to account for knocking you out. I did bandage you up a little."

"What's a few more scars?" She tried to smile, but her face hurt too much.

"Are you hungry?" Olando asked.

"Not really." She just wanted to sleep. For a long time. She'd never been this tired in all her life.

"Spark. Stay with me." Sara held her cheeks tightly, staring into her eyes. "You can't sleep again. I'm worried about you."

"But I'm so tired." She felt her eyes slipping closed.

Sara let out a little cry, her voice shaking. "I don't know what else to do."

Sahmara felt bad for leaving Sara alone, but she couldn't help it. She craved the darkness behind her eyelids. Except there wasn't darkness. A man and a woman stood before her, smiling. At first, she thought it they were her parents and she ran for them, arms open wide. But the closer she got, their faces were wrong. Their skin bright, like the sun shown just under the surface. Their eyes were a swirl of colors, changing with every breath.

"You have been a good servant," said the man in a voice that boomed so loud that she feared her ears might burst.

Sahmara halted her forward rush.

"You fought well for me today."

"For you?" Her voice came out a mere squeak.

"You bear my servant's sword."

Not only did she have the bow of the Mother, she now had saddled herself with the sword of a man apparently sworn to Hasi. She wanted to cry, but tears took too much energy. She settled for just being tired and empty instead.

"You have nourished us well this day," said the Mother. "Now rest while we battle our enemies." The Mother kissed her forehead and then everything went black.

Warm bodies pressed against her. The ground beneath her was hard. She dislodged her arm from under her side to push something itchy from her face. It scraped against wood. They'd put her in one of the wagons. Was she injured? Sara had said something about cuts. Who were these people sleeping so close by? The itchy thing turned out to be hair from the person in front of her. Her senses slowly kicked in. His scent was familiar. So where the breasts against her back. Why were all three of them in a wagon and where were the supplies that were supposed to be here instead? And the other wounded. Surely there were more than herself who had been hurt on the road.

A faint rosy haze in the sky foretold the dawn. She tried to wedge herself out of the cocoon her bedmates had woven, but only managed to wake them instead.

They both rolled over with wide grins on their faces. "You're back." Olando wrapped his arms around her. Sara showered her cheeks with kisses.

"This is all very touching, really, but I need to visit the bushes before I burst." Sahmara pried them off of her and dashed for the nearest private space as fast as her aching muscles would allow.

When she had finished, she made her way back to the

wagon. It was the wagon the Atherians had been pulling. That explained why there hadn't been a pile of supplies in it. The soldiers that had been riding were now dead and the other contents must have been spread to the other two wagons.

Olando came to her side. "You've been out for two days. We feared you wouldn't wake up again."

"I was just tired."

He shook his head. "No, it was more than that. You were so pale."

"I'm fine now." She glanced around at the camp full of men. "How many did we lose out there on the road?"

"Five. Though, they tell me that was before your arrows flew and long before you started to swing your sword."

"I don't remember much of that."

"That happens." He nodded. "It all becomes a blur in the midst of battle."

She had a feeling it wasn't that exactly, but it was close enough.

Sara joined them. "How are you feeling now?"

"Sore, but much better."

"Good. Now that you're awake, we'll head into Omasii, but I want you to stay in the wagon."

"A little walking might help loosen up her muscles," said Olando.

"How about I have something to eat, and then we'll see how I'm feeling?"

They both looked at her. "If you think that would be best," said Olando. Sara gave a hesitant nod.

The occupants of the camp started to stir, either woken by the sound of their voices or the lightening sky. The men set about putting out the remains of their fires and packing their gear. Biscuits, without any mold, Sahmara was glad to note, were handed around. Sara snuck some of the cheese from their own stores onto Sahmara's biscuit and also handed her a strip of the dried meat.

"You need to regain your strength."

Sahmara wasn't going to argue. Now that she was standing,

and the chill morning air had fully woken her, she was ravenous. Olando gave her half of his biscuit as well. She ate it without any regrets.

She noticed men beginning to mill around her, and thinking they were merely forming up to move out, thought little more about it. It wasn't until she recognized that they were all men from the road from the day before that she began to wonder what was going on.

"We're glad to see that you are back among us," said one of the two she'd last seen before she'd passed out.

"John," said the blond one, pointing to himself. "Ramsey." He pointed to the other one. "Mind if we walk with you today?"

Sahmara looked to Olando. He grinned. Confused, she shrugged. "I suppose."

They fell in beside her as the wagons started to roll. Men with bandages on their arms, heads and legs filled in around them. Roy lead the others up near the front wagon. Sara sat on the seat of the wagon beside her with one of the soldiers at her side. While she did maintain a distance from him, she didn't appear to be frightened.

Olando squeezed in beside her. She wasn't used to so many bodies crowding around her as she walked. It was as if they were all vying for her attention, none of them willing to give up an inch to another.

"What in the Mother's name is going on?" she whispered to Olando.

"You put on quite a spectacle out there. They say you moved like Hasi himself."

She snorted. "How would they know how Hasi moves?"

"Truly, Spark, we only had a few lessons together, where did you learn to use a sword?"

She tried to recall the power that had flowed through her back on the road. She'd prayed and the gods had answered. Had Hasi taken her body as his shell in the mortal world? Had he awakened memories of Zane's morning practices in her own muscles? Maybe he'd freed Yanis to live again through his sword. Perhaps it was a little of all of those.

"I've not taken lessons from any other," she said truthfully.

"Then you are truly blessed by the gods."

Yanis had been blessed too, a soldier of Hasi, but he lay in a shallow sandy grave. Zane was a prisoner. Roy held little respect from his brother or his own men. Either Hasi was weak or his champions were sorely lacking. She didn't want to be lacking so it must be the other. That would also explain why he and the Mother had lost their hold on Revochek.

The gods needed blood and there was a city full of Atherians ahead. Hasi had said they were off to battle. If they had any hope of winning in either realm, it would be best to provide blood and act while the Atherian god was distracted with his own fight.

"We need to move faster," she announced.

"Why? We've been watching the city but we haven't seen any other patrols," said John.

"I need to talk to Roy." He would understand. She threaded her way through the crowd of men and made her way to his side. The men around him gave her space, even Agis.

"Why did we wait here after Roger's men arrived?"

He scowled. "Because certain men wouldn't hear of traveling until you were ready."

Sahmara glanced over her shoulder to the twenty-some men that had been walking with her. "You should have made them move out. We were needed in Omasii yesterday."

"Were we now?"

"Yes, we were." A sense of agitation came over her. Couldn't Roy feel it too? He was supposed to be Hasi's priest.

"And why is that?" He paused mid-step. The men around him faltered, dodging awkwardly aside so as to not run into the two of them. "Do you have some information you'd like to share? We all fell for your poor girl act, but after the tales of that last battle, we know the truth."

"And just what truth is that?" The second wagon rolled by. If she didn't move soon, the men who had been with her would bowl them over.

"That you're an Atherian spy. You're going to lead us into another disaster like that town where Yanis was betrayed. You even fooled him." He thrust a finger into her chest. "But now we know. And don't think we're going to fall for it."

Her mouth gaped open. "Have you not witnessed me killing Atherians? Quite a few of them, I might add."

"You've been quite convincing."

The first of the men she'd been traveling with began to flow around them. They gave her a questioning look and walked slower as they passed.

"That's the stupidest thing I've heard in a long time," she said finally. "When we first met, you said Hasi gave you the gift of seeing the truth of people. You saw me for what I was. Or was your gift a lie?"

He sputtered. "You now stoop to insulting my god?"

"He's apparently my god too. And no, I was questioning you, not him. I'm quite positive *I* know what Hasi wants. He's made it quite clear. Has he not done so with you?"

More bodies moved past them. Sahmara didn't see their faces, they were all blurs. Her pulse quickened and her vision narrowed. Only Roy remained in focus. His lips smacked together wordlessly and his gaze darted up and down her body.

"Yes, we should move faster," he said and then held up his robes and ran to the front of the line.

Sahmara swallowed hard as the dizzy feeling faded and the world came back into focus. Olando stood by her side. Ramsey waited nearby. The others had all passed.

"Spark, are you unwell? Maybe you should ride in the wagon for a bit."

"I'm fine. I just had to speak to Roy for a moment." She started off before the line left them behind.

"Looks like you were doing more than talking. I've never seen a priest move so fast," said Ramsey.

"We should all move fast." The sense of urgency remained.

CHAPTER SIXTEEN

Omasii was little more than a clump of homes and an inn within a walled circle of wood. The gate was intact and the thick sharp stakes of the wall unharmed. The buildings were whole and people could be heard inside.

Unidentifiable bodies hung from the walls outside, their feet tied to the posts, the rest dangling within reach of wild beasts who looked to have been hungry. The smell of the dead made her stomach churn.

They'd stopped the wagons below the rolling hills filled with crops and grazing animals and approached the town on foot. It didn't warrant the term city, not compared to Antochecki.

It wasn't until she spotted guards sporting Atherian sigils on their armor that it was clear the bodies didn't belong to the enemy. The urgency from the gods became clear. For a town so small, there were a lot of soldiers.

Murmurs of the number of bodies and speculation of how many might remain alive inside ran through the men. Roy stared at the gate, only breaking away to glance at her now and then. Was she supposed to do something, give him some sort of sign?"

The cold grey sky opened up, releasing a torrent of freezing rain. She met Roy's gaze. That was enough of a sign for both of them.

Her cloak only kept the rain at bay for a few moments. Water ran down her neck into her shirt, soaking her to the bone. Sleet built up on her helm, seeming to funnel freezing rivulets onto her face. Sara stood beside her, teeth chattering and hair clumped like black icicles over her shoulders. They couldn't stay out here. They needed to act now or they'd all be too cold to fight. She said a prayer and pulled her bow from her back.

Sahmara released an arrow over the wall. It arced high and came down just on the other side. The Atherians yelled of an incoming attack. John and Ramsey looked to her. She nodded. If Roy wasn't going to give orders, someone had to. They each gathered up a bunch of men and ran for the gate with swords drawn. Olando stayed by her side as did Sara, both with their swords drawn.

She released arrow after arrow, prayers flowing from her lips without a second thought. Just as the men reached the gate, it swung open. Haggard men in plain clothes stood inside, their hands bloody and each bearing a knife. Two men lay at their feet. They joined the flood of men rushing into the town. Sahmara ran after them, her guards ever present at her side.

People rushed from their houses, weapons of all sorts in their hands. They attacked the Atherians with naked hate, regardless of their own unarmored bodies. Sahmara put the bow on her back and drew her sword. She looked at the bare steel for a moment, deciding if she was willing to be a vessel again so soon. She could feel Hasi just outside her, waiting to flood in if she but offered herself. He was furious and her head ached from just being *near* his fury. She didn't invite him in. The Mother was with her. One god was enough for now.

Men ran through the streets, her men, slaughtering Atherians. Her arrows protruded from many of the bodies near the gate. Here and there one of the townspeople or her soldiers lay on the ground, unmoving. Many more of the prone bodies did not belong here. Men shouted, fighting for their lives. And then, the shouting fell off, becoming distant and then ceasing altogether. The rain let up, turning to a weak drizzle. Men slowly reappeared, some limping and others bleeding, some leaning on another. Townspeople gathered before Sahmara and

Roy, who she found had come to stand beside her. They praised him for saving them with his soldiers.

For a moment she thought he was going to eat up every word, but he looked to her and then to the sky. "Give your thanks to Hasi. It was he who led us here."

Sahmara nodded. Just outside her body, she could feel the god's strength gathering, a powerful force like the air being sucked from the town. Her feet became so heavy it was hard to lift them from the ground. Chills ran over her that had nothing to do with the rain.

An elderly man stepped forward from the crowd. "Come inside, please. Let us offer you shelter and see to your wounds, at least until you are dry." Offers of hospitality spilled from the townspeople, each gathering two or three soldiers to them before melting into the houses.

"The Atherians have left me with extra room," said the old man. "I welcome the four of you to my table."

Sahmara would have preferred to leave Roy standing in the cold, but she nodded. Her awareness of Hasi and the Mother abated, allowing her body to move unhindered.

The four of them followed him into one of the larger homes. It was plain, more so than Sara's had been, but functional. It had a large main room with a loft above. Two wide beds taunted her. But she was wet and it would do no one any good to get the blankets damp as well.

"Come, warm yourselves." The old man stoked the fire, sending a wave of welcome warmth through the room.

"Thank you," said Roy. He sat on the bench beside the table, warming his hands.

"You'd best take off those wet things. You'll warm and they'll dry much quicker that way." He pointed to hooks on the wall by the door. Sahmara pulled off her helm and set it on the floor, then hung her soggy cloak on the hook. Sara followed suit.

"Oh, I didn't realize we had women among us," said the man. "Go on upstairs. There should be some clothes for you there. My wife and daughters had a nice wardrobe once, before the looting. They took all we had in the way of jewels but they didn't have much use for dresses." He grinned, revealing yellowed and missing teeth.

"The soldiers that were here today," said Sahmara. "Was that all of them?"

"They come and go pretty regular. Not much for them to do here. We're not a big city. They enforce their rules, have their fun with us and then move out after another wave moves in."

"Where do they go from here?" She tried to envision her father's map.

"North and south, same as the road takes them. These was new, just settling in. The last batch moved on two days ago."

"Well at least we know *they* won't be coming back," said Olando.

"So we could have another patrol moving in at any time," said Roy.

"They're usually here a week or two. Just enough to rest up and get bored. That's the part we dread most."

The sight of the bodies on the walls came back to Sahmara. She shuddered. "At least they left you your crops and herds."

He nodded. "We made sure to feed them well, even if it meant those of us left went hungry. Course, our storehouses are empty and we'll all likely starve to death this winter."

Roy shrugged off his robes. "We'll do what we can to keep that from happening." He hung them on one of the empty hooks. His leggings and thin linen shirt clung to his body. "We brought food with us." He motioned to Olando. "Go and fetch us something to share with our host."

Olando didn't look very pleased to be sent back outside, but he went, pulling up his sodden hood as he went through the doorway. The door closed behind him.

"Ladies," Roy said, "get changed." He pointed to the ladder.

Roy seemed most in charge when he had pliable men to order about. In these particular orders, Sahmara couldn't find a reason to argue. She and Sara went up the ladder polished smooth by many hands. The wood shown in the most used spaces, catching the light of the fire as they climbed.

The previous occupants of the loft had hung a cloth divider in the back corner, allowing for privacy. Sara went first, flinging her wet clothes outside the cloth and onto the wooden floor. Sahmara hung up the dripping garments along with her own. Wrapped in a blanket from the bed, she went to the two trunks along the wall and opened them. The soldiers had done a fine job of rummaging through the contents. Not a single stocking was neatly folded. While she would have preferred something the old man had to offer for practical reasons, the thought of donning a dress for just a little while wasn't exactly repugnant. Her fingers slid over the various types of cloth, feeling her way through someone else's entire wardrobe. The old man's family hadn't been as well off as her own, but neither had they been poor. She pulled a handful of nice dresses from the trunks and laid them out on the bed. One was torn on the bottom of the skirt, a ragged tear as if it had caught on something sharp. There was no blood, which seemed a good sign. It was a lovely deep green that reminded her of moss in the springtime. Not minding the tear, she set that one aside for herself. Naked, Sara peeked out from the cloth.

"What do we have?'

Sahmara held up each dress in turn and judged Sara's reaction. A soft yellow one had coaxed a smile from her lips. Sahmara tossed it to Sara along with dry underclothes.

Minutes later, Sara emerged. "Spin around, let me see," Sahmara said.

"Is that really necessary?"

"That I should have a moment to appreciate how beautiful you are? Yes. It's necessary."

Sara smiled. "All right then. Find me some slippers and I'll spin for you. My feet are freezing."

Sahmara reached down to the bottom of the trunk. She pulled out a pair of very worn but whole, slippers the color of dirt. Sara put them on, grimacing.

"They crunch my toes."

"Would you rather have bare feet?"

"We'll see." She took a few steps, resting her weight on her heels. It rather looked like she was walking on ice.

"I can hear you laughing."

"I wasn't."

Sara cast her a skeptical look. "Well?" She held out her arms and turned around slowly.

The dress hugged her hips but sagged at the top. Still, it did her far more justice than the clothes she had been wearing.

She got to her feet and gave Sara a kiss on the cheek. "I'd hug you, but I'm still all wet."

"Get changed then, foolish woman." She gave Sahmara a gentle push to the curtain.

Had they been alone, she would have changed in front of Sara, after all, they had nothing to hide any longer. But with the men in the house, she felt more comfortable behind the curtain. She set the blanket aside and pulled on the small clothes she'd brought with her. Feeling less vulnerable, she emerged and stepped into the green dress. Sara helped her pull it on and lace it up.

"Sit down. Your hair's a mess." Sahmara pointed to the narrow bed.

Sara dutifully sat. "You know, it's not going to matter. It will be a mess again tomorrow. I don't have a proper comb. I didn't think to take one when I packed."

"Oh shush. We happen to have trunks full of women's things. I'm sure there's a comb in here somewhere."

Sara looked longingly at the trunks. "You think so?"

Sahmara rifled through the other trunk but still came up empty. "Could be the soldiers took it. Nevermind. We'll make due."

"I was thinking of just cutting it off like yours."

"Not another word about that." Sahmara ran her fingers through the curls, untangling the knots and pulling the curls into neat twists.

"See, you're beautiful." She sat next to Sara.

"Thank you. I didn't think I'd ever be beautiful to anyone

ever again."

"Nonsense." Sahmara took her hand.

The door opened below. "I brought dinner."

Olando's voice brought her to her feet. Sara yanked on her hand. "Hey, sit. Your turn."

"I don't have hair."

"Yes, you do. Sit."

Sahmara sat and allowed Sara to run her fingers over her scalp. The fuzz had grown enough to rub through Sara's fingers. The feeling was so relaxing that her eyes drifted closed.

"You're still recovering. You should rest." Sara whispered in her ear. "Lie here a while."

"But I'm hungry."

"Then come eat and then back to bed with you."

"But I don't know if I can sleep alone." She'd become so used to curling up next to another warm body that the thought of a cold bed alone, even a real bed, was unwelcome.

"Don't worry. I don't relish the thought of sleeping alone either. Not in a house with strange men."

"Then let's eat." Sahmara pulled Sara up from the bed and climbed down the ladder.

"Well now. Look what we have here," cackled the old man. "Who knew I had a pair of fine ladies under my roof?"

"Fine would be a bit of an overstatement," Sahmara murmured.

"I consider you quite fine," said Olando, taking her arm and leading her to the table. "Now please sit and enjoy dinner."

She wanted to giggle, and if it weren't for Roy among them, she might have, but his demeanor kept her on edge. Whereas before he'd held her in a spiraling level of disdain, now he just seemed uncertain, like he was expecting her to cause him to burst into flames or bring the heavens down upon them all.

He officiated their meal with a solemn prayer to Hasi and then sat at the head of the table. They feasted on slightly stale bread, salted pork and raw carrots. Their host asked them questions about where they were from and how long they'd been fighting. He wouldn't share any tales of what the Atherians had done to his family or why they'd chosen those they had to hang over the walls, but the shadows that haunted his face told them what they already knew. The Atherians had treated this town little different than any other, except that they'd left this one whole and standing, though probably only because it was a convenient waypoint between larger towns.

While Olando and Sara cleaned up the meal, Sahmara intended to make her way to the ladder, but Roy stopped her by the fire. "Hasi is a man's god. You look a woman today, so how is it that he speaks to you?"

Did she want to tell him that she carried a man's sword? And if she did, would he attempt to take it from her? Did Hasi wish them to get along or had he given up on Roy? Unsure of what to say, she watched the flames.

"I'm his priest. I've dedicated my entire life to him, yet, today, I saw him in you. A woman. He looked at me through your eyes. How is that?"

"I don't know."

"I think you do."

"It's between me and Hasi."

"Have you made some sort of deal with him?"

She laughed. When had either god made any deal with her? They'd taken, but they'd also given. Yet she'd had no say in either transaction.

As annoyed as he looked, she decided that she'd better answer in some form. "In my experience, gods don't make deals with men. Or women," she added. "They do what they want to get what they need, and we either do their will or we don't."

"In my experience, those that don't suffer for it."

"Then you understand that I do not wish to suffer."

"What I don't understand is why he chose *you*." He waved his hand from her head to her feet.

She stood up straight and stared into his eyes, wishing that Hasi again looked out through her own just then, but he must have been busy elsewhere. "I prayed. He answered. Maybe you should try it sometime."

He scowled. "Prayer? I'm a priest. It's what I do."

"Then maybe you're not praying hard enough. Or using the right words. Or meaning what you say. I don't know. Hasi wanted us here yesterday. He needed something then. Maybe it was the deaths of the men we killed today. I don't know. He wasn't that clear."

His voice dropped to a whisper. "Out on the road. What the men said about you, that you fought like a woman possessed. Were you?"

"By Hasi himself."

"They say Yanis was the same from time to time. I thought they were just being superstitious, common peasants, most of them. I'd seen plenty of men filled with the fury of battle, but that one, he was different. Maybe they were right."

"I would have liked to have known that man."

Roy nodded. "He was different then, before the betrayal. I believe he lost his faith that day. His men slowly followed suit. You," he shook his head, "seem to have reawakened what was lost among us."

She didn't know what to say.

Olando came to her side. "Sara tells me that you need to rest. We've had a busy day."

Sahmara nodded.

Roy gave her a questioning look. "He gives much but takes equally." He turned to gaze into the fire, his shoulders sagging.

She wondered if she should tell him that she was the Mother's creature first, but it seemed almost cruel. Two gods behind her, was it a blessing or a curse? She had a feeling he would only see it as a further insult to his faith. Only he knew how truly devout he was. She'd seen him pray, and she'd seen him lead men into battle with an invocation to his god. He certainly seemed to take offense at anyone questioning Hasi or his will. But did that make him a good vessel?

How had Yanis felt after battle? Had he been as tired as she? As much as she wanted to ask Roy, he looked to have shut her out for now to contemplate the flames.

It didn't matter because Olando was already leading her to the ladder. "I think, for tonight, my dear lady, that ya shall sleep in the loft. Our host may find our usual sleeping arrangements distasteful."

"I think you are correct."

"Need I tell ya to keep your hands to yourself this night?"

"I do remember my manners, thank you."

"Good." He took her cheeks in his hands and tilted her head to kiss her forehead. "It is nice to see ya dressed as a lady."

"Funny, as much as I thought I missed dresses," she fluffed her simple skirt, "I find myself longing for the comfort of my recent wardrobe. It would be difficult to fight in a dress."

"Then perhaps one day we will end this war, and ya will no longer need to fight."

"We can hope."

Sara shooed Olando away and beckoned Sahmara up the stairs, following after her. "You've had your meal. Now to bed with you." She made quick work of removing the dress from Sahmara's body, leaving her in a linen shift.

Sara turned so that Sahmara could do the same for her. "I'm thinking I'll try the blue dress tomorrow," she said wistfully.

"We may be moving out tomorrow."

Sara turned around. "But, I thought we were to winter here."

"Winter is weeks off. Roger just wanted us gone."

"But he divided his army. Isn't that foolish?"

"I'm sure he kept the best for his own," said Sahmara.

"Still, that seems an unwise move."

"Time will tell." Sahmara shrugged and pulled back the covers.

Sara climbed in next to her and pulled the covers over them both. "You think that we will keep moving?"

Sahmara sought out the place just outside her where the Mother and Hasi resided. The urgency remained.

"Yes."

Sara sighed, blowing warm air against the back of her neck. "You could stay here if you wish."

Sara was silent for so long that Sahmara wondered if she'd fallen asleep. "No. I will go where you go."

"You are free to do as you wish, you know that, right?"

Sara's arm snaked around her waist. "I wish to stay with you."

She pulled Sara's hand up to rest on her heart. "Then I am happy."

Morning found them entwined in each other's arms. The men were busy being loud in the main room, none of them seeming to dare come up the ladder.

Sara sat up and stretched. "I smell food. Warm food. Two full meals in a row."

She looked so at peace here, like she belonged. As much as it pained Sahmara to offer again, she did. "I can tell you'd not mind this place. I'm sure our host would be happy to have you stay on. He looks like he could use a woman around to take care of him, and I doubt he'd be much of a bother in any other sense. He's a bit old for that sort of thing."

Sara pulled the top blanket around herself and sat there with her eyes closed.

Sahmara got up quietly and slipped into her regular clothes. At least they were dry now. They felt right on her skin, moving with her in ways that a dress never could. As pretty as the dress was, it reminded her of why so many women sat stiffly, scowling at everything and moving only their arms and even then, as little as possible. The old man's dresses hadn't required the constraining undergarments her mother's fancy dresses had, but still, they were for sitting around and being pretty, gathering herbs and flowers, perhaps baking bread and washing dishes or milking a goat and gathering eggs. Dresses were for Sara. Sahmara was done with them.

She folded the dresses neatly and put them back in the trunk, except for the blue one. She set that one out on the bed next to Sara. She straightened the bed as much as she could with Sara still on it and then cleaned up any other sign she had been up in the loft. She rather doubted the old man could climb the ladder himself. If Sara slept up here, she'd be safe enough. At least from him.

A quiet gasp came from Sara's parted lips. Her eyes opened and fixed on Sahmara.

"What is it?"

"I was praying."

Sahmara nodded. "I set the dress out for you."

"Pack it. I'm to come with you. You need me by your side."

"Oh do I now?" She was glad both that Sara had truly given thought to her decision and that she'd asked to bring the dress. She rather looked forward to seeing Sara in it someday.

"The Mother has said so."

Did the gods speak to everyone now? "Did she?"

"Dear Spark, you need me." She smiled, walking lightly over to her discarded clothes and put them on. "You were right, our host could use me here, the town could, but I've also seen your path and that is the one I am meant for."

"The Mother showed you my future?"

"Not exactly." She kissed Sahmara on the lips. "But I have felt it."

Her blood quickened and she returned the kiss, pulling Sara against her.

"Are you ladies going to join us or do we get to eat all the food?" called Olando.

Sahmara held the kiss a moment longer and ran for the stairs. Sara followed with the blue dress under one arm.

"I see you are back to being young men again," remarked their host. "Though, you miss, are a very pretty young man." He winked at Sara.

Sara sketched a quick curtsy. "Thank you, fine sir."

He grinned gleefully, then his gaze rested on the dress in her arms. "What do you have there?"

"Would you mind terribly if I took this one? I mean, I'd pay you for it. It's just that I don't have one, and it looks like it would fit me perfectly."

"It was my little Jeanie's. Not that she was so little anymore, but she shared a name with my first wife. Pretty girl, much like yourself. Keep your coins. I'm glad to see it bring a smile to a woman's lips."

"Oh thank you." She dashed over and gave him a quick peck on the wrinkled cheek. He flushed red.

Sara seemed different somehow, surer of herself. And approaching a man on her own was a big step for her. Her progress made Sahmara warm inside. So did thinking about the kiss they'd shared up in the loft.

Olando leaned over and whispered, "So what were you two doing up there so long this morning?"

"None of your business."

"My dear Spark, you're blushing."

"I am not." She prayed for the heat on her face to go away. Neither god came to her rescue.

He gave her ear a quick nibble while no one was watching.

Sahmara cleared her throat, sending Olando back to his well-mannered self and catching Roy's attention. "These people will be safe enough for a few days. We know no other soldiers will be coming from Antochecki. We need to stop their flow from further South."

"But that puts us farther from Roger and Crag," said Roy.

"Then we are farther. What is the difference if we were to winter here or elsewhere? We would still not be with them. We will leave word here of our next destination. If they need to locate us, they will be able."

Olando looked between them, his brows lowered and head cocked but remained silent.

"I suppose that's so," said Roy.

"We have weeks before the snow hits hard. We can cover much ground in that time."

Roy gazed at her thoughtfully. "You sound very sure of this."

"I am."

"All right then." Roy got to his feet and packed his things. "I'll let the others know."

Olando leaned in close. "You're giving the orders now?"

"It would seem so."

He pulled back a little to look her in the eye. "That Yanis speaking through ya?"

"Not exactly."

"The gods then." His gaze dropped to the sword at her side. "He was a man of Hasi in his own right."

She nodded.

"What games are the gods playing, dear lady?"

"It's no game."

His voice dropped to a whisper. "Ya should go with Roy. I have no wish to offend the gods. And two of them favoring ya?" He shook his head. "I pray from time to time, but I'm no true follower, devout, faithful. Surely they frown upon me. Upon us sharing a bed." Olando paled. "Forgive me."

"There's nothing to forgive." She took his hand in hers. "It's just me. I'm nothing special."

"As ya say."

"Olando."

He regarded her warily, his winking playfulness gone. Gently extracting his hand from hers, he finished his meal.

CHAPTER SEVENTEEN

Roy waited at the gate. The men gathered there around him. Sahmara, Sara, and Olando joined them.

"Where too then?" asked Roy quietly.

It amused her that he wished to appear in charge when clearly most of them favored her, even with her lack of experience. "South. Follow the road."

"Is that wise?"

"If we wish to keep forces from flowing North to the cities we've freed, then yes. Your brother can hold them off from his position while we clean them out from ours. The road is how they are moving."

"But we have so few men."

"Then we gather more, or we strike quickly as we did here."

"You didn't have a hand in that rain, did you?"

"That wasn't me. Not to say it wasn't them." She glanced at the sky, even though she knew for a fact that the gods did not reside there. They were all around them, just outside their bodies. It occurred to her just then that if she could invite Hasi into herself, perhaps others could as well. They just had to open their minds.

Was that true or was it Yanis's sword that allowed Hasi access? "I need to speak with you privately, along the way."

Roy bowed his head and seemed to shrink in on himself. "If you say so."

His god spoke to her, at least she could give him the concession of being in charge. "Move them out. The sooner the better."

He straightened and turned to face the others. "We head South. We'll be taking the wagons with us. If you need to store extra gear you've acquired, you are welcome to do so but you'll want your cloaks if you have them, layers if you don't. It's not going to get any warmer. We move into the heart of the enemy's holdings. They will not give ground lightly. You will need to be on watch at all times and be ready to fight, not weighed down with belongings."

The men nodded. They began to stow their gear on the wagons, dressing in layers of clothing and securing the cloaks about themselves. Some used blankets. Everyone carried a weapon, either sheathed or not. Sara took her place on the wagon beside the driver she didn't mind. Ramsey and John found their way to Sahmara's side as the gate opened. Olando lagged a few steps behind as they marched out onto the road.

Though no one spoke to her directly, Sahmara walked with them for a time before she excused herself to join Roy.

She'd only gotten a couple steps ahead when she noticed Olando suddenly beside her. "Do ya need me to come with ya?"

"No, why?"

"Ya hadn't been getting along at all and now he happily takes orders from ya?"

"I'm not the one giving the orders, and I wouldn't call it happily."

"They come from your lips, in your voice," he said without looking at her.

"I'm just the messenger."

"Messengers don't have god-blessed weapons or invite gods into their bodies to fight."

She sighed. "I don't know how to explain it, but I'm just me. I want you beside me like you have been. I'm no different than before."

"As ya say."

She knocked into him. "Quit saying that."

He didn't push back. His steps slowed. "Are ya going to Roy then?"

"I'm seeking his council. That's all. I expect you to share my blanket tonight."

"Yes, my dear lady."

She let out an exasperated sigh. "Keep an eye on Sara. I'll be back soon."

She wove her way through the men to Roy's side. He increased his already lengthy stride until they were alone.

"Have you ever spoken with Hasi?" she asked.

"Directly?"

She nodded.

"No. Gods do not speak to us in the words of men." He kept his gaze forward as they walked, his pace steady.

"What if I told you that they did?"

He glared at her out of the corner of his eye. "I'd think you were boasting."

"I have spoken to the Mother and to Hasi. They both draw power through me."

Roy stumbled, only catching his footing just before falling into the dirt. "Careful what you say, woman."

Glad for his slower pace, even if only momentarily, she took the opportunity to catch her breath while he regained his step. "If Yanis could do this, and myself, can others?"

"There are the holy Ma'hasi, and I would imagine there are others who hold favor of one or the other."

The mention of Ma'hasi brought her thoughts to Zane. For all the training and blessing that he swore had been placed upon him and his brethren, she could not recall seeing any real hint of Hasi behind his eyes. Then again, she'd only seen him in practice. Surely if Hasi had filled him when her home had been overrun, her family would be safe. She'd seen Zane alive. He was far better trained, his body honed for such swordplay, than she. He would have fought and few would have survived. Perhaps it was when he slept as she had that he'd been taken.

She'd been taken. Why with Hasi's blessings, had he not found her in all this time? She stared at her feet as they walked. The sword at her side weighed heavy, slowing her already shorter stride.

177

Her thoughts wandered to meeting Reva on the beach, of the old woman sucking her blood. There had been an exchange, a deal of sorts made at that moment. That was clear enough, but she'd had no such time with Hasi. She'd taken up Yanis' sword. She'd never asked for his assistance, never even prayed to him. She'd prayed to the Mother. She'd been open to him, a waiting vessel.

"I know how it happened for me, but can these others," she nodded toward the men trailing behind them, "also become vessels for Hasi?"

"I am a priest, and yet, even I only have words to hold sway over the likes of men. I cannot make them anything more than what they are. If I could, we would not be where we are today." He waved his dirty hands at the path they walked and the armed men behind them.

"But can they, the men themselves?" She chewed her bottom lip, lost in thought.

"What are you asking?"

"You heard John and Ramsey speak of the battle on the roadside."

He nodded.

"Then you understand how a god can grant power to a man."

"Yes, I suppose that is so."

"In granting that power, the god also gains it through the lives that man takes."

"Surely they are not so literal."

She shrugged. "That's been my experience. You may have better words to embellish it."

He pondered this for a moment. "So if we were to invite the gods into many men, all with similar power to that you were given, our meager force would be much greater."

"Exactly."

"I must admit, Spark, you are more than I expected."

She found herself fighting to keep up with his pace again. "We'll see about that."

"So what do you propose?"

Did he really expect her to have answers? If she did, she wouldn't have been asking. Then again, perhaps he enjoyed pointing out what she didn't know. Sahmara gave him a good long glance from head to toe, hoping she had even a hint of the power of Hasi behind her eyes as she did so. "You're the priest, preach."

"But I don't understand how you have done what you did. You hold the answers."

She shook her head. "I'm no priest."

"No, I fear you are something more. Something bigger. Let us hope the Atherians feel that fear as well."

"Some of them already have."

Behind them the wagons creaked, men coughed and the horse's hooves clomped on the dirt road. Birds chirped in the distance and a soft but chilled breeze stirred fallen leaves.

Roy stared ahead. "Many more will need to if we are to make a difference."

"Then the gods need more men. You saw how much they took from me the last time. We can't afford to wait days between battles while everyone rests, or even just me if this doesn't work."

"You did not invoke the gods at Omasii?"

Her hand brushed over the sword at her side. "I didn't need to. The men had the situation under control quick enough."

"That was wise of you."

"Perhaps it was cowardly. I will admit that being a vessel was not a pleasant experience either during or after."

"No." He paused to rest a hand on her shoulder. "I don't think that is the case."

For the first time, she saw acceptance in his gaze, though be it of his own role or hers, she couldn't guess.

"Start with a man you know. Olando. See if you can explain to him what he must do. If you cannot get him to cooperate, there is little chance it will work with the others."

"You may be right," she said.

"And if we need you before then, your plan will have to wait."

"Let's hope not." She dropped back, letting one man after one march past her. Finally, she found herself back at Olando's side. He looked straight ahead.

She did not relish the thought of being attacked before any of them were ready. If she wiped herself out, there would be no progress for days. She needed more than one man to start with.

She tapped John and Ramsey on the shoulders. They fell in line with her and Olando.

"You," she said to them, "witnessed how I fought on the roadside."

They nodded.

"And what happened to you afterward," muttered Olando.

"Yes. Unfortunately, one is tied to the other." She cleared her throat, ready for them to think she was crazy. "It was Hasi, acting through me."

John grinned. "You've been hanging around Roy too much."

"Hardly, we just started actually speaking beyond insults yesterday."

"We've seen your skill with the bow. It stands to reason that you've had experience with battle before. No one is that good without a lot of practice and time on the battlefield," said Ramsey.

"The bow was a gift from the Mother. She guides my arrows, far more so than my aim."

"You're just being modest."

"Or pious," added John.

"Or truthful," said Olando.

He might be uncertain around her, but at least he seemed to be attempting to help her win the others over. Maybe he just needed some time to adjust. She hoped so. She missed his grins and twinkling eyes.

"If we are to win this battle for Revochek, we need help. The gods are willing to help us because they also need us."

Olando laughed. Maybe he wasn't out to help her after all. "The gods care little for the actions of men."

"It's because of men believing that, that they have lost believers and as such, men and women who feed them the power they need to keep our country safe."

"We're hardly safe," said Ramsey.

"And that is your fault as much as any other man," she said, glaring him.

He scowled. She feared she might lose them.

"I can't do this by myself. You saw how much that fight took from me. If I am dead asleep for days and another attack arises, are you all enough to overpower the Atherians through mortal means?"

"We've done it before," said John, looking as offended as Ramsey.

"And your numbers are thousands less. We are losing, day by day. Are you enough to keep the Atherians at bay even if we slowly push them from our country? Their cities have lost nothing. They have families, harvests, horses, supplies and riches. We have ashes, tragic tales, and wounds that will ache every winter or rain."

The three of them walked on, silent.

John spoke first. "What would Roy have us do?"

"He would have you do as I say. He can't give you the knowledge that I can in this. Yes, he is a priest, but this is different. And I can't promise that it will work, but you have to try anyway."

"Spark, what are ya saying?" asked Olando.

"I'm saying I'm not a priest, but I'm probably going to sound like one." She laughed nervously.

"Would we fight as ya did?" asked Ramsey.

"Yes. Did any of you witness Yanis fighting as I did?"

Olando looked thoughtful. "Once, I think. The men thought he was injured in battle because he wouldn't wake up for days, but they could find no large wound upon him. Is it the sword?"

"Perhaps, but I hope it is the willingness of the man instead."

"And if it's not?" asked Olando

"We'll be passing the sword around."

"That could be awkward in battle," said Ramsey.

"Then let's hope that's not the solution."

"All right then, so what would you have us do?" asked John.

"Realize that the gods need you as much as you need them. They are right here." She held her hand inches from Olando's heart. "Just here. Waiting. Not touching, not visible. They are wishing you would let them in so they can gather what they need to make us all safe again."

"So why don't we all just gather around and reaffirm our belief in Hasi, and then he can toss the Atherian's out?" asked Ramsey.

"They are not in this same world with us. They exist just outside of it. They have their own. They also have the god of the Atherians to contend with. His people believe in him. Really believe." She gave them all a hard look. "They give him power through their belief and our blood as they rampaged through our country. The deaths of our people have brought the demise of so many more and maybe of Hasi and the Mother herself if we don't help them."

"Can the gods truly be killed?"

"Do you want to find out?"

"Well, no."

"Then I suggest doing some searching within and praying."

The hint of a smile whispered over Olando's face. "Ya don't make a very good priest."

Sahmara sighed. "I wanted Roy to talk to you, but he thought it better that I did. I can see that was a mistake."

"I'm glad ya did," said John. "I wouldn't have believed much he said anyway. He does a lot of talking, but not much convincing. We saw ya, though. That gives your words true meaning."

She wanted to hug him for making her not feel so stupid but didn't want to give Olando any other reason to pull further away.

"So what do we do?" asked Ramsey.

"I'm not sure." She pondered that, wondering what she had done to warrant the Mother's interest. She'd been alone and tired, on the verge of giving up. Empty. Not full of faith or making deals or down on bended knees. She hadn't even remembered the correct prayers for the Mother's sake.

"Be empty. Offer yourself to Hasi. No deals, no bargains. Just honesty."

"But I like women. I don't wish to become Ma'hasi," said Olando.

She wondered if he was making fun of her and Zane. His face conveyed no clues one way or the other. "You were not offered as a Ma'hasi child. You are you. He will either accept you or not. Payment is all he takes. Strength and ability are what he offers. It's really quite simple."

"Nothing about gods is simple," said Ramsey.

"I'm not going to argue that point, but for the sake of this matter, don't complicate things. It's a straightforward arrangement. Once accepted, you can choose whether to invoke him or not when a battle arises. I would suggest only a few of us do at a time. We need soldiers available at all hours and those that are vessels of Hasi will be down for days."

"As ya were," said John.

"Yes."

"I see."

"How will we know if he has accepted our offer?" asked Olando.

"He will speak to you."

"Now ya do sound like a priest," he muttered.

"No, he really will speak, in words like you and me."

"To ya maybe."

"I'm no different than you. I was empty and the gods filled me. That is all."

The thought of many of the men sharing her gifts bothered her. She had power for once. Men followed her lead when she was the only one. Now that they knew where she got her skills and that they may be the same, she would be one amongst many. Yet, as one of many, they might clear the country of the enemy and get to go home. As one, she may watch them all die or they may die while she slept off the god drain. There was no room for her to be special.

The three of them became quiet as they marched. John drifted away first. Ramsey shortly after. Eventually, even Olando left her side. Though Sara sat in the wagon not far off, Sahmara had only felt that alone once before, when she'd been on the beach before she'd met Reva. Were they going off to pray or getting away from her crazy, raving self?

By the time Roy called a halt, none of them had returned. She saw them. They weren't gone, but they remained on the fringes of the milling men. At least they weren't talking to one another, pointing and laughing at her.

Sara sat next to her, offering a narrow wedge of cheese from her stores. Sahmara took it and nibbled.

"Where is Olando? It's not like him to leave your side."

"He's praying, I hope."

Sara cocked her head. "Praying for what?"

Sahmara explained what she had talked to the men about.

"So the men should call upon Hasi and the women on the Mother?"

"What women? There is only you and me."

"I am a woman, am I not?"

"Yes, of course."

"Then I will do my duty and call upon the Mother." Sara kissed her cheek and wandered off.

Sahmara sat alone. The men who had marched near her stayed in one group and the ones who had marched near Roy sat in another. The visible divide put her on edge. She got up and walked within Roy's men to seek him out.

"Well?" he asked.

"It's not an immediate thing. Four people are trying it now."

He glanced at those closest to them and squared his shoulders. "Let me know the results."

Was he dismissing her? She wasn't about to cede the upper hand, not just yet anyway. "If even one of them is successful,

I'd like to speak to some of your men next."

He scowled. "Converting more followers?"

"Uniting our camp."

He looked from her men to his and eventually nodded. "I suppose that would be acceptable."

She got up and went back to her spot. Word passed that they'd be resting here and then marching until dusk. Sahmara propped herself up against a tree and put Yanis's sword on her lap.

In her dreams, Yanis and the eyeless young priestess of the Mother waved her onward, further down the road. Yanis stared at her waist. She looked down to see his sword hanging from her belt. He smiled and nodded. The girl felt her way over and hugged Sahmara, wrapping her tattered fleshy arms around her waist and pressing her bird-pecked face into Sahmara's stomach. She smoothed the hair upon the girl's head and then brushed the sand from Yanis's cheek. He caught her hand and held it there. His flesh was cold and his eyes hollow, but she wasn't afraid. They were dead, that was all.

A yell rushed her from her dream and yanked her back through the heavy layers of sleep to the clanging of swords and battle cries of men.

It was Sara who had yelled, only inches from her face now and shaking her by the shoulders. "Spark, we need you."

Sahmara shot to her feet, taking in the chaos around her. Men were everywhere, too many to count and most in armor that didn't belong to her people. An arrow caught her in the shoulder right beside her bandage. She cried out. Sara yelped.

"Get behind the tree. Now," yelled Sahmara as she broke off the shaft just above where it entered her flesh. She emptied her mind of the pain and prayed hard without a second of hesitation. Both the Mother and Hasi stood before her, their eyes glowing with spiraling color. Their faces were gaunt and angry. They were so hungry she could feel it in her gut, a gnawing pain that knew no bounds.

"There are so many," she said.

"You have done well," they both answered.

"Protect Sara."

"She can protect herself if only she asks."

Sahmara nodded and then opened herself to their power. The wave of hunger and hate knocked her to her knees. Dizziness followed. Back against the tree, and in the middle of battle, she took a deep breath and swung her sword at the nearest target.

"Sara," she yelled. "Pray." She tried to get around to the other side of the tree to see if Sara was even still there, but there were too many bodies in need of her sword. Her arms and hands tingled as the gods drank the blood of her enemies. Over and over she swung and thrust, dodging, charging, dancing over the dead to seek out more offerings for the gods.

Beyond her, she caught a glimpse of a man, spinning with a whirling blade, utter determination on his face. She recognized John's armor. Dead lay about him like fallen trees after a forest fire. If Hasi looked as such through John, it was no wonder men scrambled away from her now. She hunted them down, thrusting her sword through their hearts, over their throats, and between their ribs. Fear shown in their eyes and the reflection in them was not her own.

A scream behind her halted her charge. She darted away from her next target, dashing over the bodies that lay between her and the scream. With a single purpose, she barreled over the distance and found Sara pressed to a tree, her short sword on the ground at her feet. A man held her there, dangling, by her throat. He spun to meet Sahmara, tossing Sara aside, and raising the dagger he held in his other hand.

She knocked it away from him, along with his hand, in a clean slice. He screamed. As much as she wished to take his other hand and then his head, Hasi and the Mother only wanted his blood. Her sword pierced his throat, emerging from the back of his neck. His mouth gaped open, reminding her of her dreams of Yanis and the girl speaking wordlessly. This man didn't have their urgency, only gasping and then death. She hoisted Sara to her feet.

"I told you to pray."

Sara backed away from her. "The gods are so powerful. I…"

"Go to the wagon and hide there."

"But there are so many."

"Then follow me."

Sara grabbed her sword and followed. The path to the wagons was a bloody one, but Sara remained safe in her wake. She scrambled up inside the first one they came to.

"Your shoulder, how are you fairing?"

"I feel nothing." And it was true, she'd forgotten about the older injury and the new one. Sahmara glanced down at the broken shaft in her shoulder, pinning her cloak to her body. Blood glistened around the shaft. If it had soaked all the way through to her heavy cloak, surely she must feel something, but the gods shielded her from mortal concerns for now. She had little doubt she'd feel it later and get a tongue lashing from Sara for it too.

She sped over the fallen, not looking to see which side they hailed from. It didn't matter right now. Only feeding the gods mattered. Soldiers massed in clumps. She approached the closest one and started in on them. Slowly, she worked her way in to find Olando in the middle with three other men. None of them wore the frenzy of Hasi, but their swords flashed all the same. Olando looked pale, blood dripping from wounds on his neck and on his arms. His cloak masked any other injuries. He was skilled, but there were too many. Sahmara set about evening the odds.

The battle dissolved into bodies to stick her sword into and those she needed to save. The gods seemed to direct her blade to the correct targets, stripping any doubt from her. The men she relieved stayed at her back, cleaning up anything she missed. She worked her way toward John.

Between the two of them, they mowed down forces while the others filled in around them. The gods sang within her, filling her with more energy than she knew what to do with. Her arms and legs moved on their own accord, her vision homing in on the targets before her now that she knew Olando and Sara were safe behind her.

When the last of the bodies fell, the energy within faded to a more manageable level. She worked her way back to the wagon, relieving the wounded of life along the way. It wasn't until Olando tapped her on her good shoulder that the gods released her.

"Spark, it's time to rest. You need to let Sara look at your shoulder."

"How many did we lose?"

"Not near as many as we would have without you and John."

"Ramsey?"

"I haven't seen him."

"Tell the others, Roy's men. Tell them what I told you."

"But it didn't work for me."

"Try again." She let his arms take her down to the ground and then the sky went black.

CHAPTER EIGHTEEN

A man she didn't know sat by her side with a sword in his hand. Sahmara glanced around to discover she was laying in one of the wagons. The clomping of the horse's hooves on the dirt road and creaking of the wagon wheels eased her mind. They were moving.

"John and Ramsey, are they all right?"

"John woke a couple hours ago. He's up in the next wagon with Ramsey and the healer. Ramsey took on most of a patrol on his own last night. Was truly a sight to see."

She tried to sit up but the pain in her shoulder took her breath away.

"Oh no, ya best just lay back there or the healer will have my hide. She's got it packed full of something that she found this morning. Made her real happy. Must mean good things for ya."

"I need to speak with Olando."

"He's up with the priest. He said he'd be back by nightfall to check on ya."

At least he was doing as she'd asked. Though, she would have liked to see his face. "Are there any others, like Ramsey?"

"No. Just the three of ya. Don't know what we'd do without ya. Was an amazing sight, that."

They needed more. At least John was back among them for now. Hopefully, Olando and Roy could convert more.

She tried to remember the man's name. "Flyn?"

He nodded.

"Can I get something to eat and drink?"

He handed her a strip of dried meat and her water jug. "Olando said you'd be wanting these."

"Thanks."

She lay there, watching the clouds float by, listening to the wheels turn and chewing on the salty meat. Flyn helped her sit up a little so she could drink without soaking herself, though she ended up rather wet anyway.

Once her stomach was mollified, her mind focused fully on all points of bodily discomfort. Each bump of the wagon on the road was agony until it finally came to a halt. She slid out of the wagon to relieve herself. Sara found her and helped her back into the wagon.

"How is it?" Sahmara asked.

"Your shoulder wasn't as bad as I expected. The gods have shown you favor."

"Hurts an awful lot."

Sara settled down next to her and began to remove the bandage. "You used your arm an awful lot. I'd expect you'll feel far worse than the last time."

Sahmara took stock of her aches. Though she knew for a fact that she'd killed far more men than the first time, she didn't feel as sore, other than her shoulder.

"It looks better than this morning," Sara announced.

"Ouch." Sahmara winced as Sara poked around the edges. "Stop that."

"Stop being such a baby." She playfully swatted Sahmara's hand away. "Those herbs did a heap of good. My mother always swore on them, best things for open wounds. I've used them on many of the other wounded as well and don't have many left." She rewound the bandage. "Perhaps it was the Mother's grace that led us through the flowering field to begin with. I wouldn't have recognized them if not for the flowers."

Sara turned away to check on Flyn, who had a bandage wrapped around most of one thigh. Once she was finished, she sent him off get something to eat. Finding them alone on the wagon for the moment, Sahmara took Sara's hand. "What did you mean when you said the gods were too powerful?"

Sara's gaze dropped to her lap. "I prayed like you said. I really did. I saw the Mother. She was beautiful. But also terrifying."

"I know what you mean."

"Do you?" Sara stared at her empty hands resting in her lap. "You fight for her. You let her into your body. She is in you. I've seen it. Your eyes become hers."

"No, they don't."

She'd seen her reflection in the eyes of the enemy. It wasn't her own face, but it wasn't the Mother's either, nor Hasi's. It was a mix of them. The gods peeking out from her eyes, their hunger distorting her face. She was herself and them at the same time.

"They do." Sara watched the men standing around the wagon, talking quietly and sharing rations they'd seized from the Atherian wagon.

Sahmara said, "I can't control that."

"Can you control anything when they are in you?"

"Yes." She remembered the terror of knowing Sara was in danger. "I wanted to keep you safe. They wanted to charge forward and claim more blood."

Sara smiled. "You did both."

"Compromise."

"So not total control then."

"I suppose not," Sahmara said.

Sara drew her knees up to her chest and wrapped her arms around her legs, resting her chin on her knees. "What does it feel like?"

"What did it feel like for you?"

"She poured herself into my flesh, all cold and spiky, hungry, and craving blood. It was…" Sara shuddered, rubbing her hands over her arms. "Colder than a mid-winter night. I couldn't keep her inside."

"I guess I didn't notice that so much as the dizziness and the single-minded vision. But no, that is Hasi more than the Mother. She didn't have a cold feeling for me. The craving blood, though, yes. It was unsettling at first, then I just stopped thinking about it. Being in the middle of a battle does that for you, changes your priorities. Living was mine."

"I'm sorry. I wanted to, it was just…"

"It's all right." She patted Sara's foot, the closest thing to her. "You have a kind heart. It's not ready to be tainted by such hunger."

"You're not disappointed in me?" she asked quietly.

"No. But I would like to know you're safe. If you won't accept the Mother within you, then stay near someone who is or hide."

"I'm sorry I distracted you."

"You didn't. And if you hadn't woken me when you did, I might have suffered far more than an arrow to the shoulder."

Sara leaned over and hugged her carefully. "I'm glad that's all it was."

"Me too."

"How is Olando?"

She looked away again. "Not well."

"Why? What happened?" Her heart began to race. "Was he hurt?"

"Bruises and a few cuts, one nasty one to his neck, but no, it was more his pride, I think. Hasi didn't answer him."

Sahmara wished she could see him, but he remained out of sight. She'd have to deal with him later.

Flyn and the wagon driver returned. The line resumed its southern march. Sara moved to the front of the wagon to sit near Sahmara's head so Flyn had more room to sit between the piles of gear that also shared the wagon.

Sahmara rested her head on Sara's lap. It was a great improvement over the bag of rice she'd woken upon. Sara stroked her hair, running her soft fingers over Sahmara's scalp in soothing swirls that almost took her mind off the pain in her shoulder.

"What of Ramsey?" Sahmara asked.

Sara gazed further up the line. "He watched over both of you until the patrol hit us."

"He did well enough on his own, though?" She wished it

didn't hurt so much to sit up, she desperately wanted to make sure all the familiar faces still walked the line with them.

"As well as he could."

Her stomach clenched. "What do you mean?"

"I was hoping to give you more time to recover first."

Sahmara tried to sit up again anyway, to see the wagon where Ramsey and John rode, but Sara shoved her firmly back to the floor.

"He was badly wounded." Sara bowed her head. "I don't know as he will make it. There were just too many and even Hasi couldn't protect him."

Sahmara's swallowed hard as tears welled in her eyes. They weren't invincible. Even with the god's power filling them, they could be struck down.

Was it Sara's herbs or the god's favor that speeded the healing? "Is he healing well too?"

"Yes. The herbs are working. But he...suffered many injuries."

"I want to see him."

Sara still held her down. Her hands may have been soft and her body beautiful, but there was muscle there too. "You need to rest."

"I can't rest." The urgency of the gods tugged at her, agitating like a hundred hairs caught inside her shirt, rubbing, tickling, prickling. "I have too much to do."

"Spark." Sara's face turned stern. "You will rest. Tonight, when we stop, you can move to his wagon. It will do neither of you any good to move you there now."

"Then bring me some men."

Her brows rose. "Excuse me?"

"Not for that." Sahmara shook her head and laughed. "I need to tell them what I told the four of you. We need more soldiers of Hasi. Now, especially with me and Ramsey wounded."

"Olando is already doing that."

"And he wasn't able to accept Hasi himself. Not that I doubt his intentions, but I think I might be more effective."

193

She pursed her lips. "You might be right. Still, I'll not have you wearing yourself out."

"Sara, I'm riding in a wagon. I'm not pulling it."

"All right, fine. But only a few and then you'll rest. You hear me?"

"I do. Go on and find me some men."

Sara gave her a quick kiss on the lips. "Just this once."

Sahmara laughed and watched her go, her hips swaying even under her cloak.

She'd just about drifted off when Sara returned with five men in tow. Three of them watched Sara's backside more than the wagon and nearly banged into her and each other when she came to a halt. Sahmara scowled at them.

They all noticed, the two in front turning to snicker at the ones in the back. Sara shook her head at all of them. "You all should know better. None of you are getting any of this." She pointed to herself and then went to sit on the bench seat at the front of the wagon.

Flyn came to sit next to her, helping to prop her up so she could better face the men walking behind the wagon. "Not fair of ya, Spark, keeping her all to yourself," he whispered in her ear as he gently pulled her up.

"I don't." She gritted her teeth and kept the screech of pain in her throat so Sara wouldn't hear. "I share with Olando."

"Again, not fair."

"Too bad." She appreciated his humorous attempt to distract her from the movement, but they had more important things to discuss. She looked the five men over as they walked while she and Flyn bounced. The driver apologized for the stones in the road.

She only placed a name to one of them, James, a short, stocky man with a wild, dark beard.

"Have any of you spoken with Olando?"

James and another raised a finger.

"Then you know what I'm about to tell you."

"That you can make us like John and Ramsey and ya self?" asked the man next to James.

"That's up to you, but I can tell you how to make it happen if you want it to."

They all nodded eagerly.

"Well then, listen up." She gave some thought to what she had told the first four and tried to put her words a little more priestly-like. Just a bit, so they seemed more believable, more like they were used to hearing. After she'd mostly finished, she realized her mistake in their glazed eyes. "Let's go back a step."

She put her instructions more bluntly. "Pray and mean it. What you do today will affect us all tomorrow. If it doesn't work for you, then pray again. If it does, go amongst the others, to your friends, and tell them what I have told you. I need to rest. I can't explain it to all of you."

"Why not tell everyone at once?" asked James.

"Because I don't want those who Hasi has answered against those who Hasi has not. You need to remain unified. You need to work together, not begrudging those that Hasi answers and those he does not."

"So we're back to the love one another stuff then?" asked Flyn.

"If you aren't going to take this seriously, then begone with you." She shooed them all off.

James and a man with dark skin like Olando stuck around. "They will believe. They have to. We'll make sure they do."

"Make sure, nicely. I'll not have anyone acting against another. We have enough enemies."

"Rest well, Spark," said James.

They set off after the others. Sahmara watched them wander off, melding into the other men behind them or speeding up to walk ahead. Flyn lifted her head from the bags and blankets he'd set behind her and slowly lowered her back to the floor.

"Not to sound like the healer, but you should rest. I have some thinking to do, and you watching me is just distracting." He winked.

Sahmara chuckled and closed her eyes, letting the sound of men and horses walking lull her back to sleep.

She woke to a night sky. Stars twinkled above. She slid from the wagon. Men mingled around low fires, eating and laughing and talking quietly. She spotted Olando and Sara sitting near Roy and went to join them. They all looked up, startled as she entered the circle of light.

"Are ya well enough to be about?" asked Olando, concern plain on his face.

"Is John not up and about?"

"He's still complaining about being very sore."

"It's only my shoulder now. Not bad either." She smiled at Sara. "Those herbs are working wonders."

Sara beamed.

"How is word spreading through the men?" she asked.

"Slowly," said Olando. "I've been talking to small groups as ya did with us. "Some seem to believe, others laugh me off."

"Even after seeing John and Ramsey in action?"

"The men think they are merely very skilled with a sword. Seeing Ramsey fall shook even some of your followers," said Roy.

Her face grew warm. She had followers. Even Roy admitted it.

"Even those blessed by Hasi can fall," she said. "That doesn't mean that his acts were any less heroic, and more importantly, sorely needed."

"You will need to explain that to them," said Roy, shifting his robes as though wearing them now made him uncomfortable. Maybe he felt the same urgency she did. She didn't wish to upset their newly formed alliance by asking.

Sara shook her head. "They should know it. Are they daft?"

"No," said Roy. "They are men. They know swords and they know the men to stick them into. The workings of gods and women are mysterious. Both are desirable in their own ways when it is convenient."

Sahmara sighed loudly and went back to her wagon. Didn't they understand that this was what the gods and men needed to take back their country? Were they really so concerned with ale, wine and women, that the ways of the world meant so little to them? She wanted to slap them all. Instead, she turned back from the wagon and walked among them, not speaking so much as watching and being seen. She sought out John and sat by him for a short while.

"Are ya well?" he asked, looking her over.

"I am better. Hasi has favored me." Though standing and walking were taking their toll, even she knew she'd be back on the wagon soon enough.

He smiled. "Me too. Though I fear not as much."

She noticed how he sat rather hunched over, his elbows resting heavily on his legs. "It seems to be less wearing with each time."

"That's good to know. I don't know as I'd willingly do that again, knowing the pain it would bring me." He rubbed his left wrist with his right hand, massaging up his arm and back down.

"Don't dwell on that. Instead, think of the lives you saved and those you took."

"True." He nodded. "It's hard to think outside of myself when I hurt, though."

"Understandable. That's why we need more like us. Have you spoken to the others?"

"Yes. Several, and I'll continue to do so."

"Good."

She got to her feet and then couldn't catch her breath. She gasped. A vision of men in the night overcame her. She felt herself falling but could do nothing to catch herself.

"Spark," John yelled. "Someone get the healer."

Footsteps pounded around her. "No," she grabbed John's leg. "Ready the men. We're about to be attacked."

"It's night. The Atherians wouldn't move in the darkness any more than we would. It's not safe."

"They aren't concerned with safety." The weakness started to fade, but her breath still came in gasps. "They want us dead. Quickly. Get the men to arms."

"As you say, Spark. We're still fetching the healer." John shouted orders and waved at several men. They all took off running, though he stayed by her side.

"Find Olando and tell him to bring my bow."

He helped her to her feet, where she stood, swaying, pinpricks of darkness still swimming in her vision.

"Ya can't see in the darkness to fire your bow," he said.

Nerves on edge, she snapped at him, "Don't question me."

John shook his head but dashed away.

Men ran past her. At least they were taking action. She closed her eyes and breathed deeply in and out several times until the spots subsided. One of the men paused beside her.

She realized it was Flyn. "What should I do?" he asked, frantically peering into the darkness.

"Pray. And while you're doing that, put out the fires. We don't need to give them any advantages."

"But how should I pray?"

"Seriously and like your life depended on it. It does."

He ran to the nearest fire and kicked dirt onto it.

Olando was by her side within minutes, sword, bow and quiver in hand. "Ya aren't ready for this, dear lady. Hang back this once."

"Perhaps. We'll see if any new blessed emerge. If not, I will need to."

"We don't even know how many there are. Who spotted them?"

"I did. The Mother sent me a vision." The gods must be growing stronger, she considered, if they were sending her such an overpowering vision without any consent on her part.

"Then how do ya do know how many there were?"

Sahmara closed her eyes, recalling the brief glance of the future that the gods had thrust upon her. "Because I saw them. The Atherians are angry. Their god's wrath is in the air. He's firing them up and sending them headlong into the darkness after us."

"Ya know all this from a vision?"

"A vision from the Mother, yes."

"As ya say, Spark."

She took his face in her hands and rested her forehead

against his. "Olando, I need you to believe."

"I'm trying. I know ya are blessed. I've seen it, but those blessed by Hasi are trained from birth, like your Zane. They aren't shepherd boys."

She kissed him soundly until she felt him relax in her arms. "They are. Hasi cares not from where you came, only what you can do for him. If you are willing, he will use you. And by using you, we win. You understand?"

He placed his hands over hers. "Tell me ya didn't convince them all this way?"

She chuckled. "Only you."

"Good."

"Now help me get the quiver over my shoulder," she said.

Sara ran over just as Olando rested the quiver against her back. Her stern voice made Sahmara glad she couldn't clearly see her face. "What are you doing?"

"Getting ready for a fight. That means either you stick close or you hide. Which is it?"

"You're hiding with me, Spark. Tell her, Olando. Tell her she can't fight."

Olando looked between them. "I'd rather she didn't, but we may need her."

"I need her." Sara's voice shook. "If she ends up like Ramsey, I don't know what I would do."

"You'd heal me, just like you're healing him," Sahmara said firmly. "Now decide."

"I'll hide. I'll not be a distraction for you."

"Olando, make sure you hide her well."

"Me?"

"I trust you'll take care of her," she said.

"But what about ya?"

"Find me when you've done that."

"As ya say, my lady."

They ran off. She lost track of which direction they went in the darkness. Men gathered around her, weapons ready. Roy was among them, a sword in his hands. He looked to her. Was she supposed to give some sort of speech? She wasn't their leader. She was only a girl desperate enough to invite blood-thirsty gods into her body.

Sahmara stood on the log. She only had one word for them all. "Pray."

One by one, they put their heads down, mouths moving. At the edges of her sight, they faded into the blackness. She hoped they were all doing as those close to her were. Though, she pictured some, like those she'd spoken to earlier by the wagon, to be staring at the stars and rolling their eyes or mumbling about her being crazy under their breaths.

John pushed his way through them to her side. "What would ya have us do?"

By *us*, she knew he meant the god-touched. "Wait a moment and see what happens once the first Atherians are upon us.

"How will we know if we need Hasi?"

"You will know."

He nodded.

They stood in the darkness, waiting, hearts pounding, listening for any sound. All she could hear was the whispering of men praying. It eased her heart a bit to see that Roy stood among them, dutifully praying.

Olando showed up, peering at the others. He looked at her and then bowed his head.

The silence stretched on. And on. Doubt niggled at Sahmara.

Had she imagined the vision the gods had given her? Had she merely been lightheaded? Maybe the herbs Sara had used were making her see things.

Then she heard it, footsteps crashing through the underbrush. Metal against metal and men yelling. And then her men lifted their heads and their swords. Many of their eyes glowed, a spiraling twist of colors. Their mouths opened, and a horrible shrieking cry came from them. Sahmara looked to John. His eyes matched theirs. Should she open herself as well or let them take care of the attack? Should she sit this one out? Her fingers tingled. She saw that she was clenching her hands so tight that her nails had drawn blood on her palms. The gods demanded she take part.

Sahmara closed her eyes, and released her breath, inviting Hasi and the Mother into her flesh. By the time she inhaled, they were there, filling her, fueling her with abundant energy. The blood in her veins hummed. She leaped from the log with her bow in hand and led the men into the woods, not waiting for the brunt of their attack to hit. They picked off the front line one by one, Hasi's blessed beside her.

They pressed on, through the trees, over a hill, and across a field. The moon lit the battlefield as they went. The gods aimed their thrusts and her arrows true. She pressed further until she saw the lights of a city. They were close. To which city she didn't know, but the Atherians were pouring from its walls. They swarmed over the fields and through the orchards atop the gentle hills between the walls and the fields. Lightning flickered overhead though there were few clouds in the sky. Bolts drove downward, connecting with the ground, and occasionally a man. Fires erupted in the fields, flying through the dried remains of the harvest. The Atherians raced at them as though driven by their god himself. Their eyes were black and their faces contorted with anger. They fell, one by one.

She raced onward, over the fields and hills and between the trees. Her bow rested on her shoulder, the quiver empty and slapping against her back as she ran. She couldn't stop. Her legs under the control of the gods. Men ran along with her, Roy and James at the front, their feet flying over the charred remains of the fields. Olando was beside her, his eyes aglow. She grinned to see it. Her shepherd boy was among the chosen.

John arrived on her other side. They covered ground until the gate came into sight. The circular symbol on the gate nearly made her stumble despite the gods driving her body forward. She stagger-stepped until her feet untangled. She knew this place. Sloveski. Home. She was home.

The walls still stood, though many of the timbers were charred. Bodies hung from them much like they had in Omasii.

She did not stop to see if she recognized any of them.

This was home.

The Mother tingled within her, lending her speed and lightness of heart, averting her eyes as she passed by the body-strewn walls and through the blackened gate. Wayward Atherians darted toward them, some half-dressed and some without even a weapon. They all fell in the midst of Hasi's chosen.

"Ephius is desperate, mite, said the Mother. *Sending out the last of his rats to the slaughter in the hopes one might stick a sword in the blessed one."*

Sahmara threw her head back and laughed. *"Which blessed one?"*

"Exactly, mite. You've done well. Go on, take your rest now. We'll speak again soon."

Her entire body floated for a moment, so light she was sure her feet left the ground. She'd never felt such love and freedom from any worry. This was what the priests said the afterlife was like. Was she dead? She was sure that couldn't be so. The Mother would have told her if she was dead.

She became aware of others standing nearby, watching her. Olando and John stood there with wide eyes. Their own eyes. Their faces were their own as well. Blood splattered their skin and clothes and cuts colored their bodies. Olando's neck was bleeding again. Yet, their mouths hung open to see her. What did they see?

The lightness faded and the weight of the ground sucked at her feet. Her sword grew heavy in her weary arms. Her eyes begged to close.

She was home. Come morning, she would find her house, her parents, her friends. She'd learn where Zane was and get him if he wasn't already freed. Her nightmare was about to end.

She laid on the ground. It was the comfortable spot, like a featherbed. Her arm made the most wonderful pillow. And she closed her eyes, envisioning her father's face when he saw her tomorrow. Maybe she should borrow Sara's dress. That would make him happy. Her mother would smile and hug her and then complain that her hair was too short and her skin marred by the sun and scars. But they would laugh over freshly baked sweets and all would be well. They'd tell her of the attack on her home and how Zane had been filled with Hasi and killed so many until he slept like the dead and was stolen from their home. How they'd all be searching for her.

She sighed, contented, feeling their arms around her. Tomorrow all would be well.

CHAPTER NINETEEN

In the light of morning, wagons rolled into Sloveski, bringing Sara and the wounded. Many of the god-touched were sound asleep, lying wherever exhaustion had dropped them. Those that were awake set about collecting the sleepers and securing them inside a building Sahmara recognized as the home of a friend. Sadly, it seemed there was no one home to protest their invasion.

Heavy curtains became blankets. Beds held as many bodies as would fit and more overflowed onto the floors. Sara and Roy moved among them, bandages in their blood-stained hands.

Sahmara was overjoyed to see Ramsey lying amongst the sleepers, body still covered with wounds, but his color had improved. Whether Hasi had a hand in that or not, she didn't dare guess.

After the blessing of the Mother the night before, she'd slept soundly and comfortably, her entire body healed. Well-rested was no longer a state she was familiar with, yet the peace of the Mother still flowed through her, much lessened than the night before, but still there like a quiet summer morning. If she listened just outside herself she swore she could hear birds chirping and water rushing over smooth rocks. The soft scent of lavender filled the air around her, masking the smells of sweat and blood she'd grown used to.

Olando and John shared a bed with two others, so deep asleep that only their gentle snores set them apart from the dead. She tucked her blanket around Olando and kissed his cheek. Everyone was sleeping or busy, no one would miss her for a few hours. She took her sword and bow and slipped out of the house.

There were no coaches to carry her uphill to the street where she lived. No smiling vendors called out with promises of free samples to tempt her stomach. Their carts and wagons absent, leaving the streets wide and naked. The windows of the homes and shops were shuttered and the doors were closed. If anyone was still alive here, they were hiding out of sight. Antochecki had harbored survivors, she hoped Sloveski was the same.

Sahmara's step quickened as familiar surroundings enveloped her. Her father's shop, the front wall burned, but the others still standing, gave her hope. Walls could be rebuilt. His trade routes had gone nowhere. As long as his storehouses were still full... He might need some new wagons and a few horses to pull them. Those things could be hired out if she couldn't help supply them. And, of course, she would help. She knew things now. Useful things.

Her sword and bow would be of help to him. She grinned, imagining his face when she offered to travel with his caravan to guard it. And she could. She would. Her mother wouldn't hear of marrying her off now anyway. There was no help for that. Might as well do what she knew, what, with the help of the gods, she was good at. She could be useful to her family and gods at the same time.

The walls to her home were still standing, unmarked. She ran for them, trying to call for her mother and father but finding her voice lodged behind the lump in her throat. She dashed through the open gates only to skid to a stop. Nothing more than a jumble of burnt timbers and blackened stones waited for her.

All the things she'd once called precious had been destroyed. Her mother's carefully tended gardens trampled to bare dirt in some places, grown wild in others. The statuary shattered and strewn across the grounds. The stables were razed to the ground, her beautiful horse gone. Not a single servant or guard or hint of her parents waited for her here. Just a vast cold emptiness that seeped into her flesh, erasing all memory of the glory of the Mother she'd enjoyed the night before.

"Why did you bring me here if there was nothing left?" she asked the wind.

Her feet refused to leave, instead dragging her through the ruins of her former life for the better part of the morning. Tears wouldn't come. She wanted Olando's arms around her right then. Sara's too. She wished she were sleeping on the ground with their warm bodies pressed against her, nourishing the dream of returning home that she'd held onto for so long.

Now the dream was over. She couldn't unsee this destruction no matter how hard she tried. She'd known she couldn't go back to what she had been, but to go back to something was far better than what she was left with now. Nothing.

The lives she'd sent to the gods, even in their vast number, weren't enough to fill the void that opened within her. Yet, she wasn't ravenous like the gods, endlessly demanding more. It was as if she'd forgotten hunger altogether. All the glorious feasts of her life had turned into a single bowl of bitter gruel. She pushed it away and left the walls that sheltered the ruins of her dreams.

As she stared down the street the way she'd come, the door to a small cottage opened. She walked toward it, wondering what life still lived behind it. A young man crept out, glancing up and down the street with each breath. His clothes were torn and patched and his long sandy hair unkempt. He fell into step beside her. "Is it true?"

"The Atherians are gone, if that's what you're asking."

"Glory to the gods."

She stared straight ahead. "Indeed."

"Are you from here?"

"You knew these people?" she asked, pointing at the gates from which she'd come.

"Oh yes. My father worked for him. A good man, he was."

"Was? He's gone then?"

"Sadly, yes, along with any of the household that couldn't sneak away when the soldiers came."

Faint hope rose up in her chest, sending her heart into a fluttering race. "Did they? Did some of them escape? Did you talk to them? Any of them?"

The man sighed. "I only know of one man who worked in the gardens. He ran off when he saw the soldier's coming. I recognized him from gazing over the walls when I was young." He glanced at the walls behind them. "He pounded on our doors, shouting a warning as he fled. Because of him, my sister and I, who hid under the floorboards, survived. I can't say whether that man still lives or not. I haven't seen him again."

"No others then?"

"We put the bodies to rest, the ones they left us, anyway. I can say for sure that the lord and lady of the home were among them.

Her stomach seized and bile rose in her throat. She lost the power to move, her feet firmly rooted on the street. Yet there were no tears in her eyes. It was as if all moisture had left her body, leaving her a brittle shell. She fought to regain her voice.

"What about a Ma'hasi? Have you heard any word of that man who once protected a girl in that house?"

"My father told me stories of that pretty girl." The man smiled, revealing dimples in his thin cheeks. "I often saw her over the wall, smiling and laughing, her fine dress spread over the bench under the tree where she often sat in the afternoon. I don't think she ever saw me, her attention was on her visitors or the flowers in the garden around her. The man in white was always with her."

He shook his head, dropping his gaze to the cobbles. "We didn't find either of their bodies. The Atherians took slaves south, the strong, young men, he might have been one of them. Her, I can't say, maybe taken in the other direction."

They stood together for a few moments of silence before he pointed toward the remains of the castle. Black soot marred the grey stone of the towers that rose above the battered remains of the grand houses that had once sat in its shadow. "It was worse up the hill. They had no mercy for the rich. Took everything, carted it off in their own coaches with all the fine horses bearing the load."

"Your father?"

The man shook his head.

"Sorry to hear that."

It was all gone. Everything. Everyone. Her feet began to move again, one in front of the other, but her mind and body were still back behind the walls, weeping her soul into the ashes.

"We've all lost someone," he said quietly. "You as well, I imagine?"

She nodded, walking onward, staring ahead without seeing.

He fell back. She heard him knocking on doors, sharing the news of the change of fortune for those who still survived.

The Atherians had washed through Sloveski like a tidal wave. Washing the city clean of royalty, riches, and livestock. Their god had grown fat on the blood of her people and his people rich with spoils. Revochek would never recover those losses.

She eventually made her way back to the house full of wounded and sleeping men. It seemed as though nothing here had changed while she was gone, nothing but the gaping void that now resided inside her.

John stood guarding the doorway. His brows drew together as he looked her over. "Spark, are ya well?"

"Well enough," she muttered, walking past him and into the house.

Roy gave her a questioning glance as she passed through the room where she'd shared dance lessons with her friend. Sleeping wounded men lined the dirty tiled floor that had been so clean as to not spoil a white, satin slipper. Nails dotted the bare walls where fine paintings and tapestries had hung.

Sara spotted her and rushed to her side. "Where have you been? No one could find you."

She forced a smile and patted Sara's arm. "Sorry to worry

you. I went for a walk."

"But there could have been Atherians hiding out there. It's not yet safe to go out alone." Sara wiped her bloody hands on an already red-infused rag hanging from her belt.

"I had my sword and my bow." As much as she'd wanted Sara with her when she'd first seen her home, now she desired only to be alone, and to sleep. The world had become a gaping chasm that threatened to eat her whole, and she no longer had the strength to face it with open eyes.

"And the gods. I'm sorry, it was silly of me to worry." Sara gave her a quick peck on the cheek and went back to work.

The gods. They'd been grateful. She'd felt it last night, but even grateful gods couldn't bring back the dead or rebuild a city. She went to the room where Olando lay, removed her sword, bow and quiver and curled up next to him in the spot John had vacated. If she fell into the chasm, he would catch her. He would be there, protecting her as he always did. Alone, but safe, she closed her eyes and focused on his steady breathing until the horrible reality she'd discovered that morning gave way to the empty blackness of sleep.

In her dream, the young priestess hugged her tightly with her one arm and then reached up to her own neck. Despite the fact the girl was barely waist high, Sahmara felt the girl place the knotted necklace of the Mother around her throat. The rough cord scraped against her flesh. The smooth wooden beads offered respite from the scratchy fibers. The girl bowed low before her. She watched, stunned as the girl then disintegrated into black feathers that fluttered into the sky upon a gentle breeze. When she finally tore her gaze away from the cloudless and sunless sky, Yanis stood before her.

He sat her upon a rock that hadn't been there a moment ago and worked his long fingers through her hair. Grains of sand fell from his sleeves onto her shoulders as he worked.

But she didn't have hair, not long enough for his fingers to work with for sure. She knew this. Yanis began to waver, going in and out of focus. His fingers on her one moment and gone the next. She sank into the rock like it was a giant open bag of grain. She started to cry out.

Yanis gripped her arms hard and pulled her back up to sit upon the rock. It again was solid beneath her. He put his hands firmly on her shoulders and kissed her forehead with sandy lips. Bewildered, she sat still while he again wove his fingers through her hair, tugging gently. His ministrations filling her with pleasant memories of having her hair brushed with long unhurried strokes. She found herself sighing with pleasure.

When he finished, he stood back, looking her over. Yanis nodded, a smile creeping over his face and lighting his eyes in a way she'd never seen him in life. Just as she'd decided he was quite handsome, his body fell to the ground as grains of sand. The breeze returned to carry the grains upward until not a single one remained at her feet or on her shoulders.

Sahmara couldn't breathe. She gasped as the dream spit her out and deposited her back into the bed beside Olando. His eyes, open and dark, were his own.

The dream left her disoriented as she sat up, rubbing her hands over her face. "What are you staring at?"

"You have hair."

"What?" She rubbed her hands farther upward until they met, not with the scant fingertip length she'd finally gained, but with long strands that fell well down her back. Long, clean strands that smelled of rosewater. Then her fingers struck beads. Red wooden beads. The beads of Hasi, lodged in braids beside her face.

Her fingers slipped around her neck. She gulped. The beaded cord lay against her skin.

"Olando?" she managed to squeak.

He just stared.

She sprang to her feet. She needed space, needed air. She slapped her helm on her head, grabbed her sword, bow and quiver and ran down the hall through the room full of men on the floor and out into the street. John stood there, staring at her.

"What? What is it?" she demanded.

"You have hair." he stammered. "Lots of it. And those."

He pointed to the beads in her hair and around her neck.

"Yes, I manage to give the gods enough blood to free the city and they see fit to reward me with a head of hair. That's just what I wanted."

She screamed at the air around her. "You hear me? A city full of hungry people, winter coming, my family murdered, my house burned to the ground, everything gone, and you give me hair?"

Sahmara propelled a host of obscene gestures at the sky. "Well, that's just great. At least my ears will be warm while I starve to death this winter. So kind of you, really." She stormed away from John who stood with his mouth hanging open alongside the other faces that had appeared in the doorway to gawk at her. She didn't know where she was going, only that she had to go somewhere far away from the stares.

A brisk walk brought her to the fountain where she'd spent many an afternoon chattering with friends like a flock of songbirds on a sunny day. The clear water gurgled down the statue of the Mother bathing an infant as if nothing had changed.

Her mother had also loved to enjoy her afternoon sweets here with her own friends, enjoying the open air she swore kept her healthy. Sahmara had watched boys here, handsome and well-dressed, following older brothers or fathers on their way to the castle or the market to conduct business. Her heart had been given and sundered in mere moments more times than she could remember in this courtyard.

But there was no one to gossip with, or share the warm sunlight, or a thirst-quenching cup. The children that had frolicked through the mists, singing silly songs were orphans or dead. She glared at the statue with the same amount of venom she imagined Yanis felt while his men ate his beloved horse.

He'd let himself be turned from Hasi and the god had let him die, yet he was still his servant into death. The winds had taken him. He'd been forgiven in the end. Would they let her die too? Did she want to? Eventually, perhaps, but she had Sara and Olando and maybe even Zane out there somewhere.

Her family might be gone, but she wasn't alone. The gods couldn't bury the dead or heal the city, but her people could. Eventually. From the beads adorning her body, she gathered the gods weren't finished with her just yet.

Her finger tingled in answer to her thoughts. Sahmara wasn't sure if she should be angry or grateful that the gods had seemed to overlook her outburst. She still was uncertain when her first vision came back to her, tickling her memory until it took color and flesh, and she smelled the sour sweat of the slaves. Slaves that had been driven south.

All of Revochek wasn't yet free.

CHAPTER TWENTY

Sahmara returned to the house with the same speed with which she left it. A pull settled within her belly, setting her nerves on edge. She was going the wrong way. Zane was still in chains, and she could feel him out there, deep in her gut.

John stepped back, giving her plenty of room to enter without saying a word.

She sought Roy out. He stood over a bed full of wounded men, tending to them. "You'll be sending word to Crag and Roger?"

He turned, and for a moment she thought he was going to rebuke her for speaking to him in front of the others, but his eyes went wide and he merely nodded.

"Good. I have some business to attend to. Keep watch over Sara and Olando for me. Make sure they remain here."

He nodded uncertainly. "How long will you be gone?"

"I don't know."

"And you're going alone?"

"Yes."

"What if we need you?"

"You have John. The others should be waking soon, if they aren't already."

He waved his hand at her head. "What *is* all this?"

"Talk to your god." She spun around and left. She would have liked to have grabbed her jug but that was in the room where she'd left Olando, and she really didn't want to answer any questions from him right now. Jealousy would only be the half of the grief he'd give her. Sara would be a welcome travel companion, but she was needed here as were John and the others. She'd be better able to follow her vision without the distraction of company anyway. She headed south, letting the Mother guide her feet.

Afternoon slipped into night before she realized that in addition to her jug, she didn't have her blanket or her bag or anything to eat. She also had the slithery sensation of the Mother laughing at her. She pulled her cloak around her and spent the night inside a deserted cottage.

She woke to a grumbling stomach and a pull in her gut, urging her to be on the road. A few shriveled berries from a bush along the way served to break her fast.

Zane needed her. That was the pull she'd felt by the fountain the day before. He was among the slaves. She was certain of it.

She all but ran down the trail that veered off the road. It turned from hard dirt to soft sand that pulled at her boots. Pine needles poked her face as she tried to duck past the heavy branches. A deer burst through the underbrush onto the trail, near scaring her half to death. It stopped to stare at her before dashing off. Wherever this pull was taking her, it wasn't a place men often traveled.

What would Zane say of Olando and Sara? What did she want him to say? The thought of sharing Sara with him stopped her cold in her tracks. Zane was special. Her first. The memory of being in his arms had allowed her to accept Olando. But the smell of his leathers wasn't near as strong in her recollections as it had once been.

Would she give up Olando and Sara for him? She considered turning around, avoiding that question altogether by never finding him. That would be the easiest answer.

But she'd seen him in chains. No amount of sweet kisses from Sara or adoring words from Olando could erase that image. She continued down the trail.

The beads in her hair slapped her shoulder with each stride, keeping rhythm as she walked. The loose strands blew into her face and tangled in the branches and stuck to her forehead and lips and eyelashes. She'd forgotten what an annoyance long hair could be. She paused to remove her helm and quickly pull the unbound portion of the mass into a quick braid and tucked the end up into her helm as she settled it back onto her head.

By mid-afternoon, her stomach demanded more food than the berries. Loathe to set aside her onward progress, Sahmara drew an arrow and walked onward, ready for whatever might become a meal upon the trail.

A rabbit fell prey to her arrow before the sun sunk too much lower, which meant stopping for a fire and time to roast it. She grabbed the skewered animal and kept walking until the sun fell behind the trees, drawing long shadows over the landscape.

She traveled a short way off the trail while gathering wood and tinder and set about lighting the fire as she'd watched others do night after night. It took longer than others had, but she managed. After all she'd seen and done on the battlefield, the distasteful task of skinning the rabbit seemed trivial. She set it to roasting. The absence of men talking around the fires, of Olando and Sara at her side, hit her deeply. Were they worried about her? She regretted not saying anything to them, but it was too late now. Darkness fell quickly, leaving her with only the occasional popping of the firewood for company.

The barest hint of dawn triggered her eyelids to spring open. A light frost had decorated the underbrush with a fine white glimmer. As if released from a cage, she shook out her cloak, stomped out the few glowing embers, grabbed her things and then darted back onto the trail. The pull was intense now. She had to be close.

Sunlight warmed her face and shoulders, driving out the chill of the morning. The vision of men in chains came upon her again. Was she supposed to free them all? Could she? Sneaking one man out was one thing, but all of them? How much did the gods ask of her?

As she walked, she noticed the sounds that had kept her thoughts company had faded away. She wished she had Olando's silent step. Each of hers seemed to echo no matter how softly she walked.

"That's far enough," said a male voice in Atherian. He came forward on the tree-lined path, sitting high upon a black horse and covered in a heavy cloak. A thick orange beard covered half his face and all of his neck. "What are ya doing sneaking about?"

It had been awhile since she'd used her sparse Atherian vocabulary. She made a show of giving his horse a once over while piecing the right words together in her mind. "Having a look around."

He took in her sword and bow. "You one of Brown's boys?"

"Yes."

"There been another escape?"

She shrugged. "Checking the borders."

"Seen the supply wagon from Sloveski? It was due yesterday. The men are grumbling."

She shook her head.

"Circling back to the main road?" He nodded west.

"Soon."

"If you see that wagon, tell them to get a move on."

"I will."

He turned the horse around and made his way back up the trail.

Once he was far enough ahead that she figured he wouldn't hear her, she drew her bow and set an arrow to it. A quick prayer signaled its release. The arrow struck him square in the back. He fell hard. The horse danced aside.

Sahmara finished him off with her sword before he could make any noise. After a quick glance around to make sure she was alone, as well as to settle her nerves, she retrieved her arrow and rolled him further off the trail. When she returned, the horse stood there looking at her, its reins dangling in the sand.

"You'll do nicely." She hopped up on its back and patted its long neck. It had been so long since she'd ridden a horse that it took a short while to get used to the feel of it again.

The trail headed downward, emerging from the brush into red soil, rocks, and scrubby low growing plants. The horse picked out the narrow path that threaded between them with little effort.

A village lay before her. People moved about, their heads down, scurrying as if they couldn't complete their tasks fast enough. Their clothes were worn, but otherwise, these people appeared in far better shape that those she'd left in Sloveski. Atherian guards moved among them, well fed by the looks of them, and giving every moving thing a critical glare. They wore swords at their sides.

The well-worn road passed through the village and further downward. She sat tall upon the horse and ignored the men walking beside her as she passed. They ignored her in turn.

The horse had a mind to turn into the stable. She gave it a swift kick in the side. "There'll be time for that later."

The road led her toward the clanging of metal on rock. Shirtless men trudged along in chained lines of six, their breaths puffing white in the morning air. They passed rocks from one to the next until the last man placed it in a cart. The carts were drawn off by teams of giant muscled horses who strained to pull the cart up the hill to the site of what appeared to be a large structure in the making. Up on the flatland, other men in chains placed the stones, directed by Atherians with whips and clubs. Those men were directed by three men in blue robes with shaven heads and eyes lined with heavy black smears as thick as fingertips: Atherian priests.

The Mother cackled in her head. "*Won't be needing that, will they, Mite?*"

Hasi didn't seem to find the humor. His voice thundered, making her head throb with each word. "*He dares build a temple in our lands? Crush every stone into sand. Do it. Do it now!*"

"*And how would I do that? I am only one woman.*"

"*Grow more hands,*" Hasi ordered.

Sahmara counted the men with whips and clubs spread amongst the slaves. Too many men, not enough arrows.

Her quiver suddenly became heavier.

"Thank you, but I can't shoot them all before one of them gets to me. There are too many."

As if he overheard their silent conversation, a thickset middle-aged man left his charges to approach her. He peered at her from under bushy eyebrows. "What is it?"

"Brown doesn't want more to escape."

He scowled. "It was only two, and that was weeks ago. They were killed. Will we never hear the end of this?"

She shrugged.

"So what are you doing?"

"Watching."

"That's our job."

She leaned low and glared. "Watching you do your job."

His scowl deepened. He spun around and resumed his post.

She rode through the quarry, looking for Zane and any opportunity to strike that wouldn't lead to her immediate death. The pull she'd felt all the way here had vanished, but she knew he was here. The gods wouldn't have led her here for no reason. Unless that reason was to destroy the temple, but Hasi hadn't seemed to know about that. The absence of anger on the Mother's part, though... She might have known. They wouldn't bring her here without giving her Zane though, would they? Surely not after the devastation that had overwhelmed her in Sloveski.

Her scalp itched. Maybe they would. The gods didn't seem to grasp how rewards worked.

Lost in her musings, she nearly rode right into a line of chained men who were attempting to dodge the whip of their guard. The horse avoided them without any help from her.

Matted locks of long blond hair caught her eye as the whip caught his back. Zane fell to his knees. Grime and gauntness marred the handsome face she so fondly remembered. The men on either side of him helped him to his feet. His bright blue eyes were sunken and empty as he glanced at the horse under her and then back at his feet, cringing as if he expected a whipping from her as well. Blood dripped down his back and into the dark stained waistband of what may have been the tattered remains of his white leathers. The men scurried back to their work, dragging Zane with them.

She wanted to cry, to hold him, to ask the gods to return him to his glory, but first, she had to free him. She dismounted and walked over to the guard, standing next to him silently.

He glanced at her out of the corner of his eye once, twice and a third time. "The temple is coming along well enough?" he asked.

"Slowly."

He rested his hand on his whip. "Too slowly?"

Sahmara held out her hand and nodded.

"I can do my job," he said.

"It would seem not."

He reluctantly handed her the whip.

"Get in line with the others."

His mouth dropped open. "But...I..."

"You had your chance. Brown wants an example for the others."

"No. Please." He held up his hands.

"Begging for the whip?" She unfurled it and out of habit, said a prayer.

Hasi answered. His rage flooded through her with a force that nearly knocked her to the ground. She grabbed for the horse to keep herself upright. Once the initial wave passed, her focus narrowed to only the guard and the whip in her hand. She'd never used one before, but Hasi seemed to have plenty of experience. The leather snapped in the air and then again across his chest, then his face. Her arm flung back, she marveled in the power coursing through her.

Without anyone directly attacking her for once, she took a moment to feel the god within her, his giant muscled form, squeezed into her thin human flesh. Lightening-like energy flooded through every vein in her body. Every sound was sharper, colors brighter, the sweat on the terrified guard's forehead glistened like diamonds. The chained men were both beautiful and pathetic. Should she strike them down for deserting her or free them to worship once more? They'd never worship here. No one would.

This temple would be flattened by the end of the day, not a sign of the offensive structure would be left in existence. Her blood burned and the sky rumbled. Clouds flowed over the sun like waves over sand. An icy wind gusted, pasting her cloak against her body. The wind changed direction, spinning, swirling. The sky grew darker. Rain plummeted to the ground. Hail joined it with the force of stones fired from a slingshot. Men yelled all around her, running to and fro, seeking shelter in the open pit of stone.

"Kill them. Kill them all."

Sahmara gasped as she drew her sword and plunged it into the chest of the bloody guard on his knees before her. She lunged for the nearest man in chains. A pain the likes of which she'd never felt grabbed hold of her heart and squeezed. Hasi faltered within her.

"Free will, brother. Remember the rules."

"Free will nearly got us both killed, dear sister."

"But the mite did her duty, just like I said she..."

Something long, metal, and right in front of her caught the reflection of lightning.

She forced a single word to her lips. "Sword!"

The bickering of the gods within her faded as did their paralyzing grip on her body. Able to move again, Sahmara used Hasi's strength to block the blade with her own. She drove her attacker back. A cart full of stone halted his retreat. She finished him off quickly. Her entire hand and arm tingled from the feeding rabid gods.

More men came out of the blowing rain, their clothes whipping against their bodies, swords, spears, and whips in their hands. Even with the help of the gods, there were too many.

Would Olando and Sara forgive her for charging off alone to her death? Olando would take care of Sara. He had to.

With a heavy heart, she held her sword in front of her, ready.

A stone flew from her right, striking one of the armed men

on the side of his head. He staggered and wavered there. Another stone came flying from behind her. Then one from the other side. Within seconds, more stones than hail flew through the air. The guards fell, toppling onto one another, some running blindly into the gusting torrents and vanishing from view. A roar rose up around her and then the rhythmic clanking of chains. Clumps of men rushed past her to plunder the soaked bodies. They stood up with weapons in their hands and vicious grins on their rain-washed faces.

One of them must have found a key on one of the dead. He freed himself, and then the others in his line. His mates fled, leaving him to stand with the key in his hand, peering into the darkness. Sahmara approached him with her hand outstretched.

"Give it to me. I'll free the others." He gaped at her and handed it over without hesitation.

She knew he saw the god-touch upon her and figured she best well use it. "Follow the road upward." She pointed behind her. "Take as many others with you as you can. There is a village down the road. There will be Atherians to slay, but they have food and shelter that will be yours."

He ducked his head quickly and then dashed off. She heard him yelling for others to follow him.

Here and there rocks flew and men cried out. She fought her way through the wind toward the sounds and when she found living men in chains, she freed them. Rain worked its way under her cloak and into her clothing and onto every inch of her skin. She was pretty sure the only dry place on her body was the very top of her head under her helm. The dirt and stone underfoot turned slick with pooling water. She stumbled, her foot catching in the hidden ruts from the heavy carts. Her ankle throbbed as she marched onward, making sure the quarry was empty of living men before heading back to the road that led upward.

Once she crested the pit, the wind caught her sodden cloak and nearly knocked her backward. Around her, men cowered on their knees amidst puddles of water and hail, arms over their heads, crying out for mercy. Her men.

Thunder rolled through the clouds and lightening stitched the earth and sky together like a blind seamstress. A ground-rending crash made the stone shudder underfoot. She spun around to see a great funnel of wind flowing from the sky to where the beginnings of the temple stood. Like Hasi's giant finger, the wind toppled the walls as if they were nothing more than a pile of pebbles.

She yelled into the wind. "Enough."

The power within her surged until she feared it would rip her asunder, and then it was gone. The hail stopped and the wind guttered out. The rain lessened to a gentle drizzle and the blackness in the sky faded to a murky grey. The lightning ceased and the thunder grew distant.

"On your feet," she yelled at the men. "Food and shelter lie ahead." She hoped those who had gone before them had beaten the storm and were well on their way toward overpowering the village.

CHAPTER TWENTY-ONE

The god-touch had leeched all the energy from her body. She wanted nothing more than to join the men lying in the mud, but the promise of a bed and dry clothing kept her on her feet and one of them moving ahead of the other.

Some of the men around her had gained weapons, others still held palm-sized stones in their hands. Bloody, bedraggled, shivering and soaked, they plodded down the road until the village came into view. The sight of real shelter seemed to breathe life into the husks of men around her. Their steps became lopes as the mob picked up speed. Bodies lay outside of buildings and in the streets. Men from the quarry fought in groups, some still chained and others not, against the Atherians who had taken over their village.

Seeing their chattering teeth and beaten bodies, she brought her sword to her hand. She wasn't sure what good she would be without the help of the gods, but if men in this condition could fight, she could too. Sahmara swung at the first man to lunge at her. Her arms and legs surged into action, twisting her away, blocking his sword and then returning his attack. The blinding energy of Hasi was gone, she was certain of that, but his actions must have left an imprint on her muscles. Even if her mind didn't consciously know what to do, her body did. Maybe Hasi just didn't want his vessel broken while he was out of it. Selfish as the gods had shown themselves to be, the thought did not surprise her.

Men fought beside her as they did in the quarry, only now most of them had steel rather than stone. They'd tasted freedom and were desperate for more. They washed through the village, cleansing it of Atherians and tossing their bodies into the streets. The clanging of swords faded and men began to mill about, weapons hanging from limp arms.

"Get inside, eat, rest," she told them. They wandered off as if in a daze now that the fight was over.

The big man she'd taken the horse from had mentioned waiting for a supply wagon. As much as she wanted to find a bed, pallet, or even bare spot of floor to sleep on, the threat of fresh men with horses able to ride off and bring reinforcements kept her on her feet. Barely.

She kept herself moving with the search for Zane. She hadn't seen him since he'd been whipped. Battered men lay in the street alongside dryer and better dressed Atherians. He couldn't be among them. The gods wouldn't be so cruel.

She took off her helm and shook out her sodden hair as she walked. Her fingers caught on Hasi's beads as she tried to untangle the remnants of her hasty braid. Seeing hair beside her face seemed so unfamiliar, wrong. She considered sawing it off to a more manageable length with her sword.

"Don't even think about it. I'll not have my priestess looking like a man. It's bad enough I have to share you with my brother. I found you first."

Sahmara froze. *"Priestess?"*

"You wear my beads, do you not?"

"Not by choice."

"Stupid, mite. We work well together. Your people benefit as much as my brother and I do."

"I didn't agree to this. What about free will?"

"Would you prefer I strike your beloved down right now? He would not be alive if not for the favors of my brother and I. How about all those men you left in Sloveski? The men around you right now? That charming little healer and the sheepherder?"

Sahmara glared at the air around her. *"So you buy my cooperation with threats."*

"No, silly mite. I buy it with your love, even if that love does not include me." The Mother wrapped her in arms she could only

feel inside her skin, warm and made of light. The weight of her soaked cloak fell away as did the clamminess of her wet clothing. Her weariness melted into the ground far below her feet as if she were floating above it. Feather soft lips kissed her between the eyes.

She became aware of men standing along the road, others coming from doorways and around buildings, all of them staring at her.

"Look at them. See them as I do."

Fire lit around each man, no, not fire, a glow, as if they stood in front of the sun. Some shone brighter than others, their glows ranging from deep gold to pale sand. A thin trace of red danced at the edges of some of them.

Hasi's voice joined the Mother's. *"Protect them and see that their faith is strong so that we can do the same."*

Her voice trembled, barely a whisper even in her own head. *"But I was never meant to be a priestess."*

"You were never meant to leave Sloveski, dear mite, but things are not always how they were meant to be. They are what they are. Now go, bring peace to them. We will be here if you need us."

The blinding brilliance of the Mother and Hasi faded. The glows of the men around her did not.

She surveyed them all. She pointed to those lit by the deepest gold. Those without visible injury or appearing ready to collapse on the spot were very few. "You, get these bodies out of the streets. Take care of our own. Burn the others." She stared them down until they darted into the streets and began their task. "The rest of you should be resting. Atherians still lurk about. While they aren't the force they were, it will take time to root them all out."

One of the men in the street hefted the body of one of the fallen onto his broad shoulders and stood to face her. "Not that we're not grateful, but who are you?"

She opened her mouth, not sure what to say. Who was she? No great captain, no one with an army, or experience, or anything other than the clothes on her back, the weapons at her side and a few belongings in a bag in a house back in

Sloveski. Spark? A priestess?

A sudden weightlessness filled her and words flowed from her mouth that were not her own. "I am the voice of the Mother and the arm of Hasi. My name is Sahmara."

He bobbed his head. "Thank you, Sahmara." The red around his glow grew wider and more vibrant.

His words echoed down the street, flowing from a hundred mouths and surrounding her with a warmth that rivaled the Mother's. Tears came to her eyes.

One voice stood out above the rest. Zane came forward, peering at her, step by step until he was standing before her. "Sahmara?"

She nodded, all words were gone again and her throat so tight it strangled any that might have considered forming.

His gaze swept up and down her body as if she were a three-headed calf. "Sahmara?"

She was used to the wide-eyed awe of men seeing her with the god-touch, but she didn't have that right now and this, the look on his face, was something else. The glow about him reminded her of freshly tilled soil. Even beaten and weary, he was better off than most of the others who milled about, watching them with great curiosity. The red glow had multiplied throughout the glows around her, but his remained devoid of a single speck.

She put the helm back on her head to free her hands. "Are you well? Not hurt I mean. Of course, you're hurt. I saw you whipped."

He cocked his head and took half a step back.

She put her hand to his cheek, wondering at the wiriness of his beard. He'd not had that before. But of course, he couldn't shave while a prisoner. What would it feel like to kiss him with that beard? Did she want to kiss him?

It had been so long, she'd endured so much, but it had always been the thought of seeing her family and of being back in his arms that had spurred her onward, the vision of him in chains had haunted her. She'd wanted to see him free. And now here he was, right before her.

He took another step back. "You're alive."

She stood there, hand outstretched, Zane just out of reach. "Yes? Would you rather I were not?"

"No. I mean...it's just..."

"Unexpected."

"Well, yes."

She put her hand down. It brushed against the hilt of her sword. A warm tingle ran through her fingers and up her arm straight into her heart. Hasi remained silent, but she felt him there, listening and watching.

Sahmara took a deep breath, remembering Olando's words. There was no one better to question Hasi's sworn servant, to discover the truth. She steeled herself for it, whatever the truth might be.

"How long were you in that camp?" she asked.

"Too long. Since a few days after they took you."

"You mean after you *let* them take me."

His mouth dropped open. "There were a lot of them. What did you expect me to do in a room full of armed Atherians?"

"Call upon Hasi. You were one of his. He would have helped you."

Zane snorted. "It doesn't work like that. The odds were against me."

"Did you even use your sword?"

"Of course, I did. I wasn't going to let them take me without a fight."

"Take *you*?" She laughed. It was Hasi's laugh, hard and edged with the blades of a thousand men. She drew her own and pointed it at the chest she'd caressed with adoring fingers. "On your knees."

"Sahmara."

She jabbed at him, just enough to draw blood. "Now."

He dropped to his knees to the dirt, holding up his hands. "I didn't mean-"

"A single word when you spoke your oath to me," said Hasi through her.

Zane violently shook his head. His voice shook. "No. I

mean, yes, I did. I did."

There was the look she'd grown used to, though his was the terror that she'd seen in the eyes of the Atherians before she struck them down. She didn't want to strike Zane down. Yes, he'd failed, dismally, but she didn't want him dead.

But Hasi kept her arm straight and strong, unwavering. The tip of her sword hovered over his heart.

"What say you?" asked Hasi.

"You're actually asking me?"

"He is as much mine as yours."

Maybe this priestess arrangement wasn't so bad after all. She looked to those who remained outside. They'd gathered around, forming a loose circle. Red glows bloomed throughout them

"I was taken to Atheria, a slave. You know what they do to slaves?"

He nodded, glancing at her before dropping his gaze back to her blade.

"I eventually escaped. Yes, me, pampered, stupid Sahmara who had never held a weapon, escaped all on her own. I had a vision of you, here." She pointed down the road toward the quarry. "You were alive. I came here to save you. You, the man I loved."

He did look at her then. The barest hint of red flickered at the edges of his glow. "You did save me. All of us."

"I did, yes, but with help." She tugged at the beads in her hair and patted those around her neck. The inward embrace of the Mother and Hasi gave her comfort and strength. "I was young and stupid to have loved you."

She shook her head. "You took nothing beyond polishing your sword seriously, did you? Your family handed you off to the priests. You didn't want to be a Ma'hasi."

"Does anyone?"

"Yes, and you'll make sure of it." Sahmara put her sword away.

Zane scrambled to his feet. "What do you mean?"

"You disappoint me. I am your charge, but you let me be

taken without spilling a single drop of enemy blood. You've angered Hasi with every action since taking the oath to protect me. As such, we've arrived at your sentence."

"We?" He glanced around, regarding her with crinkled brows. "You're going to sentence me?" he laughed nervously, looking to the circle for help.

Olando's words flowed through her mind along with the vehemence with which he'd said them. The god within her smiled. *Yes.*

"Hasi demands your hands, your feet, your tongue and your manhood for your crimes."

"Does he now?"

She felt Hasi's fury a split second before he flooded into her body. She was in front of Zane in one giant stride with her sword at his neck. "He does."

Zane gulped, drawing his own blood as he did so.

She eased back a fraction. "I, on the other hand, think you'd be of more use with your body intact."

"How?" he whispered.

"Your hands will carry a sword. Your feet will carry you through Revochek. Your tongue will speak the will of Hasi and your manhood will remain in your pants for the rest of your days so that you can focus on your task."

"Which is?"

"You will become a true Ma'hasi and train others."

He flashed a smile that would have melted her insides a year ago. "But a true Ma'hasi is sworn to protect someone."

"You've already sworn to protect me."

"But how can I do that if I'm traveling the countryside?"

"By recruiting more men to the service of Hasi, you are protecting me. You are also protecting yourself *from* me because I'm half inclined to let Hasi have his way."

Zane's smile vanished.

"You'll want to begin by praying." She shoved him toward the nearest building.

Three men nodded to her and followed him inside.

"Well done," said Hasi, sliding away from her back into the

air.

Desperate for sleep and a few moments alone, Sahmara turned away. A pair of men held the door open to a building across the street. She went inside and discovered they had set aside a room for her. Clay pots lined shelves on the wall and herbs hung from the ceiling. There was plenty of space between the barrels and casks in the storeroom for her to lie down. She took off her helm and her sword, keeping them next to her. Someone closed the door and moments later she closed her eyes.

Frantic pounding on the door woke her. "Someone's coming," said a voice through the wood.

Sahmara leaped to her feet, surprised to find that though she was still exhausted, she wasn't aching or hurt or even the slightest bit damp. She said a quick prayer of thanks to the Mother, donned her helm and strapped on her sword. Once on the other side of the door, Sahmara found herself surrounded by anxious men.

"Who are they?" she asked.

"They've got wagons, armor and lots of armed men."

"How far away?"

"Close. We posted a few men on the rooftops, not farther out."

She nodded. It wasn't ideal but at least they weren't overrun already. "Gather your weapons and get into the street."

They scrambled to do what she ordered. A few men headed out before the rest. She followed them, seeing that they dashed from building to building, spreading the word. Men spilled, stumbled and staggered into the street just as the first of the line of armed men came into view. The pounding of marching feet and creaking of wagons followed a second later as the men around her went silent.

"There are so many," said the man beside her.

"The gods will help us," she said, baring her sword.

Then she saw the red flames dancing around man after advancing man. And in the midst of those flames, familiar faces. Olando burst from the line and ran down the street like a comet racing across the sky.

"They're friends," she heard herself say before she ran to meet him, dropping her sword along the way in case any of her men hadn't heard her.

Olando's arms wrapped around her, pinning her to his chest. His heartbeat thundered in her ear. "Ya left me."

"I left word with Roy."

"Exactly, ya left."

Was he angry or mad? She wrenched herself away until she was able to see his face. It didn't help. "I had to do this. I was going to come back."

He surveyed the crowd behind her. "Did you find him?"

"Zane?"

"Who else would ya leave me for?" The betrayal in his dark eyes cracked through his stony face.

She grabbed his hand and squeezed it. "Yes, and I'm not leaving you."

"He's not joining us. Sara was one thing, but this..."

Sahmara laughed. "He's not joining us. In fact, he won't be joining anyone ever again."

A wavering smile softened his lips. "Spark, ya kinda scare me. Should I feel bad for the man?"

"No. He's intact, just devoted to Hasi, now."

"Hopefully more so than before?"

"Oh yes. Hasi himself will make sure of it." She kissed his cheek. "What's all that for?" She nodded to the men and wagons behind him.

"Had a feeling you'd cause trouble."

"So you brought an army?"

He shrugged and pointed to the men milling behind her. "You raised one?"

"Yours is better dressed." She grinned, glad to have him by her side again.

"I don't know, I can see you and the Mother enjoying going off to war surrounded by half-naked men."

Sahmara snickered. "I prefer them fully clothed and with armor. You on the other hand..."

Olando's eyebrows rose and he grinned. "My dear lady, what is this from ya?"

A second red flamed figure barreled through the men pouring into the village. Sara reached them, breathless.

"You're well?" she asked between pants.

Sahmara nodded pulling Sara into a one armed embrace.

Sara glared at Olando. "You were supposed to wait for me."

"Ya took too long to get out of the wagon and ya run too slow."

She lightly smacked his chest. "My legs aren't as long. You could have carried me."

Olando sighed and looked to the sky. "Why two of them?"

Sahmara led them toward the wagons that Olando brought. "Is Roy here too?"

"He's holding Sloveski with a small force. They drew sticks. They all wanted to come after ya."

"That's silly."

"Ya brought their god back to them and through them, their lands and homes. That's not silly," said Sara.

Around them, men from Sloveski mixed with the men from the quarry. A bare-chested man came over with her sword in his arms, his gaze on the ground. "Ya dropped this."

"Thank you." She took it from him and watched as the red edges of his glow surged as he backed away.

"This is going to take some getting used to."

"For all of us," said Olando, eyeing the men watching her. "So what do the gods ask of ya now?"

Sara tugged at her arm. "I don't care what they ask. You're getting some sleep. In a bed. A real one. You deserve it."

"But those that are injured-"

"Need you well and rested." Sara looked up and down the street.

With both of them back beside her and Zane sent on his way, she realized that at least at this moment, the gods weren't driving her onward. The prospect of a bed and the opportunity to share it with the two people she loved was a very alluring one. But the sentence she'd just passed on Zane gave her pause. She reached out to the gods.

"You may expect Zane to be celibate, but I surely hope you don't demand it of me or you can both find another priestess."

The Mother laughed. *"You recall me saying that things aren't always what they are meant to be?"*

"I do."

Hasi rested his hands upon her shoulders. A disconcerting vibration of power emanated from his fingertips into her skin. *"In your particular situation, embodying both male and female desires does align with the role you will fulfill for us. My sister accepts your healer and I, your swordsman."*

"He will be pleased you didn't consider him only a sheepherder."

One of Hasi's swirling eyes winked. *"Well, he did have a hand in bringing you to me."*

"And I am to bring many more to both of you then?"

"As long as you keep the light alive, we will keep them safe." The Mother kissed her forehead.

Sahmara gasped as a vision halted her meandering steps. She saw herself, as if from a bird's view high in the sky, speaking to men and women gathered around her. Flashes of her and groups of people, those dressed in rags and those in great finery, Olando and Sara surrounded by red fire always nearby, flashed in front of her eyes. In some of the flashes she stood near broken buildings, in others towns with sturdy walls, laughing children in the streets and lush gardens. Sometimes she was as she was now, and others silver threaded her hair, the red beads in her braids standing out brightly. The last glimpse showed her hunched and walking with a cane, a shriveled man and a white-haired woman on either side laughed at something she'd said.

Tears ran down her cheeks as the vision faded. The gods slipped from her body and drifted back into the air, returning her body fully to herself.

Olando grabbed her hands. "What's wrong?"

"Nothing, absolutely nothing." She kissed his cheek and wiped at her tears.

Sara gave her a strangely knowing look. "Showed you did she?"

Her mouth gaped. "How do you know that?"

"The Mother showed me this place. When she told me you'd need me. And she told me what I'd need to do."

"What exactly is that then?" Sahmara pried one of her hands from Olando's confused and concerned grasp to take on of Sara's.

"Come on, I'll show you." Having spotted what she was searching for, she led the three of them through the crowd. She spoke with a man outside the door of what looked to be a simple two-room home. After a brief exchange, he grinned, darted inside and left with an armload of clothing.

"Until we leave, this is yours." Sara pointed into the home.

"Ours." Sahmara pulled them both inside with her.

"He," Sara gestured to the man who had left, "will start spreading the village's supplies to those in need. Now, to bed with you. No arguments, you're going to rest. Mother's orders."

The men might be sharing supplies, but there was so much else to do. People needed her. Hasi and the Mother needed her. Her mind spun with all she'd seen and the nudging urges from the gods. So much destruction to heal and so many people to reach. Weariness weighed heavily upon her.

As happy as she was to see Olando and Sara, her eyelids begged to close and the one large bed covered in blankets looked so inviting. She set her helm on a wooden table and the sword next to it. She shed the quiver next, and then the bow. Her fingertips tingled as they ran over the carvings. She stared at the gift from the Mother she'd carried for so long. Armed men and women, tiny and detailed, covered the surface, and in the middle, in a deep red stain, stood a woman. Her.

She pointed at the red figure and stammered, "Can you see that?"

Olando peered at it. "I've always seen a woman surrounded by warriors, but..." He looked from the bow to her and back again. He shook his head. "I never realized ya were that woman. But ya are."

Sara cocked her head. "Funny, I've always seen you on it. You didn't?"

She shook her head and stepped back, desperate to close her eyes before the god-sight revealed anything else. "I think I need to lie down."

Sara elbowed Olando in the ribs. "Finally, she agrees with me."

Olando nodded. "No one is stopping ya."

Sahmara sat on the edge of the lumpy mattress and pulled off her boots. The bed was harder than she remembered beds being but so much softer than the ground. She burrowed under the layers of blankets and sighed wistfully.

The bed dipped as the sudden weight of Olando and Sara joined her, one on each side. Their familiar smells and the warmth of their bodies eased her worries. The gods would have their demands and the people of Revochek many needs, but she was Sahmara, safe and loved, and she hadn't had the luxury of being selfish for so long. Just this once, everyone else could wait until tomorrow.

ABOUT THE AUTHOR

Jean Davis lives in West Michigan with her musical husband, two nerdy teenagers, and two attention-craving terriers. When not ruining fictional lives from the comfort of her writing chair, she can be found devouring books and sushi, enjoying the offerings of local breweries, weeding her flower garden, or picking up hundreds of sticks while attempting to avoid the abundant snake population who also shares her yard. She writes an array of speculative fiction. Her novels include *A Broken Race*, *Sahmara,* and in February of 2017, *Trust: Book one of The Narvan*. Her short fiction has appeared *in* The *Brewed Awakenings II* anthology, *The 3288 Review, Bards and Sages Quarterly, Theian Journal*, Acidic Fiction's *Corrosive Chronicles* anthology, *The First Line, Tales of the Talisman*, and more. Follow her writing adventures at
www.jeanddavis.blogspot.com

Made in the USA
Lexington, KY
22 June 2019